T0207911

THE
LEGEND
OF THE
SNOW
MONSTER

MYRTHA L. MCKINNEY

authorHOUSE®

AuthorHouse™
1663 Liberty Drive
Bloomington, IN 47403
www.authorhouse.com
Phone: 1 (800) 839-8640

Published by AuthorHouse 01/22/2016

ISBN: 978-1-5049-7368-7 (sc)
ISBN: 978-1-5049-7367-0 (e)

Print information available on the last page.

Any people depicted in stock imagery provided by Thinkstock are models,
and such images are being used for illustrative purposes only.
Certain stock imagery © Thinkstock.

This book is printed on acid-free paper.

Because of the dynamic nature of the Internet, any web addresses or links contained in
this book may have changed since publication and may no longer be valid. The views
expressed in this work are solely those of the author and do not necessarily reflect the
views of the publisher, and the publisher hereby disclaims any responsibility for them.

Myrtha McKinney, a native of Indiana, now living in Clarksville, Tennessee, is presently attending Trident International University online to obtain an MSL by May 2016. She is a past reporter, editor, and poetry author. The Legend of the Snow Monster is her second book offering after The Black Side of the Fence in 2013. She has been writing for over forty-five years and has appeared on television shows, radio programs, and poetry readings in her hometown of South Bend, Indiana. Myrtha is the proud parent of five adult children and six adult stepchildren. Writing credits include The Black Side of the Fence, published in 2013, and poetry published for poetry.com, Stellar Showcase, and helium.com.

CONTENTS

PROLOGUE

Once upon a time, on a cold dark continent, sat a small village ringed by tall, foreboding mountains that isolated the village from the rest of the world. The village lay at the foot of the tallest mountain called Mount RaNinjitsi. A sinister peak that appeared when the clouds lifted from the face of the mountain, which gave the mountain its name when interpreted meant "Terrible Mountain." A twin peak on the other side of the wide valley called Mount RaNinjitsi was just as foreboding as its twin, whose name when interpreted is "Dangerous Mountain."

Fog hung over the dense forests with faint trails running through it like a shroud, rising toward the heavens, blocking the sunlight, which barely reached the forest floor.

Vegetation ran wild and sprawled across the forest floor like a woman's dark, thick and tangled tresses. Summers were short and intense while the winters were long and harsh. Storms occurred often and snowfall buried the village for many weeks. Hunting was difficult and food was scarce.

The villagers foraged in the woods and worked small farms. Hunting parties were rare now and the women tended the gardens and took care of the farm animals, like sheep, goats and a cow or two.

Yet there was something different about this village though, something sinister" even evil. The children hardly frolicked and stayed close to their mothers' hems. Somber faces held something else not common in children-fear. Laughter sounded strange when it occurred and the mothers jumped and looked around furtively, and the child would cover their mouths as if they had done some wrong.

The women looked old with worry lines; their cheeks were hollow, and their eyes huge in their thin faces. They huddled in whispering masses, eyes darting around, never resting long, except upon the dense forests. Heads tilted, listening, cringing when they did hear what they had been listening for. Then they would snatch at children suddenly gone tense, and hurried for the door of their cottages and firmly closed the doors and slammed the crossbar in place.

The village had a terrible secret and it haunted their daily lives. It took the joy of life, harried them every waking moment and filled their nights with tortured dreams. Sleep often evaded the villagers until exhaustion claimed them in the wee hours of the night. A curse on the village was the curse, the curse of their fathers, and their fathers before them.

The legend of the Snow Monster was a mystery very few people in the village really knew completely. They only knew that his roaring and growling, heard daily, filled them with terror. As far back as memory went they provided tribute of food to the Snow Monster that lived atop Mount RaNinjitsi.

Old Major Thom, the oldest villager and resident historian, told them often of a time when the village was not terrorized by a "Snow Monster." A time when the village was prosperous. The villagers laughed at him, cursed at him, called him crazy, and threw stones at him. They were so very poor, and all they ever knew was their very own mean-spirited poverty.

Mayor Brown knew Old Major Thom told the truth. He was neither rambling nor crazy. Unusually rambunctious after they had to carry their nightly offering of food to the foot of the mountain, Mayor Brown often broke up small pockets of disturbances. Seeing food needed to feed, their families go to someone else, especially the Snow Monster, filled the villagers with rancor. Mayor Brown shooed the young people away and sent Old Major Thorn home. It was just another thing he did on his nightly rounds of the village.

He understood and did not hold it against them. Mayor Brown's father decided to hunt the Snow Monster and kill it after a severe winter left their food supplies very low. Pleas from his mother did no good. His father was a very proud and stubborn man and refused to listen to anyone. He set off alone to hunt and kill the monster that threatened his family. No one has seen him since. His mother tried to hide her broken heart from him but he watched her pine away for his father. He watched her die lonely and bitter.

They heard its growls throughout the night roaring through the mountains echoing until it filled the whole valley with its terror-filled sound. No one ever claimed to have seen the monster. They knew only that when they returned to the site of their contribution to the monster, the food was always gone. There were no tracks to follow, but there were signs something had been there. Broken branches and rotting food littered the ground into the woods. That was the only clue to the mysterious monster that haunted their minds, their thoughts, their very lives.

Chapter 1

Starvros Makes a Decision

Mayor Brown sighed heavily as he made his nightly round of the village. He came around the corner near the village meeting lodge and found a very angry crowd of villagers waiting for him.

"What is this?" he said surprised.

"We need to talk to you Mayor Brown," said the blacksmith, Dirk.

"Yeah," affirmed the crowd of men.

Mayor Brown noticed Bobbo the candle maker, Clyde the baker and George the horse handler in the crowd of men.

"We need to have a meeting," said others in the crowd.

Mayor Brown saw some of his neighbors and a few relatives in the crowd. The mumbling and grumbling grew louder. He raised his hands to quiet the crowd and promised to meet with them later that evening.

Mayor Brown did not want the villagers too worked up. They might do something they would regret, later. He knew the blacksmith, Dirk was a hothead who could set them on a path leading to trouble for the village and it was his job to protect the villagers from themselves and others.

Mayor Brown trembled when he heard the growls echoing through the mountains.

He hurried to complete his rounds and retreated safely to the lodge for the meeting.

The lodge filled with every adult male in the village, a cacophony of noisy voices raised in anger, met him when they entered the lodge.

The Mayor groaned and said, "This is not going to be an easy meeting."

He quickly opened the meeting and asked if there was a spokesperson for their concerns.

"Mayor Brown we don't need a spokesperson for this meeting," said Dirk, the blacksmith. "You know very well why we are here. Every man in the village is here. We are tired of taking food from our families to feed the Snow Monster. We barely have enough food for ourselves. If this winter lasts any longer, none of us will survive. We want to know what you are going to do about the Snow Monster."

Mayor Brown thought that Dirks' work over hot flames and dealing with the hot irons of his craft made him loud and harsh, but maybe that was just Dirks' way.

Dirk stood five feet nine inches tall, taller than the men in the village whose average height of five feet seven inches tall barely reached Dirk's shoulders. His broad framed and muscled body came from working his craft, as a smithy. He had huge hands with thick fingers. A mane of thick unruly black hair with long side burns framed an angular face with a wide, low forehead. His eyes small, black and cruel looking below heavy black brows that met together in the center of his forehead missed nothing. They moved constantly taking in everything around him. A swarthy complexion from the heat of the anvil and the cold mountain air gave him a fierce visage. His thick, short neck sat atop his shoulders giving the impression of a great bull.

Mayor Brown shuddered. He could not look at the man for long a sense of unease about the smithy settled beneath the surface of his consciousness.

'Now Dirk you know there is nothing I can do about the Snow Monster, alone." said the Mayor, shifting from one foot to the other.

"We have been down this road before" You grumble and complain and blame me for your troubles but when I ask you to hunt the Snow Monster and kill it, the grumbling become excuses," said Mayor Brown. "By the way Dirk are you speaking for everyone here, or just for yourself?

If you're speaking for everyone, then organize a hunting party and help us find this elusive Snow Monster and kill it," said the Mayor.

Once put on the spot the smithy began backtracking, "I- I didn't say I was speaking for everyone here. l was just expressing my frustration," Dirk blustered.

"Yeah we're all frustrated," said Bobbo.

"I'm not frustrated, I'm angry and I'm afraid!" said the butcher, Josef.

"Mayor Brown, we do not know what it looks like. We do not know where it lives. How are we going to hunt a thing like that? It is spooky the way it takes our food and does not leave any tracks, said Gustavo" the village stores keeper We are low on food and I will have to start rationing the food if this winter lasts any longer," Gustavo continued.

"We know about this people," said the Shaman running his hands through his thinning hair and fingering the many amulets tied around his neck.

"'We are not getting anywhere. We keep rehashing the same things. We are not solving the problem. Centuries shackled to a curse not of our making, our fathers, our father's father, and our ancestors have been in this room talking about this same issue. They did not solve the problem and neither have we," the Shaman said, as others nodded in agreement. He heard echoes of assent around the room.

"Aye, Aye, the Shaman is right," fluttered through the room from several in the crowd.

"Quiet down, men. Yes, the Shaman is right, but it does not help when we have to go home to children who are hungry and a wife who looks at you with regret in her eyes. A wife who feels like you failed to provide for her and the family. What excuses can we give her when all we work for goes to a monster who takes the little that we can scrounge from this accursed valley and leave us with barely enough to exist? Tell me, how do you live in fear every day? How do you live a life knowing that the little you have is taken from you by a cold, unfeeling, greedy, monster every day that our ancestors send to us to live good.? I speak for all of us in this; I am tired, frustrated, fearful and afraid. What do we fight against; we are ignorant of the Snow Monster and his ways. We blindly followed the dictates of the curse as all of Circle Valley has for over five hundred centuries, Tell me, what can we do? Do any of you have the answer?" Karlief's questions, met with silence.

Karlief was the Master Gardner. He planted the crops and saw to their dispersal to the families in Circle Valley. He was tall and slender, tanned from the summer sun, and weathered -looking about the face from the harsh winter weather. His hair was curly and brown, his eyes as brown as his hair. He had a huge broad nose that filled his face above thin lips and high cheekbones. He had long slender fingers on big hands. The fingernails darkened by continuous working in the soil.

Dirk intervened with a scathing indictment of the men at the meeting.

"What is this; you wanted a meeting a few hours ago. You men were on fire about getting rid of the Snow Monster. Where is all that bravado, now? You are foolish and weak. Only Dirk is brave and strong. I am the best hunter in the village. If I had men with backbone, I am sure I could rid Circle Valley of the Snow Monster. Nevertheless, every time there is a call to action you complain like women! We will never get anything done if we keep backing out," Dirk stated loudly. All the men fell silent at Dirk's scathing remarks and hung their heads, not meeting his cold eyes.

Starvros waited until the meeting was underway. He opened the big heavy wooden door to the lodge and quietly slipped into the back. Starvros hoped the wind gusting through the door would not give away his presence. The men were intent as they discussed it-the "Snow Monster." Starvros knew he had to do something. He could not continue to live this way. He must find a way to convince the villagers to hunt the Snow Monster, kill it and free the village from the curse.

Starvros cringed at the back of the room, finding a hiding place that allowed him to see and hear the men as they continued to discuss the Snow Monster. Starvros heard the loud growls echo throughout the forest, reverberate off the mountains like clanging cymbals, and closed his shabby shutters to the sound.

'Would there ever be a day or night he would not hear those growls echoing throughout the valley?' Starvros wondered.

The snarls rose to a pitch as they moved higher up the mountain and gradually faded away. The silence was almost eerie, but welcome.

Starvros' poverty ate at him daily. It drove him to the meeting tonight. He knew as a youth in the village he was a meddler in "Men's affairs," but this could not wait. It was life or death for Starvros. He had to take this chance. For him there was no more time for grown men's conventions and village rules. Starvros knew very well that when it came to him there was a different set of "rules." Starvros' initiation into the village, the custom for all the young boys in the village who came of age, did not happen for him. Starvros waited for the villagers to invite him along on a hunting party after the disappearance of his father and then his mothers' death in rapid succession, but no one came. Game, scarce because of the Snow Monster, required the villagers to go longer distance into the mountains for food but they did not include Starvros. He waited, and waited, and then anger rose in him at the unjust actions of the villagers.

Starvros knew what they would do to him for meddling in men's business. He needed the men in the village to take action or he would not survive another winter in Circle Valley. Starvros settled in his hiding place to wait for an opening to speak his mind.

Starvros had never been in the lodge before. It was not grand, but stark, the rafters were visible enabling Starvros to see cracks where the wind and snow sifted through the beams. Birds had found their way in and he could see several nests in the rafters. He also saw a hornets' nest high upon the wall where it met the roofline. The walls of cut logs filled with mud, pine needles and pine tree sap, explained the strong pine scent in the room. A huge stone fireplace faced him and a roaring fire filled the room with heat, only it did not reach Starvros where he sat in the back of the room near the entrance.

A large table centered in the room surrounded by various sized benches and stools, seemed huge to the small lad. On the walls, hunting gear hung at various levels and all kinds of animal pelts covered the walls giving added aura to the huge room, by blocking much of the air coming through the cracks in the mud and pine tree pitch. Ancient spears and a few lances with their blunt tips hung on straps lashed to the walls He noticed beaver pelts and bearskins, deer and fox, as well as wolf and cougar pelts strewn carelessly about the place. Fierce looking heads of animals long vanished from their woods looked down on him from their perches on the highest sections of the walls and over the huge fireplace mantle. Bear traps and fishing gear of all kinds, and large and small wooden cages lay atop tables to his left near the entrance. Various sized snow- boots, shoes and gear he did not recognize sat in wooden boxes along the walls and a huge box of wood for the fireplace stood by the entrance. He saw a smaller box of kindling and the torches burning in perches along the walls.

Starvros' anger rekindled at the men of the village. He could only catch field mice and small birds with a make shift trap that looked ineffectual compared to those in the lodge. Starvros had been so intent studying the interior of the lodge he did not realize the room had grown silent.

"This is my chance," he said. He rose from the back of the room and stood in the center aisle. "We must hunt the Snow Monster or we will all die. We have no choice!" he said into the quietness.

All heads turned. The Mayor looked into the dimness and recognized the orphan boy whose mother died last winter. Left to fend for himself by the villager they frowned with guilt at his temerity. Not one of the villagers took him into their homes as is usual when a child is an orphan in the village. Everyone looked everywhere but at the small boy standing before them.

"Damn you, lad!" yelled Dirk. "'You get out of here!'

"This is men's business you little upstart! Who do you think you are trying to tell men how to live?" Dirk continued.

The veins in his short neck stood out and his swarthy face looked even redder as anger at the intruder flushed through him with intensity.

Starvros pulled himself to his full height for one so small.

"I am seventeen summers and I am part of this village and have a say in what happens to the village. I will not leave until I've had my say." Starvros uttered bravely, though he trembled from head to foot.

"Rogue," snarled Dirk. "I told you to leave!"

He advanced toward Starvros, fists clenched tightly.

Starvros backed away from the man surprised at his anger. Starvros hung his head and started to leave the meeting. He stopped when the Mayor called his name.

"Starvros, come here lad," the Mayor said.

Starvros turned and slowly walked toward Mayor Brown through a sea of murmuring voices, stepping cautiously around the angry man in front of him, almost blocking his way to the Mayor.

"This lad'" said Mayor Brown does have a voice in this village. Well lad, do not stand there gawking. Tell us this idea you had to help the village" Speak up, speak up." said the Mayor with laughter in his voice.

Starvros began hesitatingly, peering at the angry faces surrounding him.

"I-I have h-heard o-of the S-Snow M-Monster. I have heard its roars from my cabin and I covered my head in fear. However, the time has come for us to end this curse.

That monster has taken m-my f-father and my-my mother! The cost of the curse is too much to pay with age-old reasons we no longer remember. If we do not unite against the Snow Monster, I fear the whole village will not make it through this winter, or any other winters." Starvros said as he found his voice.

The Mayor's mouth opened and closed at the speech of one so small and frail!

"That's a mouthful," snarled Dirk. "Now that you have had your say, get out and leave the business of the Snow Monster to grown men of the village to work out!" he spat out contemptuously.

"That's enough, Dirk," said the Mayor.

Others in the crowded room sided with Dirk, murmuring their comments in assent.

"We can capture the Snow Monster," said Starvros, desperately trying to get them to understand what they must do.

"Capture the Snow Monster!" echoed all the men in the room.

"You talk like a fool," the butcher said, throwing up his hands.

"Just let him talk so we can get back to men's business," said Gustavo.

"No!" yelled Dirk. "I will not let him speak. He is a meddler in grown men's affairs. Put him out of here since he does not have the sense to leave. Go! Get out of here with your loony ideas!" Dirk advanced toward Starvros.

Starvros backed away from Dirk to the door. Starvros stared at Dirk, eyes wide. He turned and opened the heavy door and burst into the cold night. Panting, he fled home to his small cabin and bolted the door with its thin crossbar. He knew if Dirk followed him, the frail door would not hold against his big burly frame. He waited, but no one came. He sat on the bed in the corner of his small cabin and wiped his face.

"I will build a fire and then I have a lot of thinking and planning to do," Starvros said into the darkness.

"If no one will help me, then I will do this alone!" he continued.

Starvros stood and walked to the fireplace, which took up one wall of his cabin.

The bed took up another wall and a table and chairs were in the center of the room. The pitch had decayed in several areas of the cabin walls and Starvros had stuffed them with rags and the pelts of the field mice he hunted. Still the winter cold seeped in and Starvros always felt cold, always seemed hungry, and always lonely. Except for Moira his childhood friend, he was alone.

Tika saw the boy run from the lodge. She wondered why he was there. What had sent him from the lodge in such a hurry? As she drew nearer to the lodge, the door burst open and Dirk stood in the doorway. His frame filled the doorway. Tika stopped in her tracks like a deer just before a killing. She held her breath hoping Dirk had not seen her. However, he turned his head sharply in her direction.

"Tika," he smiled showing his surprisingly good teeth. "What are you doing out in this cold night air?" He spoke lightly, swallowing the anger that had risen in him because of the young upstart, Starvros.

Tika winced. He always talked loud and irritatingly when he saw her, talking more at her than to her.

Tika decided to ignore him and asked, "What was Starvros doing in the lodge? I saw him run out of there like the Snow Monster was chasing him." Tika said.

'Take that insinuation!' she thought, as she smirked at Dirk.

Dirk frowned, looking through the slits of his eyes.

'She will be ripe for bedding in a few years,' he thought. 'I have already approached her uncle about marrying her. He will not refuse me. I am the best man in the village. I am taller, stronger, and a better hunter than all the men in the village. When I marry her, I will tame that mouth. Because of her beauty, she has been able to wrap that uncle around her finger, but not Dirk. Not since Abbey Laurel, he had not given his heart to another woman. Dirk sighed. He must stop his thoughts. It did him no good to think of Abbey Laurel. When he did think of her, his hatred for Starvros grew until he wanted to ... Stop Dirk! 'Do not say it. If you say those words, you will never be able to pull yourself back from the brink of madness.' As his thoughts continued to berate him, Dirk barely heard Tika's next question.

Tika realized Dirk was in some kind of mental quandary and she wanted to divert his attention in case he was in such deep thoughts about her. She saw the way he looked at her and she did not like it.

"Is my uncle in the lodge, Dirk?" Tika asked loudly.

"Oh, oh, yes he is. The men folk were having a meeting," Dirk said pulling his mind back to the present with difficulty.

"Really, is that why my uncle is so late coming home? The cook sent to fetch him home before his supper gets too cold. As meager as it is, it needs to be eaten warm," said Tika. The cook was one of the village women who came to cook and clean for them. Mayor Brown had not remarried since the death of his wife and Tika's mother many years ago when Tika was a small child. Yet she could get fussy when he was late in coming home. Nodi did not want to be out late because of the snow monster, and she had her own brood to feed. She often sent Tika to find him. She knew he would come right away if Tika asked him. He tended to dawdle with the village men discussing "the topic- the Snow Monster."

"'We are finished with our meeting. We were interrupted and I doubt we will solve very much tonight. Here let me escort you into the lodge," said Dirk.

He tried to grab her hand but Tika turned aside and brushed past him holding herself tightly as she rushed ahead of him into the lodge.

'When you are mine missy, you will not brush me aside so easily,' Dirk thought.

Tika shuddered, not from the cold, but from the realization of Dirk's intentions for her, she stiffened and silently vowed, "never!"

"Uncle, she said loudly, her voice squeaking.

"I've come to fetch you home for your supper before it gets too cold."

All eyes turned again to the entrance of the room and the men drew deep breaths at her beauty. Well known by the villagers they all smiled and greeted her. Many of them had received baskets of goodies from her uncle's kitchens with a promise they would continue to come if they did not divulge it to her Uncle. The villagers often saw Tika roaming the woods for herbs, wild vegetables, fruits, berries and nuts and feared for her life. The Snow Monster roamed the same trails. That uncle was too easy on her, they felt, but they would not tell him so!

"At least he has a supper to go home too," snorted Gustavo.

"Aye," said others. "We are lucky if we have some goat cheese and bread."

Mayor Brown ignored the barbs, greeted his niece warmly and kissed her on the cheek.

"This meeting is over. You all go on home. You have kept your families waiting long enough. We are not going solve anything tonight," said the Mayor echoing Dirks' words.

Tika looked at Dirk and found he had not taken his eyes off her. She looked away quickly.

"Mayor Brown, May I walk part of the way with you since my smithy lies so near your own fine cabin?" said Dirk.

Tika groaned.

Mayor Brown looked at Tika, puzzled by her attitude.

Dirk was the best man for Tika. Dirk would protect her. He was easy on the eyes to look at and she would live in comfort and not squalor like some of the villagers. It was the best plan for her future he could devise. She should be happy for his attentions. He determined to give her a good talking to after supper.

"Dirk, we would be delighted to walk with you, wouldn't we, Tika? Asked Mayor Brown.

"Yes, Uncle," she said lowering her eyes and turning her head to the side. A vein pulsed in the side of her temple showing her agitation, but she spoke no further.

Everyone filed out of the lodge and the last one out locked it up tight. They trudged through the snow in the darkened night to their homes grumbling all the way.

As Mayor Brown's party reached his home, they heard the howling of the Snow Monster, echoing though the mountains above them.

Tika shuddered. She was always very watchful, yet the howling filled her with dread as if she sensed in some way the Snow Monster knew of her treks in the woods. Tika had the uncanny feeling they were destined to meet, and she was terrified.

Dirk leaned toward Tika and whispered in her ear. "I will protect you from the monster whose growls disturb your pretty head, little one. You do not need to be afraid when you are with Dirk."

Tika edged away from him and ran into the house without a backward glance at Dirk or her uncle.

Mayor Brown looked at Dirk and said apologetically, "She is young Dirk, give her time. Do not rush her or you will lose her."

Dirk bowed to Mayor Brown. He turned, headed toward the smithy where his cabin adjoined to back of the shop where he plied his trade that had dwindled to tool sharpening. The horses in Circle Valley were few and he sharpened axes and made knives for the men and the women.

"She has until the spring and then Dirk will wait no more!" he said fiercely into the wind as the Mayor watched his retreating figure disappear in the snow that began to fall, briskly.

The next day dawned gloomier than the day before. Snow had fallen during the night and if possible, it was colder, too. Starvros woke early. He had much to do today and he wanted to get an early start. Starvros shivered and goose bumps ran over his entire body as he struggled into his meager clothing. He started a fire in the hearth, and stood as close to the fire as he could. Starvros could feel the air rushing around the room from the gusts that seeped through the cracks in the walls.

Starvros thought a lot about the decision he made last night after his humiliating flight from Dirk at the lodge. If the villagers would not help him, then he must help himself. Starvros tried hard to remember the things his father taught him before he disappeared. He did not feel within himself that his father was dead, but he knew if he were not dead, nothing would have kept him from coming home to him and his mother.

Now, mother was gone. Starvros was puzzled by his feelings and confused. He knew very little about the elusive Snow Monster.

He was going to see Mayor Brown. The man showed him a little kindness, and Starvros felt he would listen to what he had to say without the villagers and Dirk present to interfere. Starvros knew the Mayor felt guilty about him. Starvros decided to take advantage of Mayor Brown's feelings of guilt and find the answers he needed to hunt and kill or capture the elusive Snow Monster. Starvros ate his meal of left over cheese and bread with a small cup of goat's milk.

Starvros doused the fire down to glowing embers and left the cabin. Starvros walked quickly, a bounce in his steps. His stomach muscle tightened and he could feel stirrings in the pit of his stomach. His mouth had gone dry. His eyes brighter than usual were large in his narrow face.

His hands were clammy in the cold winter air. Starvros made his way through the village to Mayor Brown's house.

Though the village was poor, they had a caste system. He and his parents were so poor they lived in the smallest cabin at the end of a path toward the backside of Mount RaNinjitsi. The Brown's, on the other hand were more prosperous and they lived near the center of town not far from the lodge in the center of the village. In addition, the smithy was right behind the lodge, separated from it by the community gardens, animal pens and the slaughterhouse/ smoke house. A river ran along the opposite side of the village where the women washed their clothes. The river, frozen solid from the winter cold often overflowed its banks in the spring from the snows that melted on the mountains and flowed into the river. The women went out daily with axes to break up the ice for water and to fish for their meals, or they would gather wooden buckets of fresh fallen snow, if the drifts were too high and they could not get out of their cabins. This winter there seemed to be no shortage of falling snow. On the other side of the river lay pastureland, meadows, wild fields and forests until they reached the base of the mountains, which ringed the valley ending in the twin mountain to Mount RaNinjitsi- Mount RaNanjitsi. Its peak was not as imposing as its twin was, yet it still filled the valley with a sense of foreboding. The mountains surrounded the village like soldiers which made an impenetrable barrier around the valley, giving rise to the name of the village- Circle Valley.

Starvros barely glanced at the scenery as he hurried to his errand. He arrived at Mayor Browns' door breathing hard from the cold. Starvros knocked on the huge, thick, wooden door.

"No one could break this door down," he uttered to himself as the door opened and he was face to face with her-the prettiest girl he had ever seen. Starvros stared at her. His mouth opened and nothing came out.

"Oh" said Tika, "You are the boy I saw running from the lodge last night."

Starvros' eyes opened as wide as his mouth. Still he could not speak. As her words penetrated his brain, he reddened in the face at the memory of his flight from Dirk. However, Starvros' focus was on the beauty that was before him. He had often seen her in the village or passed her secretly on the trails while hunting for the small game for his meals, but he never spoke to her, her beauty had a way of silencing him.

"Well, come in silly boy, are you trying to heat up the outdoors?" Tika said laughing.

"No, No," Starvros mumbled as he stumbled over the threshold into the house. "I'm here to see Mayor Brown, if I can. I want to talk to him about the meeting last night," Starvros said, finally getting his voice under some control.

His voice sounded weak and uncertain to him in the face of the great beauty standing in front of him. He knew he could never approach anyone like her, so he worshipped her from afar and did what he could to keep her safe when he saw her trekking in the woods.

Tika smiled. She was used to the way the men looked at her. It was somehow sweeter coming from the shy boy who was just a few years older than she was, she judged. He did look somewhat frail though. He was handsome too. He had a thin, narrow face framed by black, thick, unruly hair. Wild eyebrows and long lashes overshadowed his black eyes. When he came into his manhood, they would be smoldering eyes, Tika thought. He had a long aquiline nose, lips full on top and thin on the bottom, sensuous lips. His chin jutted from his angular face, and a dimple winked at you when he talked.

As a picture of a mature Starvros flooded her mind, she gasped.

'He looks young' she thought wryly, but why did her heart and her breathing quicken at the sight of him?'

"I will see if my uncle will talk to you Starvros, wait in the great hall," said Tika

He had to shake his head to free his mind from the allure of her. Starvros looked around the great hall, seeing it for the first time when Tika left the room. The room was huge, filled with a massive fireplace along the wall opposite the front door. Tapestries, and animal pelts from bears, tigers and wolves covered the wall to his left, covered with the dust of ages from of non-use-another product of the Snow Monsters' hold on the village. To his right the wall featured all kinds of weapons. Lances spears, knives, bows and arrows, and slings for throwing stones traversed the wall from top to bottom. The floor of carved stone, similar to the fireplace stones well hidden by animal pelts that littered the floor like rugs, felt soft beneath his booted feet. The windows framed by long, scenic, velvet tapestries, with gold and colored threads depicted scenes from daily life in the village; surely allowed no air through them.

"Uncle, Starvros is here to see you," said Tika, knocking and then entering his study at his summons to enter.

The Mayor was impatient at the interruption. "Starvros, what does the lad want?" he asked, brusquely.

"He wants to talk to you about last night at the lodge," said Tika.

"I don't want to rehash last night, send the boy away" grumbled the Mayor.

"But, Uncle he came in the cold…

"I said send him away, Tika," the Mayor's voice boomed loudly through the house, interrupting her.

Starvros heard him. Before she could return and tell him what her uncle said, Starvros walked boldly into the room.

"Starvros," the Mayor said, uncomfortably, "What did you wish to see me about? It seems to have brought you out on an extremely cold morning" he continued Starvros noticed the Mayor did not offer him a seat. Starvros faced the Mayor, his stance wide and his fists clenched and unclenched at his side.

"I came to continue what I started last night." Starvros said boldly. I want answers to my questions and explanations about the Snow Monster. I need to know all that you know about the elusive monster and the curse that has plagued this valley for centuries.

The Mayor smiled showing his small white teeth as he remembered Starvros' exit from the lodge.

Starvros remembered also, and spoke gruffly to cover the awkward moment. "I want to know what you know about the legend of the Snow Monster and the curse, Mayor. As a legitimate citizen of Circle Valley, I have a right to know this and I am not leaving until I get those answers!

15

"Why?" challenged the Mayor.

"I have a right to know and if no one in this village will give me the answers I need, then I will have to seek those answers another way. I thought that because of the kindness you showed me last night that you would be willing to help me today. That is why I am here," said Starvros.

"Okay, but I don't know if it will do you any good knowing all the details, it didn't do your father any good!" the Mayor snarled.

"Nor yours!" retorted Starvros.

"Your insolence will not get you what you want, Starvros. I have changed my mind. You will get no answers today. I must ask you to leave my house, now!

"What did you say, Mayor?" Starvros asked quietly.

"I said leave my house!" the Mayor repeated firmly,

Starvros turned and stormed out of the house, not seeing Tika in his rush to get out of Mayor Brown's presence. He wanted to strangle Mayor Brown. He could not understand his hostility toward him; he could not understand why he treated him as an enemy. Fuming, he trudged through the deep snow.

'Who will give me the answers I want and need,' thought Starvros.

Starvros stopped and looked around. Then he saw the Shaman's cabin, which stood on the other side of the lodge.

"The Shaman!" "Surly he knows the entire story of the Snow Monster and can give me the answers I need," Starvros exclaimed.

Starvros crossed the path and made a beeline for the Shaman's cabin. He knocked at the heavy door several times before the Shaman's sister Jayne opened the door.

She was a severe looking woman of average height, but her demeanor made her look tall and slender. She was blonde like Moira and you could see the family resemblance. Her hair was long, thick and straight. She had gathered it into a ball atop her head that helped her look more severe than the frown on her face and the deep furrows in her forehead. She also, had small green eyes like Moira yet, her eyes did not hold the same warmth, laughter and kindness as Moira's eyes. Her ears and feet were also large like Moiras' Her lips all but disappeared on a thin mouth that looked like an upside down smile. Starvros did not like the woman he saw before him in the doorway. Jayne looked down at the small lad at the door, screwed her nose at him and bellowed, "What do you want?"

Before Starvros could tell her why he was there, she brusquely told him to get away from the door.

"We do not have time for beggars today," she said. The Shaman is busy preparing his rituals. Shoo, shoo, get away from my door!"

She shut the door firmly in Starvros' face.

Starvros' eyes grew large and his mouth fell open at the closed door. "Not once, but, twice, I have been turned away from the doors of people in this village. They have no right to treat me like this. I live here too. I will not let them get away with this I will show them." Starvros stormed, as he turned toward home.

While he was fussing, a hand touched him on the shoulder and he jumped. He swung around to attack and saw Moira, the Shaman's daughter. She was no great beauty like Tika, but she was his friend, his only friend in the village. They had been childhood friends and when his father disappeared and his mother died soon after, Moira was there for him. She often brought him small portions of food from the Shaman's house

Starvros suspected sometimes it was her own meal she sacrificed to give to him. She had long straight honey-colored hair, over a rather thin long face. Her eyes were small and green in color, which belied a temperament of stinginess- she was not stingy.

Her lips were a thin line across her face, her chin pointed in her long oval-shaped face and she had big ears for a girl, which she tried to hide by covering them with her thick hair. She was tall and straight and lean, almost a boyish figure, which she hunched down at the shoulders to hide her height. She was almost as tall as he was. She had big feet, too. On a dark night, she would look evil. Her fur parka seemed too big for her and she never wore the attached hood. The cold never seemed to bother Moira.

She and Starvros spent many hours in the forests and mountains foraging and she could climb as good as he could or better. If it were not for Moira, his life in the village would have been unbearable.

"Oh, it is you," Starvros said.

"Yes, it is I," Moira said with a laugh.

"That is not funny; you could have let me know you were here," he said gruffly, trying to hide his fright.

"I did not want to break your train of thought. You were so deep in your thoughts," said Moira with laughter in her voice.

"Why are you out here?" he said looking at her curiously.

"I saw the way Aunt Jayne treated you at the door. She is such a witch. I decided to help you," Moira stated.

"How are you going to do that?" asked Starvros.

"I am going to sneak you into the house to see Father," Moira continued.

"Father would never allow his guests to be treated the way Aunt Jayne treats the poor people of this village, said Moira. "However, she never allows him to see her doing that to the people, but then he would only make allowances for her. She is his only sister. Aunt Jayne never married. She says she gave up her life to take care of her brother and his orphaned daughter. That, she says is the only reason she would be living in a Shaman's cabin," Moira said talking rapidly in the cold air.

Moira grabbed his hand. "Come on, Starvros, its cold out here!" She led him around the house to a side entrance. She opened the door and looked inside.

"The way is clear. Come in." Moira said in a whisper as she pulled him into the house and dragged him through corridors he barely glimpsed with several closed doors facing onto it.

"Aunt Jayne is at the back of the house and Father is at the front of the house.

We can go this way through the parlor to the library where Father is reading. He reads a lot." Moira continued.

Starvros saw the old world beauty of the rooms he passed through. His cabin could fit in the shaman's cabin two or three times and there would still be room left over.

The floors, so thickly covered with animal pelts that their feet made no sound as Moira stopped at a door and knocked three times, waited, knocked two times, and then knocked once.

"That's our secret knock. Aunt Jayne doesn't like me bothering father so we devised this little code so he would know it was me at the door," said Moira to Starvros.

CHAPTER 2

STARVROS WANTS ANSWERS

The door opened and the Shaman stood in the doorway with a big smile on his face.

"Moira! Who is this with you?" he said as he saw Moira was not alone.

"Father, Starvros came to talk to you and Aunt Jayne was so mean to him.

She would not let him in and she slammed the door in his face," Moira said indignantly.

"I'm sure you're mistaken, Moira. Your Aunt Jayne means well,"

the Shaman said kindly.

Moira turned to Starvros and gave him an "I-told- you-so-look."

The Shaman gathered his daughter in his arms and led the way back into the room he retreated to study the signs and wait on a message from the spirit world.

"You have such a kind heart, Moira," the Shaman said, lovingly, setting her down on the seat in front of the huge fireplace.

"Starvros, I thought we had seen the last of you last night," said the Shaman. The memory of Starvros as he rushed from the lodge at Dirk's insistence left a fresh image in his mind.

Starvros felt uncomfortable for a minute, and paused. 'No, I will not be sidetracked again. I will not run from what you think of me. I am here to get answers to my questions and I am not leaving until I get them,' thought Starvros.

The Shaman raised his eyebrows at Starvros, but said nothing to embarrass the boy further. He was a kind man who had his weak moments, and his secrets. He knew to keep his place. He had asked the Mayor to do something about the boy after his mother died. Nevertheless, to appoint a family to oversee the youth belonged to the Mayor, not him. He did not want to make waves.

'In times past, the villagers respected him. Now the youth poked fun at him and taunted him about the Snow Monster. They felt as Shaman of the village; he should have found a way to free them from the grips of the Snow Monster. The Shaman knew they would not listen to him if he did have any idea to rid them of the Snow Monster but at this point, they were only about complaining and mourning over their circumstances. If they really wanted to rid Circle Valley of the Snow Monster, they would do more than complain and blame him. They needed a reason to spur them to action. Maybe Starvros is exactly what is needful to move the villagers from their state of complacency.'

the Shaman thought as he turned to Moira, and said briskly.

"Thanks for bringing Starvros to me. We have much to discuss, so if you will excuse us."

"Why do I have to leave? I want to hear about the legend, too, Moira stated

"Moira, this is men's affairs. Please go to your room. I will call you when Starvros and I are finished with our talk," the Shaman said, quietly.

Moira left the room looking perplexed and confused, and very curious. She beat a path to her secret room where she could hear their conversation. She eavesdropped all the time on her Father's meetings. 'How can I help him with his duties, if I do not know what was going on with his flock?' Moira thought.

"Okay, Starvros. Let us get to the business that has brought you out on this cold winter morn. I can see it still has to do with the reason you broke in on our meeting last evening," the Shaman, said.

Starvros rankled a little at his words and frowned. 'Why do they fail to see that I am part of the village?' Starvros thought.

"I am a man of seventeen summers, Shaman. I belonged at that meeting as well as every other man there. I depend on no one in this village for my living and hunt my own food, such as it is. I chop my own wood for my fire and take care of the few farm animals I have. I get my water to drink and wash with from the streams in the valley. I bother no man or woman for my living. All I ask; is the same consideration from the villagers. They treat me a like an outsider. You treat me like an outsider. I do not deserve the way this type of treatment from you. What I asked for at the meeting was reasonable and it was my right as a citizen of Circle Valley. My ancestors came from this village, also. My request is to know the details of the legend of the Snow Monster!" Starvros demanded.

The Shaman sat down after Starvros' passionate speech. "You have said very well, Starvros, and all you say is true. You have a right to know about the legend. Have you approached Mayor Brown. I am sure he ..."

Starvros interrupted the Shaman, "I went to the Mayor's house this morning and was thrown out of his house without learning a thing. I am in no mood, Shaman, to be trifled with any longer," Starvros said vehemently. Starvros stared at the man before him, seeing him clearly for the first time. The Shaman was the village religious leader, doctor and all around fix it man. He was tall and slim with a regal bearing befitting his position. An aura of mystery and authority surrounded him. Starvros surmised this was because his profession passed down through the generations from father to son. He had long gray hair that he had gathered into braids with feathers and animal bones at the nape of his neck. He wore a long beard, which folks claimed he never cut. It was long and gray speckled, fully engulfing his high angular cheekbones and chin. He had small, beady eyes, black as night, and a long slender nose and a full sensuous mouth completed the look of a man of deep religious beliefs. He wore clothes made from course animal pelts and was ruddy complexioned with a face that was weather beaten, like tanned hide.

"I see," said the Shaman. "Well let's begin."

Moira sucked in her breath in her secret cubbyhole. "At last, she would hear the legend of the Snow Monster. No matter how many people she asked, no one would tell her, and all her father said was "Moira it is not a woman's business to know about the Snow Monster.

"All we can do is to live in fear," Moira thought. 'We women do not even know what to fear. It growls and we run inside our homes and shut the door and hide and cower in fear like the children!'

"The curse began long ago, about five centuries ago, said the Shaman. It is a never-ending curse, passed from generation to generation. If there is a solution to it, no one has found it to this day. Circle Valley was a prosperous village as you can see by the few larger cabins and the lodge. The village was the center of life for all the villages in these mountains. There was a King and a Queen who lived in the castle."

"A castle? Where is it? A King and a Queen? Who are they? Where are they? asked Starvros.

He had been through every part of the village and he knew there was no castle here.

"Shush!" said the Shaman to Starvros, laughing at his enthusiasm. "Let me finish the story, it will answer all your questions."

The door to the study opened quietly and Jayne stood in its opening a quiet intensity on her face.

"Jamond, what is that urchin doing in here?" Jayne asked

The Shaman turned, startled at her voice.

"Ah, ah, Jayne, Moira brought him to me. He needed some answers to questions ..." he stuttered before her like a child caught doing something wrong.

Jayne peered closer at Starvros. "You're the boy I turned away at the front door. I must ask you to leave again; obviously, you did not get my message right the first time. The Shaman needs this time to prepare his rituals. He does not need any interruptions. I make sure of that, Jayne said sharply.

I will tend to Moira, later. Leave now, quickly." Jayne spoke harshly.

Starvros looked from her to the Shaman; he would not meet his eyes but looked down at his hands.

"Leave Starvros, he spoke timidly before his sister, "we can do this at another time."

"No, we cannot Jamond! I am out of time. If I can get no answers from you or the villagers, I will get them myself. I will leave immediately from your house. I will leave this village. I will hunt for this elusive monster and get my own answers, since all the villagers cower before it and women!" Starvros uttered fiercely.

The Shaman hung his head and said quietly, "I am sorry you feel like that Starvros, but do what you must do for yourself lad."

Starvros jumped to his feet knocking over the chair he was sitting in. He stood straight and tall. A vein pulsed in his temple. His mouth, a thin line in his angular face, pressed together to shut out the fury of words he wanted to fling at the Shaman. His breathing, sounded loud in the room.

"How am I supposed to feel, Jamond? I fled from the lodge because of Dirk last evening. Mayor Brown would not see me this morning. Now you are allowing a woman to throw me out of your house not once, but twice! I have done nothing to wrong any of you. Why do you treat me thus? Tell me, so that I can understand your hatred for me.

You are a Shaman. Why do you allow this? You remain silent at my questions.

Therefore, I will leave your home on my own." Starvros said passionately, tears stinging his eyes as frustration boiled over. Starvros threw back his head and yelled loudly, and stormed from the room. Jayne followed hard on his heels to make sure he left the house. Starvros walked quickly through the large cabin and out the front door.

Starvros refused to use the back door the crazy woman wanted him to use. He wanted to rage at her. He wanted to tear her to pieces. He trembled all over. Something primordial rose in him at the thought of a woman throwing him out of the Shamans' house, again! Just one more thing he could not abide about Circle Valley firmed his resolve to leave it as soon as he was able.

Moira groaned as Starvros' impassioned appeal to her father rang in her ears.

Nevertheless, she was not surprised. Aunt Jayne ruled the house and her father, too.

Often, she saw a look pass between them she could not define. When father tried to assert himself she would cross her arms and stare at him, her mouth thin in her pale face, and he would mumble his assent to her wishes. He made a retreat to his den and his scrolls or to his laboratory, it was the only room he could lock them both out of as long as he wanted, that is until Aunt Jayne's ranting warned him it was time to come out and face her. Aunt Jayne ran the Shaman's house strictly, even picking the subjects for the Shaman to use in his rituals. He served the villagers and they were loyal to him. They tolerated Aunt Jayne, though Moira could tell they did not like her. Moira heard the front door shut with a bang and her thoughts went back to Starvros.

"We did not get answers to our questions!" she said. "I thought I would finally learn the secret of the legend of the Snow Monster!" Moira left her hiding place to find Starvros. By the time she was dressed in her winter clothes, Starvros was gone. She searched for him near the Shaman's cabin, but he was not there. She ran back and forth calling his name. She received no answer. Then, she heard her name called. It was Aunt Jayne.

"Moira, Moira, come in this minute!" Aunt Jayne said, harshly.

Moira answered her. "I'm coming, Aunt Jayne."

She knew she was in for a good tongue-lashing and possibly more from her aunt.

Moira lifted her chin, shook her hair loose from its pins and squared her shoulders. Why did Aunt Jayne always discipline her? Moira could not remember a time when her father disciplined her, or talked to her about her behavior.

Moira could not remember her mother and the sketchy information she knew was not enough. She could see the wooden expression on their faces when she talked of her mother or asked them about her. She starved for information about her, but try as she might she could not glean any further information than that she died giving birth to her. Moira did not know if she looked like her mother. She did not know her mother's people. People said she looked like the Symthes'- her father's people.

Moira barely knew her mother's name. She whispered the name into the cold winter air as if by some magic, her troubles would go away.

"Maeva!"

Moira frowned trying to hold back the tears that stung her eyes. Her shoulders drooped and she slowed her steps toward the house and to Aunt Jayne's wrath. She was not in the door before her Aunt gave her a tongue-lashing and more and sent her to her room.

"Maybe I should leave like Starvros," thought Moira, after the thrashing, she received for sneaking Starvros into the house. She had learned not to speak of these things to her father. He would do nothing but make excuses for his sister.

Moira pulled at the hair near her temples, making them stick out like cowlicks. She bit her lips pulling the tender skin away until they were swollen and bleeding. She bit at her nail beds and pulled the skin until it bled. She was learning to hate her Aunt. Yet, something in her ran from the hate. She knew if she gave in to the feelings that overcame her whenever Aunt Jayne hurt her, it would change her forever.

She would become a shadow of her aunt, cold and bitter. Moira did not want the rage that engulfed Aunt Jayne, the sickness that caused a person to harm another person for no reason, to sway her. She did not know the cause of her aunt's bitterness, nor did she know why she took her rage out on her. Moira knew only that it must stop. The only way to stop it was to leave. Moira thought for a long time and decided she would join Starvros on his quest.

"Yes," she said, excitement gripping her. It swam through her mind like salmon flowing through a stream, gathering momentum to make the giant leaps upstream. Moira felt hot and breathless at the same time. Moira forgot the pain from the bruises and welts on her body as she raised herself from her bed and ran to a table in the corner. She felt giddy.

Moira's bedroom was not pink and pretty. Moira had made it warm and cozy by taking some of the extra animal pelts, and tapestries depicting hunting scenes, and covered her walls and floors with them. It made the room dark and cave- like, illuminated only by the light from the huge fireplace that flanked one wall. The only window covered by thick gold colored fabric with gold and red tassels did not allow much light or cold into the room. Hand-stitched quilts and woven blankets, she saw the women in the village weaving daily on their looms, piled high on the bed kept Moira warm when the fire died out during the night. Moira's hunting gear, climbing gear and baskets she used to forage in the woods for herbs and berries hung randomly along the other wall. Her snowshoes, she kept in a cubbyhole by the fireplace, next to the box of wood for the fire. Her closet was a huge cupboard built into the room. It held her winter clothes including her favorite fur parka handed down to the Smythe women. Dried flowers and berries hung from the rafters scented the room, and prevented dankness that pervaded the other rooms at the top of the house. Moira did not mind that her room was away from the rest of the living quarters. It kept her out of Aunt Jayne's way.

Moira gathered ink, a scroll she begged out of her father, and writing quills from the table beneath the window that she used for writing. She was thorough in her planning. She looked at the quest from all angles. She surmised that if she told Starvros she was going with him, he would forbid her to go.

"I will wait and follow him after he leaves," she thought. "He will need extra provisions anyway. He does not have enough provisions for a journey like that. He will need my help. I am familiar with the woods and the trails through my own ramblings in the forests. I can climb mountains better than any man in the village can. I will leave this house of pain and misery. They will not miss me," Moira surmised.

Moira's plan took several days for her to gather everything she needed, secretly. Her comings and goings would be her own. Aunt Jayne usually ignored her after she had one of her episodes. She would be no problem until the rage came again and by that time, Moira determined she would be gone. Moira decided not to leave a note for her father.

She felt the blame lay at his door. She did not know why, but his apathy was worse than Aunt Jayne's sickness.

Moira's plan involved spying on Starvros to see when he was preparing to leave.

She would give him a head start, and then she would follow at a slower pace, eventually quickening her pace until she caught up with him before nightfall on day one.

Starvros' heightened color and his dark curly hair waving in the windy morning air made Tika draw in her breath as she caught sight of him rushing down the lane toward his home.

"Starvros, Starvros," Tika called.

He turned and looked, but did not see her through the haze of his rage. She ran quickly toward him.

"Starvros, I have been looking for you since you left our house," Tika said catching up with his long strides and falling into step beside him.

"Go home, Tika, I am not in the mood for women today," Starvros said sternly, not wanting to let go of the anger at the sight of her beautiful face.

"I want to apologize for my Uncle's behavior toward you, Starvros." Tika continued.

"Why? asked Starvros, stopping to stare at her. Why should you apologize for one more thing the villagers have done to me? I do not want your pity, Tika.

Like I said, go home and leave me alone. I will be all right in spite of Mayor Brown, the Shaman, his crazy sister, Moira and you!" Starvros stormed.

"You don't have to take your anger out on me, Starvros. I was only trying to help you!" Tika said, puzzled by his anger.

"I didn't ask for your help, I don't need your help. No one has helped me before. I will stand on my own two feet, alone. I will find the snow monster, alone. I will discover the secret of the curse of the Snow Monster, and I will do it alone "Go home, Tika. What I will do, I must do." Starvros said.

"What will you do, Starvros?" Tika asked.

"While anger has spurred my momentum, I am going home to start laying aside provisions for my journey. I should be ready to go in a day or two, a week at the most." Starvros averred

"You will be careful, won't you, Starvros?" Tika asked.

"I will be careful," Tika, Starvros, said, looking at her intently, as if searing her image in his mind.

Her eyes fell before his gaze and her cheeks flushed with color.

"Goodbye then, Starvros," Tika said gently.

"This is not goodbye, Tika. I will see you again!" Starvros vowed.

Tika watched Starvros as he walked toward his house. She turned and went back home. She did not want to stop to talk to her Uncle, but as she passed his door, he called out to her to join him in his study. Tika dragged her feet as she turned and joined her Uncle.

Before she could say anything, her Uncle began to talk on the subject that concerned him most.

"Tika, I asked you to come in here because I want to talk to you about your attitude toward Dirk."

Tika opened her mouth to deny it, but the Mayor held his hand up to silence her outburst.

"Allow me to finish what I have to say before you deny what we both know to be true. Tika, I am your mother's brother. The only relative she had left. I took you both in when she was sick. I provided good care for her until her death. I believe I have taken reasonably good care of you since her death. All I ask is that you consider that I am looking out for your welfare. I think Dirk would make a good husband for you," Mayor Brown said confidently.

Tika's eyes opened wide, her mouth gaped open, and she wailed,

"But I don't like-love him, Uncle. I loathe him. He is not for me, Uncle," Tika said hesitating.

"Oh, I think he is, Tika. I think you are too young and naive at this time to know what is best for you. Dirk is the best man in the village. He will give you the life you are accustomed to living. You will not lack for anything with Dirk. Everyone else is beneath him. The Shaman does not count and there is no one else," said Mayor Brown.

"I can choose for myself, Uncle, It is my life as you say," Tika said.

"Choose for yourself," Mayor Brown shouted. "You are a mere slip of a girl, just entering a new phase of your life. There will be changes happening to you. You will not understand these things and a husband will be able to help you. I am inadequate at this," Mayor Brown stated.

Mayor Brown's eyes narrowed in thought as he considered all the men in the village she could choose besides Dirk. Then his eyes opened wide as he shouted.

"Not that pauper, Starvros! He cannot take care of himself, Tika! How do you think he will be able to take care of you? He is a mere puppy compared to Dirk. Dirk is a man of strength and courage. He is the best hunter in the village. He has a living ..."

Tika interrupted him. "If you and the other villagers did not treat Starvros so badly and do for him as you do for the other boys, then he would be worthy of me, Tika cried."

"You hush, girl, do not tell me my obligations!" Mayor Brown shouted. He was a proud man and no girl was going to tell him his duties. His face, warm and highly colored, sweated in an effort to deal with his headstrong niece. His head wobbled on his short neck as if it would topple off onto the floor. His small, black eyes sparkled, and his thick, full lips were juicy with spittle that sprayed Tika as he shouted and raged at her.

Tika stepped back from his salivary juices, while shouting at her Uncle.

"No, I will not marry Dirk. I will run away before I let you marry me to that bullish man!"

"Where will you run to, Tika? Do not talk like a fool! You have nowhere to run.

Who will take you in? You will get used to the idea of marrying Dirk, my girl, and Tika, no matter how excited you get, never again presume to raise your voice to me in my own home. You will give me respect as your Uncle and you will come to realize I know what is best for you," Mayor Brown said quietly.

Tika realized she was out of control. She tried to quiet herself. She needed to reason with her Uncle.

"Why does any of that matter at this time, Uncle? If we do not do something about the Snow Monster, none of us will live beyond this winter to worry about who I will or will not marry. However, until that time, I will follow my heart. My heart does not choose Dirk. Now if you will excuse me, I will go see how Nodi has been in providing our meal for today. Nevertheless, I will think further on this Uncle." Tika said finally able to control her voice.

"You do that Tika. Think very carefully, after all is said and done, it is your future," Mayor Brown said.

Tika did not look back at her Uncle, she kept moving through the house, but she did not go to see Nodi. Her fury took her to her bedroom, her sanctuary. Tika closed the door leaning against it breathing deeply to calm herself. Her hands shook. Tika saw her reflection in the looking glass on the wall. It was oval and very ornate, and older than she was with a black carved wooden frame. It did not give a good reflection, but it was hers. The mirror reflected a face, drained of color, looking at her out of large black eyes. Her nostrils flared in her face. Lips full and shapely pouted from her anger. The narrow chin quivered from emotion and a dimple in her chin and cheeks winked with every facial movement. Spots of color in her cheeks revealed the emotions she held in check. She ran both hands through her wild raven-colored hair, which formed a peak in the center of a high forehead, flowed to her waist, as she pulled it high over her head. She then let it slip slowly through her fingers, savoring the feel of it. It seemed as if this ritual allowed the anger to slip through her fingers and soothe her nerves. Tika relaxed and began to pace the room, her thoughts darting about in all directions. Her forehead furrowed as she considered her options in light of her Uncle's declaration that she marry Dirk.

Tika realized what her uncle said was true. Her breathing slowed and she unclenched her fists As long as she was in his house she would have to do what he said.

Tika felt the influence the Snow Monster had on the village. How isolated and narrow he made their world. There was no one she could turn to, nowhere to go. She railed against the curse that bound her to a man she did not love.

Tika's room on the second floor of the large house faced the back, with two long narrow windows facing the south side of the house. Another window faced east showing the base of Mount RaNinjitsi and the forests, which densely covered its base. A fireplace filled the north wall and kept the winter cold at bay. A wardrobe filled the west wall along with a water table covered by a huge pitcher and bowl for washing. A writing table and chair occupied the corner of the west wall. A bed flanked the east wall under the windows, covered in thick patchwork quilts. The walls, well pitched that no air entered the cozy room. Thick tapestries covered the walls from floor to ceiling adding warmth to the room. A settee faced the fireplace in the middle of the room. Next to it, an ornate carved wood table stood with scrolls strewn across its surface and a shelf beneath held her prized mementoes. Animal pelts draped the floor and several hung on the walls. Wood for the fireplace was stacked inside a wooden box beside the fireplace and a fire glowed in the hearth diffusing the room with heat.

Tika barely noticed the room she loved so much as she paced the room deep in thought.

"Aha! Starvros!" she said loudly and looked around furtively to see if anyone had heard her outspoken words.

'Starvros was the only one brave enough to leave Circle Valley to find different answers to the same old problems. Starvros was her way out of her uncle's house and Circle Valley! She would join him on his quest. Maybe they could find a way out of this cursed valley, her uncle and from marrying Dirk,' Tika thought.

Tika laughed. She leaped and twirled around in the large room. Tika ran to the writing table for quills, ink and paper. The paper was fragile and yellow with age. She used the paper sparingly because once it was gone there would be no way to get anymore. "I must make plans." Tika said excitedly and then she halted as she realized Starvros would not willingly take her along with him on his quest.

'However, he cannot keep me from following him. Besides, he may need me. I am sure his supplies are limited. She admired him for his bravery. We all in the end must determine and fulfill our own destiny,' Tika surmised.

'I just want to make sure my destiny is not to marry Dirk,' Tika thought.

Tika began to write furiously, making a list of the supplies she, and eventually Starvros would need if the journey were long and hard.

"It's going to take several days to accumulate the things on my list. I must watch Starvros carefully to see when he leaves, and then I will leave shortly after him and by nightfall, I will have overtaken him and I will deal with the rest of it when I see him," Tika spoke aloud into the room, confident Starvros would not send her home.

Starvros spent a week preparing for his journey. He did not talk to any of the villagers, but stayed away from them. When they saw him, they whispered among themselves, the younger boys taunted him calling him the "Monster-slayer" and laughed derisively at him. They often threw balls of snow at him and he would run home and slam his door against a barrage of snowballs. Starvros was surprised that the villagers knew of his intentions to hunt for the elusive Snow Monster. They all thought he was crazy. He heard the comments from the adults in the village, "So is the father, so is the son!" as he passed them on the paths in the village. He ignored the villagers and went about setting his traps and fishing in the river whenever he could break through its frozen surface. At the end of the week, he took stock of his supplies and was surprised at how meager they were. He cursed his poverty, but was determined to go on. He had no choice. There was no bright sunny future for him. Only the future he made with his own hands would keep him from utter destruction at the hands of the Snow Monster and his blasted curse on Circle Valley. He could not get the villagers to see that things were getting no better. Starvros reasoned that he would have to ration his food from beginning to end, and hunt along the way as he climbed higher up the mountain. He was sure there were more animals higher in the mountains.

Starvros stood before the small wardrobe in his house; he slowly opened the door as if he stood before a shrine. He removed the fur-lined parka from the back of the cupboard. It was his father's parka, made by his mother before her death. He smoothed it out with his hands. She had used the last of the fur pelts and pieced them together as she awaited his return. Starvros saw her broken heart reflected in her eyes as she realized he was not coming home. He watched the life drain from her as they struggled to live on what his father had stored up for them before he left. After they had depleted their stores, they lived off what he could trap and catch, and what they could glean from the forest.

Starvros saw his mother sicken and die. No one came from the village to help him. He buried her himself and covered her grave with large stones he carried to her grave, alone. Anger rose in his throat. He shook himself from the memories. They did no good, now.

Starvros put the parka on and was surprised it fit him. He would need it in the mountains where the storms were more severe. Starvros put his gear into a pack he wore on his back, checking items off his list as he packed them away. Rope, climbing gear, snowshoes, extra pants and shirt made from animal hides by his mother, thick sweaters woven on the loom standing empty in the back of the room, extra mittens, dried meat, dried fish, fresh meat and fish from his week of foraging, cheese and bread. He had slaughtered the only farm animals he had left and had taken the meat and salted it with the small amount of salt he had left and wrapped it in thick hide and snow wet leaves for the journey. Most of it he left behind in the small smoke house his father built behind their cabin. A suet made by his father of honey, animal fat, nuts, seeds and coarse meal, he added to the pack. He remembered his father taking it with him on long hunting trips. He said it gave him energy. Starvros had several water bags made from the stomach of goats and dried in the sun. These he tied to a belt at his waist. He could replenish them from the many streams and rivers that flowed in the mountains, or from melted snow.

The hunting knife his father made and presented to him after the manner of all the boys initiated into the hunting ritual. He received his knife after capturing and killing the boar that the men rounded up in the woods during his first hunting trip with the adult men. He was thirteen summers that year. He passed his test and the knife was his gift after he killed the boar. Starvros smiled at the memory. His father had taught his son well. The other weapons were a spear and a walking stick. The spear was one of his father's older spears he left behind. Starvros lashed the spear across his back and the knife he thrust into a sheath at his waist.

Starvros stood in the center of the room testing the gear to see if he could move easily with it on his back. He knew traveling would be more difficult with snowshoes in the higher elevations with its deeper snow.

He was ready for the hunt. He, who only hunted small animals and field mice, was ready to hunt the elusive Snow Monster that terrorized his village, and drove him to poverty, and starvation. Realization washed over him at the task he had set for him.

"Somebody has to do it," he said to himself "Either way I am dead. If I stay in Circle Valley, I will die of starvation. At least I am doing more than complaining. I have nothing more to lose. I can do this. I must do this," Starvros rationalized, loudly.

Starvros gathered his supplies, poured water on the fire and closed the cabin. He did not bother with locks; no one ever came to his house. Starvros headed toward the back of his cabin away from the village and toward the foot of Mount RaNinjitsi and disappeared into its thickets. Starvros followed the familiar trails he knew as the thick forests closed in around him stopping along the way to gauge the distance he had traveled and to mark the path, just in case he had to find his way back down the mountain.

It was a safety feature his father taught him. He took his large knife from the sheath at his waist and made a gouge in the north and south side of a tree at eye level so that it was seen coming or going. If there was no trees then he would mark the ground by making a fresh dig in the snow and pull the vegetation leaving a bare, visible spot, or he would make a cut from the bushes to show the greening in the limbs.

Starvros prepared for his journey with more than he thought. He saw that because of his lack of experience he under estimated his unproven knowledge. His father taught him but his narrow journeys in life had not given him a chance to prove what he knew. Only experience can test knowledge, Starvros surmised.

Starvros journeyed for most of the day mostly getting the lay of the land and deciding his course of action. He was familiar with the first level of the mountain and there were familiar trails criss crossing through the forest. The trees were thicker at the lower level and the snowfall barely reached the ground overgrown with thick vegetation. Some trails had been cut away by previous hunting trips and some of the trails were already marked. Starvros knew his first few days out would be easy going because it was the usual hunting ground for the villagers. Starvros knew his trail would cross some of the villagers out hunting for meat to feed their families, but he never interacted with them. He just went on his way doing what he needed to do to feed himself. It was early morning and the sun was not yet up over the mountains. Moisture hung thick in the air. Starvros expected snow by the end of the day. He wanted to travel as far and as fast as he could before nightfall.

Starvros breathed deeply of the sharp smell of fir trees, mingled with the wet, damp smell of rotting vegetation. They crunched underneath his feet, loudly protesting his intrusion as the vegetation crumbled in the final assault upon their death knell. Small animals scurried away from their hiding places, hurriedly seeking new places away from his slow and steady advent into the forest.

Intent upon finding new trails, Starvros traveled well and far the first day. By nightfall, he was ready to set up camp and get a good night' sleep. His trek had taken him to the far side of Mount RaNinjitsi, away from the course of anyone or thing coming down the mountain. Starvros did not want to run into the Snow Monster on his first day.

He was on the backside of the mountain, but not at the first level, yet. From his calculations and observations of the mountain before he set out on his journey, Starvros surmised that there were four levels that possibly which spanned into flat plateaus. The third level was the hardest level due to less tundra and trees and more stones and rocks. The last level before the peak, he called the true mountain. He would probably encounter more storms at the fourth level and deeper snow levels as well as deep ravines, and crevices. Starvros knew fissures could open suddenly beneath your feet and that would make the going slower than he anticipated. He did not know if he would ever see Circle Valley or its inhabitants again. Starvros only knew that if he did not do this, he would die.

Starvros was perplexed about the animals. He did not know it there were dangerous animals higher in the mountains or more game animals driven there by the Snow Monster. All he knew was that there were no game animals or dangerous animals within the vicinity of Circle Valley. The hunting expeditions the men went on often-yielded less meat than they hoped. Starvros, excluded from their hunting forays, always found a small package of meat left on his doorstep after a hunting expedition. He did not know who left it for him. He thought that Gustavo, the village stores keeper might have left it for him. No one ever revealed who left the package for him, but he was grateful for it. He assumed it was Moira, his only friend in Circle Valley, who left the goods for him. Without it, he might have died a long time ago.

The villagers limited by a decree from Mayor Brown were not to venture beyond the first level of the mountain. If the larger game was higher in the mountains, then Starvros felt he had a better chance at surviving the quest he had set before him. His only danger came from the purpose of his quest- the Snow Monster, and Starvros was about to break the decree set by Mayor Brown through his journey to find the elusive Snow Monster. Yet, he felt no qualms about it.

'If they did not obey their own rules and laws concerning him, Starvros felt he had no loyalty to obey their laws either. If the laws set by the villagers cannot enjoin the lawmakers to obey them, then why should he obey them? The law is for the lawless. Someone should have intervened on his part when Mayor Brown refused to allow him to become a part of the village according to the ritual laws for boys to become men. Mayor Brown knew that Starvros' father disappeared in a search for the Snow Monster. He knew when his mother died, and yet he did not offer Starvros the initiation rites as a citizen of the village as the laws dictate. The villagers left him to his own devises,' Starvros' thoughts swirled through his mind as he continued his trek.

Starvros reached a campsite before nightfall. It was a clearing on the backside of the mountain. It was dusk, the time before true darkness descended upon the mountain. There were boulders here and there and a stand of fir trees surrounding his site. Starvros set up camp, checked his list and supplies, built a fire and made a lean-to with sticks and branches from fir trees. Starvros ate a small meal from his meager supplies. Starvros fell exhausted into blankets woven by his mother that he found in the bottom of the cupboard with his father's parka. It was as if she was helping him from the grave, with her store of unused blankets. Starvros slept as soon as he snuggled down into his blankets.

CHAPTER 3

THE JOURNEY BEGINS

S tarvros opened his eyes, his body stiff and tense, and his ears were straining to hear even before his consciousness became aware. The hairs on his body stood to attention. He struggled to clear the sleep from his mind. Something disturbed his sleep. There, he strained ...turning his head toward a sound, faint, but close. Starvros' finger felt for the knife in its sheath at his waist. He gripped the knife firmly. Pulled from its sheath the knife glistened as moonlight flowed through the cracks in the lean-to and slid down its length. Starvros, fully awake, sat up; pulled the covers away and crawled to the entrance of his make shift shelter. Eyes darting everywhere as he adjusted to the darkness, tried to make sense of the many shapes in the night landscape. Aha! He saw movement in the shadows. There, it moved again, circling around his camp. Starvros backed to the rear entrance and slipped into the darkness. Fatigue left him as his bare feet touched the cold wet snow. He turned away from the shadow, going in the opposite direction to come up behind it. His hands, cold and numb gripped the knife harder. He barely felt the snow slipping through his toes. His eyes riveted on the intruder, Starvros grabbed it from behind and brought his dagger to make the thrust through the heart as his father had taught him, when his ears heard his name screamed repeatedly.

Starvros wrestled the dark shape to the ground dropping the knife in the struggle.

His breathing mingled with that of the intruder as they fought in the snow. Starvros sat atop the intruder, winded, breathing hard, gasping for air. The intruder lay quiet beneath him.

"Will you get off me Starvros?" said Moira.

"Moira! Why are you sneaking around in the dark? What are you doing here? How did you get here?" Starvros shouted as the questions tumbled from his mouth.

"Wake everybody in the forest, will you Starvros? One question at a time but, first, get off me, Starvros," Moira shouted back at him.

Their voices broke the silence of the night. Birds chattered nervously in the trees above them. Moira could hear the slithering of small animals in the bushes around them'

"Get off me, Starvros," Moira said, more firmly and quieter.

Starvros realized he was still sitting atop her and he rolled off her and jumped to his feet.

"I'm, I'm s-s-sorry, M-M-Moira" Starvros said helping her to her feet. He brushed the snow from her, his teeth chattering. He began to shiver visibly.

Moira looked down at his bare feet, "We better get you back into your shelter before you catch a cold," Moira said laughing.

"Aye, we better," said Starvros laughing.

They both moved toward the lean-to when a shadow crossed their path. Both Starvros and Moira jumped and screamed'.

Gosh, you two make enough noise to wake the whole forest including the Snow Monster," said Tika

Starvros slumped down into the snow, pulling Moira down with him. His mouth gaped open and his eyes blinked, not a sound came from his mouth.

Moira, looking from him to Tika, struggled to her feet. She always felt inadequate around Tika, but she was surprised at Starvros' reaction.

Starvros get up out of the snow and close your mouth," Moira said sternly.

Someone had to keep his or her head. It was obvious Starvros had lost his to Tika. Moira was used to the way Tika affected the young men in the village, She wished someone would look at her that way. It made her feel strange that Tika could make Starvros act like all the other boys. She always felt Starvros was hers. They had always been friends. When no one else was there for them, they always had each other. Now things had changed with Tika's coming,' thought Moira.

"Let's go to the lean-to and talk about all this. None of us is going to get any more sleep tonight and Starvros is freezing." Moira said dryly.

"Aye, it seems Moira and I had the same idea,' said Tika eyeing the taller girl warily.

Back in the lean-to, Starvros cuddled in blankets to his chin while the two intruders settled themselves the best way they could in the small structure.

No one spoke until Starvros warm under his blankets, asked, "Why are you here?"

Both girls turned and looked at each other.

Moira spoke first. "I came to help you on your quest"' she said.

"So did I," said Tika.

"Tell me the real reason you are here or I will, No! I am going to send you both down the mountain when morning comes," Starvros said.

Tika protested emphatically saying, "You can't do that Starvros, and if you do I will only follow you from a distance. You cannot make me go down the mountain, and my reasons for being here are my own. You are not the only one who does not like what is happening in the village. That Snow Monster is affecting people in other ways than poverty and starvation. There is something more valuable being lost, - our humanity, Starvros is gone. We have stopped caring for each other. Another person's well being does not matter as we fight over food. You should understand better than anyone Starvros I believe that the reason the villagers did not help you after your parents died is because no one wanted more responsibility- another mouth to feed, so they left you to fend for yourself. Well, I am not going to allow you to handle my life in such a cold-hearted manner. Therefore, whether you take me with you or not, I am not going back to Circle Valley. I will keep searching until I find a pass out of this terrible mountain, this terrible valley. Tika breathed hard and ragged, close to tears.

"I agree with all that Tika has said. I too, have my reasons for leaving Circle Valley. Your quest was the best way I could find to free myself from my situation. My reasons are none of your business, Starvros. You know this, and you need me. I am more experienced at hunting and tracking than you are. I can climb better than you can and, Tika, since you are here, you had better be able to keep up. Your beauty will get you nowhere. Out here you need skills," Moira chimed in.

"I have not roamed the woods all my life knowing nothing," Tika shot back.

"Let us try to sleep," Starvros said. Wondering how he would keep the peace between Tika and Moira.

Moira and Tika took the hint and found places in the tiny lean-to for the rest of the night. Everyone was soon asleep from an exhausting day and no one saw the third shadow hovering around the campsite. The shadow moved away up the mountain.

Much later in the day, Starvros roused himself from troubled sleep. His dreams bothered him on awakening. A sense of foreboding hung around him like the fog surrounding the peak of the mountain, above them. Starvros left the shelter and moved to the campfire. It had burned low. Starvros realized this could be dangerous. When they were higher up the mountain, keeping a fire going all night was very important to their safety. He did not know if any larger animals roamed the same forests as the Snow Monster. He had more to think about, now. Already the character of the quest had begun to change.

"What is it now?" Starvros frowned as he heard footsteps. Moira entered the clearing. "Where have you been, Moira? I did not know you were awake. It is not safe for you to leave the camp alone." Starvros said, concern for her safety making his voice sound harsh to his own ears.

"You finally woke up, said Moira. Oh, do not start with me, Starvros I can take care of myself. You did not ask me to join you on your quest. I came on my own and I can leave when I am ready. The princess is still asleep I gather. She's going to have to carry her load, Starvros." Moira said peevishly.

"Please, Moira don't worry. I will help Tika. She is not like you," Starvros retorted.

"What do you mean by that, Starvros? She is not like me," said Moira.

"Hey, you two stop talking about me as if I am not here," Tika said, crawling from the lean-to.

"I can carry my own weight. I do not need your help. Why do you insist on seeing me as a helpless person, Moira? Just because I have good looks does not mean I am helpless. That has been the problem my whole life. People treat me like I will break. Do not underestimate me. Let us go looking for that Snow Monster. You will find there is more to Tika than you both know." She said flippantly.

No one spoke, as the trio broke camp for the next leg of their journey. Moira and Tika showed Starvros the extra food they brought and he was happy and shared that he had buried marked provisions along the trail. Starvros asked the girls to wait in the camp until he searched the area for a new trail up the mountain.

The sun came over the rim of the mountain nudging life awake. Starvros heard the noisy birds as they flew from tree to tree. He recognized jays and finches, large blackbirds his mom used to make into pies, pheasants and a falcon circling high overhead. The dank smell of vegetation rose with the heat of the sun, the snow glistened like millions of minute mirrors, reflecting the light. The tall trees could not keep the bright light from radiating through the clearing he had chosen for a campsite. Starvros shaded his eyes as he looked for a break in the forest that would signal a trail. He knew that eventually he would have to make his own trails, for no one had been to this side of the mountains in a long while. He left Moira and Tika to finish packing their gear and circled the perimeter of the camp looking for an opening leading up the mountain. Starvros soon returned to the campsite with news that he had found a trail.

They gathered their gear and renewed their journey each thinking their own thoughts, and limiting conversation to directions about the terrain, as they slowly ascended the mountain.

Starvros walked ahead of the girls using a staff to test the depth of the snow and to check for crevices or chasms that might lay hidden under the deep snow.

"We need one of those, Starvros," Moira shouted to make herself heard.

"I know, we will find them at our next campsite," Starvros shouted back.

The little group walked steadily throughout the day. After locating and setting up their next campsite they ate silently, went to their beds in a large clearing next to a clear stream and fell asleep, after Starvros located and cut walking sticks for both Moira and Tika.

Morning brought them to their second day in the mountains.

When we get higher up the mountain the air will be thinner and it will be harder to breathe, and we will have to pace ourselves and rest more or we will tire ourselves out. Be sure to take short quick breaths to conserve your strength, Moira continued.

"What makes you such an expert," Tika challenged.

"You don't have to listen to me, Tika. However, when you fall out from the lack of air, I will not lift a finger to carry you one step!" Moira said firmly and walked away.

"We will need each other as this journey becomes more difficult. They were right when they said the Snow Monster was elusive. I have found no tracks this far up the mountain that could belong to the Snow Monster. He has to seek food other than the villagers' provisions," said Starvros, to divert another argument between Moira and Tika.

"You may have to look for different signs of his movement. Remember the villagers said it leaves no tracks when it comes for the food offering," said Tika.

"You are right, I forgot that detail," Starvros said excitedly.

He paced around the clearing talking more to himself than to Moira and Tika.

"I have to look for things such as bent twigs and new leaves broken from bushes and trees. I have to notice disturbances in low-lying vegetation and the snow. The snow will shift in his presence' My father taught me this, he said, as he glanced from Tika to Moira, his eyes glowing.

Starvros could almost hear his father's voice as they sat before the fire in the evening telling him how to track animals and then demonstrating the techniques on the few hunting trips with his father. It was only the two of them and his father taught him the age-old hunting secrets of Circle Valley. He had forgotten, for he surely did not use those techniques to trap the field mice he hunted and the small birds he caught daily for his meal but now Starvros realized his Father had prepared him for this journey. So far, he instinctively used the training his Father had drilled into him on their forages into the forest to hunt for food. Starvros also knew he had fallen into feeling sorry for himself after losing both of his parents. His anger stemmed from their untimely end and his inability to accept their deaths. He blamed the villagers because they did not help him. Starvros was finding out he had to help himself. Starvros was responsible for the quality of his life; how well he lived or how bad he lived was his sole responsibility. The villagers still had their part to do but that was not his responsibility. Starvros knew that the success or failure of the quest he had undertaken was his responsibility, regardless of Tika or Moira.

"Come on girls let's break camp and begin this journey for real," Starvros, said, excitedly. A new confidence flowed in his voice.

"Now that I know what to look for, this Monster is no longer so elusive!" Starvros stated.

Starvros wait! We do have to eat something before we rush off looking for the Snow Monster," Moira said laughing at his enthusiasm.

"Oh yeah, well don't stand there gawking at me, start cooking. I am hungry", Starvros said, rubbing his hands together.

"Okay, but you stoke the fire Starvros, while Moira and I prepare the food," said Tika

Soon they were eating heartily. Completing breakfast, they broke camp carefully dousing the fire with snow. They moved rapidly through the rest of the day moving higher up the mountain. Starvros moved quickly, certain in his newfound confidence that they would not see many signs of the Snow Monster until they were higher up the mountain.

Tika pulled at Starvros' coattail. "Stop Starvros, I have to rest. We have been traveling for hours now and. I am tired."

Starvros turned in his tracks and took the scarf away from his mouth.

"We have to keep going. We need to cover more ground. I would like to travel beyond that out cropping of rock just ahead of us in about two or three more hours," Starvros said impatient at Tika for wanting to stop.

'Three more hours! No, Starvros. I want to stop now," whined Tika.

Moira looked back to see the couple stopped in their tracks. She groaned.

"What is wrong with them? Did they know we have to keep moving? There is a storm on the way by the look of those lowering, dark purple clouds closing in on the top of the mountain." Moira said with frustration. She walked back to Starvros and Tika in time to hear her whining about needing to rest.

"I told you she would not carry her load," Moira said. "'We need to keep moving"

There is a storm on the way.'"

Both Tika and Starvros turned to Moira.

"How do you know there is a storm on the way? said Tika sarcastically.

Moira pointed to the distant skyline, but it was not so distant it was almost closing in on them.

"We have got to hurry and find shelter," said Moira. "That storm is moving faster than I thought.

"Oh my! said Tika. I guess I messed up again. We could have been half way to the rock outcropping by now instead of arguing about how tired I was."

"Tired or not Tika we have to make it to those rocks. so let's get moving, now!" shouted Starvros.

The trio began moving toward the outcropping of rocks Starvros had pointed out to Tika earlier. The snow began to fall before they traveled halfway to their destination.

Moira suggested they tie ropes to each other so they would not lose each other in the storm and they continued to trudge toward the rocks no longer visible in the storm. They only knew to continue upward and slightly eastward.

Along with the storm came raging winds and extreme cold. The sharp scent of the fresh falling snow stung Starvros' nostrils as he took a deep breath. The trio moved slower, the snow weighed them down and the winds beat them back.

Starvros felt a tug on the rope and stopped to give the girls a chance to draw up beside him. Tika looked like a beautiful snow maiden covered completely in snow, Moira stood beside her panting heavily. Shouting to be heard over the blowing wind, Moira said,"

Starvros we have made very little progress in this storm. If we do not find some kind of shelter we will freeze to death out here in the open."

"Look around and see if you can find any rocks or trees grouped together where we can shelter from the remainder of the storm. From the way those clouds are sitting on the peak of the mountain it is going to be an all-nighter. I will stand here and hold onto the ropes we have tied to each other, you two fan out in opposite directions and see if you can locate a place we can hold up in during the storm. With us still attached to the ropes no one can wander off and get lost in the storm. When you make your way back to me, just follow the ropes back by looping and tugging on the rope. I will tug back to let you know to keep coming until you make it back to me and then we will decide what else to do based on your findings. Is everybody clear? You know what to do Tika? Starvros asked.

Yes, Starvros I know what I am doing and I am not tired now! Tika said as she started to move away from Starvros. I will go this way, Moira.

Aye Tika, I will go this way, be careful and use your staff, Moira said as she started in the opposite direction fanning away from Starvros as he planted his feet in a wide stance in the deepening snow.

Later, they returned to find Starvros nearly buried in snow. Both were cold and near tears, but realized if they cried the tears would freeze on their face. They dug Starvros out of the snow saying they had found nothing. They stood on a flat plateau. Starvros frowned thinking hard. Starvros stared at the deepening snow and yelled for Tika and Moira to start digging. We will bury ourselves under the snow. We will make snow structures like we did when we were children," Starvros stated.

"We are still children! Tika murmured. I do not know how we got out her in a storm playing in the snow like children, but this is not fun! This is terrifying! We could die out here!"

"Stop mumbling and dig Tika, Moira said to her harshly. This is not the time to panic! Dig girl, dig for your life depends on it!"

"When you have dug enough snow to cover yourself, take out your bedding and cover yourself completely. Use your staff as a pole in the center so that we will be able to find each other after the storm is over, commanded Starvros. Try to get as close to each other as possible."

"Starvros shouldn't we bury ourselves together so that our body heat can keep us warm?" asked Moira.

"Good idea, Moira," Starvros answered.

"We can also use all our bedding to cover us which will give us more insulation against the freezing wind," said Tika.

"I like that idea too, Tika." we will use our three staffs together to create a breathing hole and as a tool to help us get out when the storm is over," Starvros said breathing hard from his exertions,

Soon they had dug their snow structure. They each laid their packs on the snow and piled some of the bedding on top of them. They spread the rest of the bedding over them and used their staffs to lift some of the bedding into a tent like structure. They pushed the staffs into the deep snow until they could go no further. They piled snow around them to hold them steady and to keep the bedding elevated as high as they could. They knew that eventually the weight of the snow would collapse everything. They spread the rest of the sleeping gear on top of themselves tucking as much of it as they could around their boots having dusted much of the snow from their clothing as possible. They helped each other to cover up and settled in their igloo-like structure made of blankets and snow to wait out the storm.

Starvros passed around bread and cheese and they ate fresh snow for fluids. Weary from the trek in the storm, they soon slept.

Starvros woke hours later, stiff from the cold seeping through his parka. He looked around trying to adjust to the darkness. He pulled his fur mittens from his hands and felt in the darkness for Moira and Tika.

"Starvros get your cold hands off me, said Tika. I'm awake!"

I am awake, too," said Moira, "Do not put your cold hands on me, I am already freezing".

"I was checking to see if everyone was all right. Someone needs to check and see

If the storm is over," said Starvros.

"You check it," both girls said together.

Starvros began to move his staff around and around inside the igloo like structure.

"What are you doing?" Moira screamed as snow fell in upon them."

"I'm trying to open a hole to see how deeply we are buried in the snow and an escape hole, be quiet and let me do this." Starvros said, continuing his activity with the staffs, while the hole grew wider and wider.

"By using our bedding over the staff it molds the snow smooth so it does not cave in on us, "he told Moira and Tika while manipulating the staff.

As soon as the hole was wide enough for someone to climb out, Starvros removed the staff and blankets. The snow was smooth and solid and it was large enough for someone to wriggle through.

"I will help one of you girls to scramble out to the surface. As soon as you check the deepness of the snow the two of you can dig me out, and we can pack our gear and get on the trail again.

"Whoa, Starvros! We don't know if its morning or night," said Tika.

"I said, check the snow depth and dig me out. We will decide what we will do next," Starvros said, frustrated by having to repeat himself to the girls.

"Aye, Aye, Master grumpy," Tika said.

Starvros hoisted Moira and Tika through the hole in the igloo-like structure with much effort. Many grunts and exclamations later, both girls stood in the deep snow looking at the structure that housed them during the winter storm.

Tika leaned toward the hole to speak to Starvros as a tool whizzed through the hole, then another, missed her face and landed at her feet, and she heard the muffled voice of Starvros say,

"Start digging!"

Moira and Tika picked up the tools and began digging Starvros out of the makeshift structure. Starvros looked around surveying the area. The snow covered the ground with a deep layer, in the early morning light, which obliterated the trail they made the day before. Everything looked bright and new the frozen tundra sparkled in the sun light. The clouds that brought the storm had moved on. Today was a new day and Starvros was glad to be alive.

Upward and eastward is the way we shall go as we travel up the mountain, Starvros said to the girls.

"Not before we dig our supplies out and eat something," Moira said. You are always so gung ho about things but you do not take care of the details, Starvros. It is the small things that lead to bigger things in life, you know. She was a little miffed with his earlier frustration at them.

Starvros ignored the statement and began digging out the rest of their supplies. Moira and Tika helped and in no time, they were eating the meal Moira and Tika set before them.

Having repacked their gear, Starvros pointed toward the outcropping of rocks they were heading toward when the storm waylaid them.

"Let's get moving we have a lot of ground to cover before this day is over. We have to recover the ground we lost to the storm and move even higher up the mountain before nightfall. I hope you got some rest because we will make very few stops during this leg of our journey. Make sure you took care of your personal needs before we get started for those are the only stops we will make," Starvros said as he handed each girl a hunk of the suet his Father made. Eat this along the trail it will ease your hunger and take handfuls of snow for water."

Ewe! What is this stuff, Starvros? I know you do not expect me to eat this!" Tika asked

"Oh, just eat it and shut up, Tika," Moira said. Must you always make mountains out of molehills?"

"I do not know what you mean by that, Moira. I was just saying I do not know what this stuff is. What is in it Starvros?" Tika asked again.

I thought you were a mountain girl Tika, everyone in Circle Valley knows about this suet. The men always take it on long hunting trips. It is not so bad when you get used to it Moira explained.

"You still did not answer my question. What is in it?" Tika asked slowly as if she was talking to morons.

Starvros ran his finger through his hair, his face ruddy in the cold mountain air.

"We do not have time to bicker with you about what is in the suet, Tika. Eat it or not it's' up to you, but you will be left here in the mountains if you stop to eat something else. As I said before, we have a long way to go. We will start now! End of discussion! Starvros said, as he purposely moved toward the rocky outcropping sighted earlier, poking the ground with his staff to find solid ground. Moira fell in behind him and Tika followed. By tying them to each other, Starvros felt it would be a better way to keep track of one another and they could communicate by tugging on the rope to get one another's attention.

Meanwhile, down below in the village, trouble was brewing for Starvros. The disappearance of Tika and Moira was causing quite a stir. All the eligible men came to the lodge in response to the blowing of the horn of danger. Its' use startled the men and they dropped everything they were doing. The women came also, carrying babies and dragging reluctant children behind them.

Mayor Brown stood in the front of the lodge along with the Shaman. Dirk was the last to saunter in. Mayor Brown frowned at his unconcern. People milled about asking one another if they knew why the horn of danger sounded.

"Ahem, ahem, ahem. People of Circle Valley, you have been summoned here for some very grave news. Two young girls in the village have disappeared," said Mayor Brown.

Men's mouths gaped and women gasped as they clutched their children tighter to their sides as Mayor Brown's word rippled through the room. Dirk raised a heavy brow watching the Mayor and the Shaman.

Dirk exploded, enraged, "Not Tika, Mayor!" he thundered loudly.

"Yes, Tika and Moira have disappeared from the village," said the Shaman

The villagers whispered in groups.

"The reason you were summoned is because we are trying to pinpoint the last time they were seen by anyone. We need a timeline to figure out how long they have been gone," said the Shaman.

"It is your own fault," said Bobbo. "You let those girls run wild through those woods with the Snow Monster loose in those woods, too."

There were many assents to Bobbo's' words

"Aye, Aye, That's right. You tell em Bobbo!"

Mayor Brown pulled at his hair, shuffled his feet and bit at his thick lips.

"Please this is not the time to place blame. You see, they may have left with someone they know," the Mayor spoke.

"Spit out the whole story Mayor Brown, We do not have time for bits and pieces, if Tika is missing; I want to start looking for her as soon as we can get everything together. Now, tell us the rest of it," said Dirk his tone firm.

"W-We believe they left with Starvros on his silly quest to find the Snow Monster," the Mayor said in a rushed tone.

"Starvros! The orphan boy?" said all the men at once.

"Starvros? Why would they leave the village with that little orphan boy? I knew he was trouble when he came to the meeting, meddling in grown men's business.

He has gone too far. I will find him and Tika and I will kill him. He will be an orphan no more. He will be dead!" Dirk spat out.

"Dirk, we have to be rational and keep our heads. We will not hear of killing anyone," said the Shaman. Let us form a search party, go after them and bring them back to the village where it is safe. We do not know when they left the Village and we do not know how far they are up in the mountains," the Shaman continued.

"I saw Moira in the woods three days ago. She had a big sack with her. There she goes roaming those woods with that Snow Monster lurking about. Mayor, you ought to be ashamed of yourself. I've said my piece, now I'll hush, and let you men get on with it," said Bobbo's wife, Marta.

The Mayor looked uncomfortable, but managed to continue the meeting.

"We'll all meet at the lodge in an hour when you men are geared up," said the Mayor.

Wait a minute," said Grunda, the wife of Jorge the ex-horse handler. "You men can't leave us women and children here by ourselves with that Snow Monster! How will we prepare the nightly offering while you men are gone? Some of you will have to remain with us," Grunda said brusquely.

"'We won't squabble about who goes or stays. All those who want to go, meet back here soon," said the Mayor, cursing the Snow Monster for having to consider it before their families.

The men were ready within the hour and set off at dusk, just before the offering to the Snow Monster. A good-sized party of ten men assembled to find three people.

Starvros and the girls had a three-day lead on them. The men were loaded with gear and food supplies; they brought torches soaked in animal fat-and cloth. Many had hunting gear they had not used in months. There may be game for hunting higher in the mountains. A sense of excitement gripped the men as they trampled the snow beneath their feet and approached Mount RaNinjitsi disappearing into the forests at its base much as Starvros did three days before them.

'It seems the boy involved them in his quest for the Snow Monster,' thought Dirk as he searched the trails for signs of the trio's venture up into the mountain.

Mayor Brown had asked the Shaman to remain at home. He did not want the Shaman's conscience to smite him. He did not want him to tell the whole story of the girl's disappearance. He did not know the full story himself, but he did know that he had gone to Starvros' cabin to apologize to him and found the cabin cold, empty and most of Starvros' belongings gone. He had not bothered to look in on Tika. He assumed she was avoiding him because of the argument they had about her marrying Dirk. When the Shaman came to tell him about Moira's disappearance, he looked for Tika. Her room was missing many items and she had vanished. He panicked and went to the lodge to blow the horn of danger. How a mere slip of a boy could upset their world by asking one simple question about the Snow Monster caused the Mayor to fume. He was almost in agreement with Dirk to kill the boy.

The men traveled far their first evening out but waylaid by the same storm that Starvros and the girls encountered. Howbeit, in the forest the men had more protection and less snow. Dirk fussed about nature's onslaught and he worried because he knew the storm was much worse higher in the mountain, and with a three-day head start, the trio, was well up the mountain. Everyone in the rescue party had room to make their own shelter from the storm. Dirk assigned Gustavo to Mayor Brown. He wished the Mayor had stayed behind in the village. He felt he would be more of a hindrance than a help to the rescue efforts, But, he was the Mayor of Circle Valley.

The next morning, Dirk crawled from his lean to and breathed deeply of the fresh mountain air. It smelled so good you could taste the tangy pine scented aroma permeating the forest after the storm. He felt as he did when they went on hunting parties, blood flowed quicker through his veins as his pulse raced in anticipation. They would not catch them this soon, but they were on their trail.

"I will find them soon. The snow has delayed them, too. I will teach Starvros not to take what is mine. What belongs to Dirk belongs to Dirk," he muttered to himself.

Dirk yelled loudly to wake the other villagers.

"Arise, people, we must find their trail before they reach the rocks higher up above us or we will lose them altogether. They are still a good distance ahead of us. We have to make up that distance and move faster and harder than they can so that we can overtake them and return them to Circle Valley. The storm has delayed them as well as us. So let us get busy! Get your gear packed, that means everyone," Dirk continued, noting that the Mayor was not up, yet.

Mayor brown crawled from his lean-to as Dirk concluded his speech. Shaking himself awake with a day's stubble on his face his thoughts turned to Tika. 'Why would you leave the comfort of your home to come out in this?' he wondered. Mayor Brown was not comfortable. He was not a hunter. He never went on the hunting parties with the rest of the men. The villagers always gave him a portion of whatever they hunted. He was glad he was the mayor of Circle Valley. However, this time it was different. It was Tika, and she was family.

Mayor Brown struggled to his feet and approached Dirk. "You think you will catch up to them soon, Dirk? he asked.

"No, they have journeyed several days, which puts them a great deal ahead of us. They are up in the mountain and there are many ways to go. We have to rely on human evidence to find them. Because of the storms, any trails will be lost," Dirk said.

"What do you mean by human evidence, Dirk?" asked Mayor Brown.

"I mean we will have to look for physical evidence of their campsite, broken twigs and branches, evidence of meals eaten, and lastly we will be searching for clues that they went into the woods to take a dump, or pieces of clothing left behind or dropped on the trail." Dirk stated as if he were schooling an ignorant child.

"O, I see what you mean. Well, why don't we eat and be on our way," the Mayor said.

"Mayor Brown, we will have to travel double time to catch them. We will have to push the men to rise earlier and travel later to make up the distance. Everyone will have to do their part. I have assigned Gustavo to help you but he is not to carry your weight. Do you understand?" said Dirk quietly.

"Aye, Dirk I understand perfectly. I will pull my own weight. Thank you for Gustavo. I will not be a bother to him or hinder this rescue attempt. I want Tika and Moira back as much as you do. Everything sounds good to me. Do you think the men will do this?" asked Mayor Brown.

"Leave the men to me, Mayor Brown," said Dirk.

Dirk talked to the men and by mid-morning, they were back on the trail, moving in a running-pattern typical of their hunting days. The men, exuberant, began to chant as they moved rapidly through the snow.

"Time to give chase, no time to waste. Must stay the pace or lose face.

"No dogs or horses yet stay the course. We'll overtake our prey this very day."

By nightfall, the group of men reached the plateau and made camp. They were happy they had traveled so far and sat around the campfire at the edge of the plateau singing and telling old hunting stories.

Mayor Brown sat in front of his lean-to. Exhausted he knew he would retire earlier than the others would. Mayor Brown knew he did not have the stamina to lead these men. If it was not for Dirk, he knew they would not travel this far without anarchy among the men. He had a newfound respect for Dirk's skills and he knew he was right in suggesting Tika marry him. He would take good care of her. Mayor Brown said good night to the men, crawled into his lean-to and was soon asleep.

Dirk watched the tired man retreat and frowned.

"I wonder if Mayor Brown will be able to keep the pace they had set to overtake Starvros and the girls. I do not want to leave Tika in the presence of another man for too long, especially Starvros Gunther. I will keep an eye on the Mayor," "We might have to leave the Mayor behind on the plateau and go on without him," Dirk thought.

CHAPTER 4

MORE TROUBLE FOR STARVROS

Starvros and the girls, reached a new destination by nightfall Making camp became a solemn occasion as the group fell into their beds and soon slept. Morning came all too quickly as Moira, an early riser, woke the others for breakfast.

"Rise, you two sleepy heads we have much ground to cover today," she said. I have

already started a fire for a hot breakfast. I'm tired of bread and cheese!" she said laughing as Tika and Starvros crawled from their shelters rubbing sleep from their eyes.

They quickly made breakfast, ate their meal and packed their gear for the days'

journey. Starvros looked around at their surroundings. They were in a stony area of the mountain. We will find a plateau at each level of the mountain. We will try to reach a level each day from here onward," said Starvros The mountain will get more rugged as we climb higher."

"You have led us well so far," said Tika- "Lead on!"

"Yes," said Moira but, when will we see evidence of the elusive Snow Monster?

Remember he is the reason we are traipsing around this mountain in this cold and snow." Moira continued.

"I surmise we will see more evidence of his presence as we near the peak and we will be nearer the peak in a couple more days' journey. Let us start moving, we have a lot of ground to travel. It will be rugged from now on because we will be climbing

Straight up the mountain face," Starvros warned.

"Moira since this is your area of knowledge, you should take over the lead and tell us what we must do from here on." Starvros replied.

Moira dropped her pack to the ground and removed climbing gear from her pack.

"We will tie ropes around our waists as we did in the storm, Moira stated. Each of us must have an axe. "Tika did you bring an axe?" Moira asked.

"Aye, I did," Tika said.

"Aye, good. You will use the axe to hack out places to put your hands and feet. Your hands are to pull yourself up the mountain and your feet are to push yourself up the mountain, so hack out a good place to put your hands and feet so you do not slip and fall off the mountain, pulling the rest of us with you. If you need to rest tug on the rope hack a place to wrap your rope around until you are ready to continue your ascent, by tugging on the rope again. When one of us wants to rest, we will all rest. Everybody clear, and Tika that does not mean you stop to rest every five minutes." Moira averred, pointedly looking at Tika.

Tika sputtered, "Why are you looking at me? I can climb a mountain better than you can!"

They continued to make preparations and began to ascend the mountain as Moira instructed them.

Starvros stopped them suddenly. "Do you realize we have not heard the growls of the Snow Monster since we have been in the mountains?" he said, puzzled.

"Are you sure? What does it mean?" Tika said her eyes huge in her face.

"It means the Snow Monster knows we are in his mountain," said Moira,

"That's exactly what it means, I have a feeling we will confront this monster soon. Let us move on. We are not going to see him climbing the face of the mountain. I want to get off this rock face by nightfall," said Starvros.

They continued the journey concentrating on where and how they were climbing up the mountain, pausing only to give instructions. They reached a flat place as the sun set and Starvros decided they could make camp there for the night. Sitting in the camp, they could look out over the ground they had covered. Starvros saw the forests, white with snow from the storm earlier in the week. Starvros stood and peered over the edge.

"Moira, Tika, come here!" he yelled.

"What is it Starvros?" they said. "You scared us!"

"Look," he said pointing toward the distant skyline below them. "Is that a campfire?"

"A campfire?" asked Tika.

Her heart sank. She backed away from the edge her face pale, her mouth agape; she grabbed her head with both hands and moaned.

Moira also reacted in the same manner. Starvros looked from one to the other

"What is going on? You both know who is down there, don't you?" he asked them gruffly.

"It might be the villagers coming to find us," said Moira quietly.

"Who else can it be? I do not need this. I know I should have sent you both back to Circle Valley and went on this quest alone!" shouted Starvros.

You should have sent us back to Circle Valley!" "You can't send anyone anywhere, Starvros Gunther! I go where I please! You need help! Who would have dug you out of the storm? Who got us this far up the mountain? You cannot do this alone! Let me help you, Starvros? They will not catch us now that we know they are coming! We can out pace them and stay ahead of them." Moira sputtered.

"What about you, Tika?" Starvros asked turning from Moira to her.

"I don't want to go back," she shuddered as she thought about Dirk being among the villagers below.

Starvros thought a while and said to the girls.

"We will break camp and continue moving throughout the night and find shelter by morning, sleep for a few hours and resume our journey. Does that sound like a plan?" Starvros asked the girls, his anger subsiding.

They broke camp, put out their campfire and continued their journey up the face of the mountain throughout the night. By morning, they were exhausted and Starvros asked them to look for shelter where they could sleep. They had reached another flat place on the mountain. This place was wider than the last place and had trees, grass and bushes.

They unshackled themselves from the climbing gear, dropped their packs and searched the cliff side for shelter. Moira soon called out that she found a cave. Starvros and Tika joined her and they searched the cave thoroughly with Starvros going in first brandishing his axe to make sure no wild animals inhabited the cave.

"We will sleep here for the rest of the morning. The first person to awake will awaken the others and we will keep moving. We'll eat on the run." Starvros said.

The cave, wide enough for the three of them, a crevice in the face of the mountain, well hidden from view, seemed an ideal campsite for the day. The interior, dark enough for them to sleep enveloped the tired trekkers with its' dank, musky smell. Starvros said the smell would soon evaporate with a roaring fire. Near the entrance, barely visible from the landing, Starvros saw moss covered steps leading up the mountain wall.

"A stair way to heaven," thought Starvros.

"Look at those steps Moira, they look as if someone or something carved steps up the face of the mountain!" Starvros exclaimed.

"Yes it does," she said, eyes wide.

They both shook their heads.

"Nah, the Snow Monster couldn't have carved those steps. Maybe people who lived in these mountains long ago carved the steps as a route up to the peak. We will explore them later. I am too exhausted to do anything but sleep," said Starvros.

"Me too," said Moira.

"The cave is free from wild animals. We will sleep a couple of hours and resume our pace to stay ahead of the villagers. I am sure they have found our last campsite," continued Starvros.

"I'll bet they were plenty upset to find us gone, said Tika with a laugh as she exited the cave. Everything is set up for sleeping. What were you two doing out here all this time besides avoiding work?" Tika continued.

"Nothing really, I'm tired and ready for bed," said Moira, impatiently as she brushed past Tika into the cave.

"What's the matter with her!" said Tika.

Let us just go to bed, Tika. We are all tired from the pace we have set to keep away from Dirk and the villagers." said Starvros.

"Good idea," Tika said.

"We won't cook because the smell of cooking food will surely tell our location to anyone in any direction" Starvros stated.

Inside the cave, Moira had set out dried turkey meat, bread, cheese and melted snow to drink. They ate in silent musings and climbed into their bedding to sleep.

As they slept, another storm raged on the mountain. Snow fell in large flakes. The clouds settled close on the mountain and erased the entrance to the cave, as snow fell steadily. By mid-morning, the area blanketed in fresh fallen snow and ice almost blocked the entrance to the cave.

Starvros shivered under his blankets and woke with a start. The fire had burned low he surmised, when fully awake. He rose to his feet.

"I must get wood to replenish the fire," he said.

Suddenly growls and snarls rent the caves' quiet, which sent Moira and Tika scurrying from their beds into a comer of the cave screaming and moaning.

Starvros stayed rooted to the spot as he stood listening intently trying to locate the direction of the Snow Monster. He held his hand up to silence the girl's screams and moans. The snarls echoed around the cave as if the Snow Monster occupied the same space as they did and soon they died away in the distance above them.

He must have been standing right above the cave, Starvros said.

You could have fooled me, said Tika her voice trembling, I thought he had entered the cave with us. I feel very frail at this time. I wonder what I could do to a Monster like that. I must have been crazy to think I could kill a monster that sounds like that. What am I doing out here in these mountains chasing that monster. The reality is very different from planning all of this in my bedroom. Tika began to breathe quickly and the color drained from her face.

"I-I f-feel faint." she whimpered.

"She's going to have hysterics, Starvros. Grab her before she faints or tries to run from the cave!" said Moira.

Starvros leaped into action and grabbed Tika before she fainted.

Use the wet snow on her face," Moira shouted. "I will cover her with a blanket to keep her from going into shock."

Starvros half-carried Tika to the bedding she had so hastily left, and laid her upon it.

Moira covered her with her blankets, while Starvros ran to the cave's entrance for snow to mop her face. Tika came to, wailing, "I want to go home."

"No, we are not running away because we came close to the reason we are in these mountains. We only heard the Snow Monster and that is not so different from the way we have lived ours lives in these mountains since our youth," said Moira.

"You are silly Tika. Are you not the one who foraged in the woods near our home? You heard his snarls, and you did not faint! You did not run home to Mayor Brown, then! Why are you acting so foolish now! Starvros did not drag you on this quest. You came on your own, for your own reasons. This is not the time to cower and run!" Moira continued

"I agree with Moira, we came here to find the Snow Monster. He has let us know we are close to his lair and he is warning us away. We will not run away like frightened little children," said Starvros.

"'We are frightened little children," whispered Tika

''We are all afraid, Tika, but we cannot let the Snow Monster know we are afraid.

We must stalk him as our ancestors hunted and stalked animals in these mountains for perhaps thousands of years. We are the hunters of our generation moreover, we must prove to our ancestors that we are as brave as they were in their time.

I, for one believe our ancestors are watching us, cheering us on and helping us to keep the traditions of the past alive. I feel the hunter's spirit coursing through my blood. I am ready for this elusive monster. I did not come this far to turn and run at the first sign of my prey!" Starvros said passionately.

"Hooray!" said Moira. She felt happy for Starvros. Gone was the timid youth that started this quest. Before her stood, a man eager for a quest he first sought out of desperation. We will stay here. The condition of our bodies may have led to Tika's episode.

We will rest until this evening and then we will use the steps to reach the peak,"

said Starvros.

He felt embarrassed after his speech. He set about rearranging his blankets and busied himself refurbishing the fire.

"We will rest for several more hours and the first to wake will awaken the others.

We still need to stay ahead of the villagers," he said as he lay down close to the fire.

The girls followed suit and soon everyone slept soundly. Starvros woke first and saw the fire had burned low, again. What is it with these fires; they are always burning low, too quickly. I will get some wood to rebuild the fire before I wake the girls.

Starvros looked around the cave and saw only kindling wood for the fire.

I will have to go outside the cave for wood," he said

'We will have to gather more wood so we do not have to travel outside the camp to restore our wood supply,' Starvros thought. He turned to pick up his axe and when he turned around a presence stood in the cave's entrance. He could not see much because of the darkness in the cave. Starvros guessed the presence had waited until the fire burned low to enter the cave.

"Damn it! I will have to be more careful," Starvros grunted

Starvros thought the villagers had found them and he jumped backwards brandishing his axe. The presence moved forward a couple of steps and Starvros moved backwards a couple of steps prepared to throw his axe at the presence!

"Leave this Mountain. Leave now! Leave or forsake your lives," the presence said in a deep guttural voice.

"Who is it? Who are you? What do you want?" asked Starvros, the questions tumbling rapidly from his mouth.

"Leave now," said the presence, his voice rising to a pitch like the wind outside the cave.

"No, you cannot scare me. I will not leave this mountain," said Starvros.

"You have been warned!" the presence uttered.

Starvros took a couple of steps forward and the presence took a couple of steps backward toward the mouth of the cave. As it stood in the light of the entrance, Starvros could see it clearly.

Starvros gasped, his eyes widened, his mouth opened and the hairs on his body stood to full attention, his face paled and trembling from head to foot he stumbled backwards over Tika and Moira who woke screaming, jumping to their feet as the presence vanished through the open entrance. Moira could tell Starvros had seen something that sent him into shock.

"Oh, no, not again, she said. Starvros, what is it? What happened? What did you see?" "Cover him up Tika. He is in shock!" Moira ordered.

"I-I think I-I s-saw the S-Snow M-Monster!" said Starvros

"Where?" said Moira and Tika backing away from him and looking around the cave.

"H-He a-appeared in the e-entrance to the c-cave and w-warned us to l-leave n-now or f-forfeit our lives, Starvros said dazedly. H-He s-stood in the e-entrance so t-that I-I c-could see h-him c-clearly. H-He is as t-terrifying as his s-snarls' I-I was n-naive. I-I d-did n-not k-know. I am a mere slip of a boy c-compared to that c-creature. H-How did I-I t-think I-I could kill something so m-massive?" Starvros stuttered.

"Get a hold of yourself Starvros, you are stuttering like a silly child. Where are the words of that passionate speech you uttered before we went to sleep!" Moira said sternly.

"He must have seen something to scare him silly, Moira. Leave him alone," said Tika, pushing her away from Starvros.

"Oh, you would side with him when he is weak and scared, because you are as weak and scared as he is. All you have done since you came on this quest is whine, complain, and run away. Starvros needs us to encourage him to be strong, and you always do the opposite. You are not good enough for him, Tika. I hope he comes to realize how shallow you really are. He started this quest and we came along. None of us can turn back to live our lives as usual, without seeing this through to the end and that includes the villagers, too. We are different. This quest has made us different. We will have to finish what we started. The course has been set. If you are not going to help Starvros, then step aside. The Snow Monster knows we are in these mountains he knows the villagers are here, also," Moira said passionately.

"Maybe, we have turned the tides and this warning is to scare us off because the Snow Monster is afraid of us for a change. He has had things going his way for far too long," Moira ended her tirade.

"That is enough from you Moira," said Tika. I can take a hint, but warnings are a different matter. A warning means someone or something is going to do something to you if you don't get out!" Two warnings in one day mean a double threat." Tika shouted.

Tika leaped upon her gear and began shoving items into her pack, mumbling to herself.

"I am okay, Starvros," said finally finding his voice as Moira's words penetrated his dazed mind.

"Tika is very frightened, Starvros, if we don't watch her carefully she will wander off trying to find her way back to the village and get lost in these mountains or worse. Talk to her Starvros, try to calm her fears or she will endanger us all," said Moira.

"I will talk to her, in the meantime, pack our gear. We will leave this place as quickly as possible. Tika is right. We do have a double threat from the villagers closing in on us, and that presence which appeared here today. The Snow Monster

knows exactly where we are. Tika, calm yourself! We cannot turn back. We cannot go willy-nilly down the mountain. We must continue our quest. Moira is right in her assessment of the situation. I will protect you," said Starvros.

Tika sighed and turned from Starvros.

'Starvros will protect me. Ha! Who will protect you, Starvros? Moira? You were scared silly yourself. I wish Dirk were here, he would protect me.' Tika jumped at the direction her thoughts had taken, but she realized the truth.

'Dirk! brave, strong, brash, Dirk would protect her with his life!' Tika continued her packing to shut out Starvros' words as well as her thoughts.

Starvros sensed her withdrawal and assumed it to be from a deep fear within her and he regretted her coming along. He determined to watch her more carefully as they continued their journey.

Moira came to him. "Tell me what you saw Starvros?" she asked.

"Now that I can think, Moira I don't think it was a real monster, but an apparition. If it was real, it had a good chance to harm all of us. The apparition, sent to frighten us away almost accomplished its goal, if it were not for your no-nonsense words. Thanks to your encouragement, I am better. Thanks my friend!" Starvros said, grasping her shoulder and smiling broadly.

"Thank you Starvros! What are we going to do?" Moira asked

"Just as you so eloquently put it Moira, we will continue our journey up to the peak. We have no choice, despite the warnings. Let us eat something before we pack our gear and break camp as soon as possible. If we travel the rest of the evening until the morning, we will reach the peak before morning, well before our pursuers," Starvros continued.

They ate bread and cheese and drank goats' milk from their pouches in silence, afraid to give voice to the fear rising deep in their minds.

Soon they were exploring the steps, which led up the face of the mountain and came to another flat ledge. They did not stop to view the dusky sky from the setting sun heralding the approaching night, but continued on their way, exploring the mountain for steps, which made the going much easier. By nightfall, they reached the third level up the mountain. They had traveled quickly but saw on reaching the third level that it was a larger area than they realized. They made camp and Starvros assumed they could rest because they were farther ahead of their pursuers. They could see the peak more clearly from their campsite shrouded in thick black clouds.

"It seems as if the peak is always surrounded by angry looking clouds. I wonder if it indicates that storms besiege the peak. I know I have seen more storms and snow fall since coming on this quest, than I ever saw in Circle Valley," said Moira.

"That is due to the higher elevation, said Starvros. Snow higher up in the mountains barely reach the valley floor. That is why it is a good place for a village. The valley has rich fertile land and good streams, rivers fed by the melting snows and rivers high in the mountains. Circle Valley should have been a prosperous village, and it should have supplied every villager with what it needed and more to survive and even prosper, said Starvros. That is why it is so important to destroy the Snow Monster and the curse," he continued.

Moira continued to stare at the peak as the clouds shifted.

"Starvros look up there on the peak, I see a castle," Moira said, excitedly.

Starvros spun around in time to see an imposing large, gray, stone castle sitting precariously on the peak of the mountain.

"Terrible mountain, terrible peak, terrible castle," said Starvros aloud as the clouds once again closed off view of the castle.

"The Shaman mentioned something about a castle before your aunt threw me out of your house, Moira. I am still upset that he would not tell me everything I needed to know," Starvros stated.

"Oh Starvros, I believe you will find out everything you need to know on this quest." said Moira.

"I am sure you are right, Moira," Starvros answered. Let's get moving girls we have a quest to complete," Starvros said.

The trio continued on their journey traveling light and moving swiftly to put greater distance between them and the villagers pursuing them. Their travels took them around the face of the mountain rather than straight up the façade. Snow began to fall heavily as they moved around to the backside of the mountain. The snow swirled around them fiercely as the winds whipped them into small tornado-shaped wind tunnels that stung their faces and pierced through their clothing. Their movement slowed as they struggled against the wind with every footfall. They used their staffs with every move they made and had to hold on to them as the wind tried desperately to wrench them from their cold mittened hands.

The forests seemed denser on the backside and it was darker and gloomier because of its proximity to the other mountains that completed the circular range of mountains that ringed Circle Valley. Very little sun light penetrated through the thick canopy of trees and it was much colder with harsher terrain.

Tika drew up beside Starvros and spoke to him.

"Starvros I am sorry for the way I acted. I am frightened that we will not make it out of here alive." She stated softly.

"We are all afraid, Tika. This is something we have never encountered before. It is dangerous, I will admit and we do not know what dangers each day will present to us. Nevertheless, we have to be brave Tika, whatever comes our way we have to meet it with courage. I feel that is how we overcome anything that comes our way. So be brave Tika and we will make it out of this very much alive and well," Starvros said looking at her tenderly.

Moira approached them. "I see a clearing ahead you two, but do you hear that noise?

"What noise?" Tika and Starvros said together.

"Don't you hear a rumbling sound?" Moira stated.

No-o-o! Moira you must have keen hearing powers, because I do not hear anything above the wind," said Tika, annoyed that Moira had interrupted her conversation with Starvros.

Moira looked sharply at Tika, but only reiterated that she could hear a rumbling noise in the distance.

The trio stopped in a large clearing, and turned around while Moira tried to pinpoint the direction of the sound only she could hear. Moira was insistent that they not venture any farther into the clearing.

"Stay near the trees," she shouted at them.

"Why are you shouting Moira?" Starvros asked.

"Can't you hear the rumbling, Starvros? It is getting louder, Moira shouted.

Suddenly from the other side of the clearing, a dark cloud appeared on the horizon.

"What is that?" said Tika pointing toward the darkness coming toward them.

Starvros and Moira turned at her question and saw the cloud coming at them at a fast pace.

"Whatever it is, it will overtake us soon. It is too far away to see what it is. I do not suggest we stand here waiting for it to catch us out here." Starvros said.

"How good are you girls at climbing trees?" Starvros continued.

"Climbing trees!" Moira and Tika said together.

"Yes! Climbing trees. If we do not get to a higher place, whatever that cloud is, it will mow us down. I do not know if it is an avalanche or something else. At this point, the strange things that are happening in this mountain do not surprise me. It is obviously under an evil enchantment or under the same curse as Circle Valley. Move quickly girls find a thick sturdy tree and climb as high as you can. Find a branch where you can wedge yourself in so you will not shake loose or fall to the ground. The trio turned and headed for the trees while the malevolent cloud was still a good distance away. Starvros helped the girls find a tree, booted them into the tree and handed them their packs. Tie yourself and your pack to the place you wedge yourself in very well. I will be nearby as soon as I find a sturdy tree. Starvros found a tree near the girls and realized they were in a straight line facing the clearing. They could see the approaching cloud. Moira screamed, as she was the first who recognized what was coming their way. Tika screamed, also. "What are you screaming about?" Starvros shouted.

Moira shouted back, "Starvros it is a large herd of reindeer!" The largest herd I have ever seen!"

"Reindeer, how? Why are they here? What is going on? Starvros asked as his eyes adjusted and he recognized the herd of animals coming at them.

"It is a stampede," Moira said, loudly.

"They were sent to trample us to death and we are not out of danger, yet. Hold on for dear life. Those beasts can shake us out of these trees or trample the trees to the ground," Starvros said to the girls. Fear made his voice sound high and thin to his own ears.

The trio stared fearfully at the cloud as it grew nearer and the reindeer grew larger and fiercer as the fear of whatever drove them to stampede made them look hideous and terrible in intensity.

"They will be upon us soon girls, hold on!" Starvros shouted, over the rumbling sound that was now a roaring sound in their ears.

Tika whimpered, "I do not want to die, Starvros!"

"None of us want to die, Tika. Get a hold of yourself! Moira shouted, to the frightened girl. "Now is not the time to fall apart! You may have beauty Tika, but you have no common sense. How you face a situation determines the outcome. If you go through a situation crying and fearful, you will come out crying and fearful. If you face a situation with courage and fearlessness, you will come out with courage and fearlessness, Moira asserted.

"How do you have courage when you are so afraid," Tika wailed.

"Tika, courage is deep within all of us. It is in the moment, when we are facing something momentous that we pull the courage from within to help us. It is in you, Tika. Now, be brave and hold on, the herd is almost upon us." Starvros avowed.

Tika saw the visage of the massive herd coming at them. She held on to the branch she tied herself to and closed her eyes.

'If death was going to claim her today, she did not have to look at it,' she thought.

"Hold on, Moira," Starvros shouted as the herd stampeded into the forest.

The trees shook and swayed from the force of the massive herd. Starvros heard Tika's screams as trees bent and fell beneath their hooves. They thundered through the forest in a seemingly never-ending swarm of dreadful looking animals. Starvros could not take his eyes off them, but marveled at their brute strength. They were huge! One of those animals would have fed the village all winter! Starvros shuddered and his teeth clanked together as the herd pounded the tree he had latched himself onto. He had straddled a branch thicker than he was and wedged himself in tightly. He only hoped the girls were as safely wedged in their tree as he was. Snow sprayed him, kicked upon him by the hooves of the beasts. If it were not for the snow pelting him, Starvros felt this event was all a mirage, a figment of his imagination. It felt strange to him.

Starvros knew at this point that someone or something was trying to kill them. The apparition in the cave was a warning, like Tika said but this was an all out attempt to kill them. If it were not for Moira's keen sense of hearing, they would have died in these mountains. Starvros turned to watch the last of the herd plummet into the forest.

"Where are they going?" Starvros wondered aloud. It seemed like they would run right off the mountain into oblivion.

Starvros called out to Tika and Moira after the rumbling of the stampeding reindeer receded in the distance. "Tika, Moira, are you girls all right?"

"I am all right," Moira responded first.

Tika responded, "I am not all right!"

"Either way you are alive, the both of you. I suggest we stay in these trees the rest of the day and night or at least until we know there are no more dangerous animals headed our way or that the herd does not return and catch us out in the open." Starvros said

"I agree," stated Moira. I suggest we eat some of Starvros' suet or some dried meat from our supplies and drink some water from our pouches and stay here and get our bearings," she continued.

"That is a good suggestion, Moira. What do you think Tika," Starvros asked.

"You do not want to know what I am thinking, Starvros! said Tika her voice quivering. I will just remain silent and do whatever you and Moira suggest. I cannot put a voice to what I am feeling so just leave me alone," Tika averred.

The trio ate in silence, perched on their branches in the trees the rest of the day, each one thinking their own thoughts. No one broached the subject of the fearsome reindeer stampede. They watched the sunset as its rays filtered through the trees. Tiny prismatic particles of snow glistened around them as snow melted and fell to the forest floor in colors of red, green, yellow and orange. They rested and slept fitfully well into the night.

In the wee hours of the morning, Moira woke with a start. The reindeer were returning. She woke Starvros and Tika.

"Shush, the reindeer are returning, Moira spoke quietly.

Starvros turned to see a huge buck with great wide antlers leading the herd back the way they had come. Starvros sucked in his breath at the massive buck. He was beautiful and majestic. He trod softly and slowly through the snow. He was as wary as Starvros and the girls. Maybe the reindeer were not so sure what spooked them was not gone from the forest. He stood on the edge of the clearing. Starvros could hear the rest of the herd coming behind him. They filled the forest. Starvros had not seen so many reindeer at one time. They would feed the village for years to come!

Starvros did not understand. If there were so many reindeer this high in the mountains, why did the Snow Monster want their paltry offering of food every night? If he had so much, why did he want the little they supplied? It did not make sense. That is probably why it is called a curse, because it is nonsensical," Starvros continued, thinking to himself.

After a long pause, the lead buck bounded into the clearing followed by the others as they hurried over the frozen tundra toward their grazing place. It seemed to take forever for the huge herd to leave the forest and leap away into the distance.

Starvros gathered his things.

"Get down everyone, get down! We are going to follow the herd!" Starvros shouted.

"Follow the herd! Are you crazy? I am not following a herd of reindeer that just tried to kill me," Tika said emphatically.

"I do think that is asking a bit much of us, Starvros. I agree with Tika," Moira said dryly.

"Think about it girls! I can see the Snow Monster releasing those reindeer from huge pens to frighten us, again; and if he has them in pens, then his abode is nearby. This will lead us right to him, I am sure of it," Starvros said excitedly.

"Well, that part makes sense," said Moira.

"Oh, you will agree with anything Starvros says, I for one do not care who sent the reindeer. All I know is that I want to go in the opposite direction from it and the reindeer." I do not understand you and Moira. You both seem hell bent on killing your selves for this silly quest," Tika said.

"It was not so silly when you decided to follow Starvros up here Tika, what has changed your mind?" Moira said looking keenly at her.

"T-There is n-nothing like almost getting killed twice, that can change your mind in a hurry," Tika snapped back at Moira.

"Girls, girls let us not fight about this, we have to go somewhere and the herd gives us direction and proves there is something real here to find," Starvros said.

The herd has left plenty of tracks and we cannot get lost. We will follow them where they lead us. We will see what lies ahead and make any future decisions from there. How does that sound? You girls want to try it. We have to go somewhere from here. What do you say? Starvros appealed to them.

"Aye, you have spoken well Starvros. I will follow you and the herd.' Moira stated.

"What about you Tika?" Starvros asked.

"I said I would be silent and do what you and Moira want to do. I will be quiet and follow your lead. You did not ask me to come on this quest. I chose to follow you without your knowledge. You have saved my life more than once and I have been ungrateful. Forgive me. Let us get our things and follow the tracks in the snow." Tika said quietly.

Moira narrowed her eyes at her.

'What is she up to? I do not trust her agreeable attitude. I am going to watch this Missy very carefully.' Moira thought.

The trio gathered their supplies and started gingerly across the clearing. The going was easy because the many hooves of the reindeer in their coming and their going had packed the tundra down across the clearing. The trio walked in a line talking as if they were taking a Sunday stroll in the garden.

"Starvros, do you think we are in danger of the reindeer returning to trample us underfoot," said Tika.

"No Tika, I think that was for a specific purpose-to deter our quest for the Snow Monster. I can imagine him waving the animals out of a pen and starting the stampede to scare us, warn us or…

"Kill us!" Tika piped in.

"Well yes I believe that was the intention Tika," said Moira.

Tika mumbled inaudibly.

"What did you say Tika?" Moira asked. Her senses were tingling where Tika was concerned.

"I did not say anything Moira I was just trying to wrap my brain around the fact that I am out here hunting for someone or something that is trying to kill me," Tika said softly.

"M-M-M, and is that a bit of sarcasm I hear in your voice? Moira continued.

"Leave her alone, Moira. She has had a severe fright. She is not like you," Starvros said feeling very protective about Tika.

"What do you mean she is not like me? Starvros, Moira said, shrilly. She did not like the way he shielded and protected Tika. Starvros was her friend. She did not like Tika's intrusion in their friendship. Am I jealous, Moira asked? No way, No, I do not like her prissy ways and the way she gets men to do things for her. That is all. To admit to more would take her to a place she was not ready to admit. However, she was honest enough to realize she did not like the connection between Starvros and Tika.

"Leave it be, Moira," Starvros spoke sharply to her.

Moira fell silent at his rebuke and continued across the clearing.

It took all of the rest of the night and they were only mid way across the clearing.

"Girls stop. Let us tie a rope to each other in case we have more incidents. I would hate to be separated out here. I did not understand the nature of this mountain. It is much wider and more expansive that I even considered." Starvros said, as he tied ropes to himself as the lead, and then Moira, and then, Tika.

CHAPTER 5

MORE TROUBLE BREWING

The villagers reached Starvros' last campsite by nightfall. The air was cold and the men were visibly upset to find the trio gone. Dirk fussed and fumed around the campsite as he realized Starvros could not travel as fast with two young women unless they willingly traveled with him. Dirk looked at Mayor Brown with narrowed eyes.

'He was not telling them the whole story. He could not understand why both girls disappeared from the village. Moira's reasons were not his concern, but Tika's reasons for possibly running away from Circle Valley meant everything to him,' he thought.

Dirk sweated as his thoughts followed the unbidden course that set his heart pounding loudly in his chest. His head ached from thinking so much. Dirk jumped to his feet and went to find Mayor Brown.

Dirk found the Mayor sitting in the choicest spot, before the roaring fire the men had started as they set about making camp.

Dirk spoke gruffly. "Mayor Brown, we have to talk. You are not telling the whole truth. I Want to know why Tika left Circle Valley, and I want to know, now!" Dirk said breathing hard.

"Calm down, don't you give me a lot of flack about this in front of the men. I am still the Mayor of Circle Valley. Go and look over the edge of the cliff, Dirk; then come back and we will talk calmly and sensibly," said Mayor Brown

Dirk stomped his way to the edge of the cliff and peered over the side. He could see in the distance, the trail they had carved coming up the mountain. He could even see their last campsite. Slowly he backed away and returned to Mayor Brown.

"What did you see Dirk?" asked Mayor Brown softly.

"I saw our trail and our campsite. We should not have lit a fire. I did not think the little upstart was smart enough to break camp and travel through the night," Dirk said.

"If you could see it, so could Starvros," said Mayor Brown.

"That is my point exactly, Mayor Brown. He could not break camp with two unwilling captives. Mayor Brown, you and the Shaman are not telling us the whole story!" Dirk said rather loudly causing some of the men to turn toward them questioningly.

"Keep your voice down man," Mayor Brown said sternly. He grabbed Dirk's" wrist

with his pudgy hands.

"If I had told the truth, what would you have thought of Tika and Moira?" However, as your Mayor and her uncle, I have to protect Tika and Moira from you, the villagers, Starvros, themselves, and now the Snow Monster! I do not apologize for lying to you. I do not know the reason Tika or Moira decided to join Starvros on his silly quest. All I know is that they are in danger and I will move heaven, earth, and all the villagers to return them safely to their homes. I cannot let you ruin it by telling the villagers the truth. They will pack up and go home if they knew the truth and I will not risk that. It means life and death for Tika," said Mayor Brown whispering desperately to Dirk.

Dirk snatched his arm away and stood to his full height before Mayor Brown.

"Much that you have said is true. I will think more on it. I will say nothing at this point, Mayor Brown. However, when we catch them, remember Starvros is my problem. I will take care of him," said Dirk.

"No Dirk, we will not have justice based on one man's feelings. This has affected the whole village and the whole village will decide the fate of this trio, who are also a

part of the village. I blame myself for Starvros. I did not treat him according to the laws of our village and his bitterness has affected my household. I see now that you cannot remain impartial and unaffected and think the ripples of life will not affect you. I did not realize that you receive back what you give out. How you treat your fellow man has a direct impact on how others will treat you," Mayor Brown said quietly.

"You do not tell me what to do, Mayor Brown. It will depend on which of us gets to Starvros first? I will kill him with my bare hands and throw his body from the mountain, when I find him," said Dirk.

Mayor Brown felt uneasy with Dirk's confession. He could not tell where so much of Dirk's hostility toward Starvros stemmed. He sensed it was more than his feelings for Tika. He remembered a vague rumor about a lost love. He knew the men in the village followed Dirk because they admired his strength and if Dirk hated Starvros, so did they.

Mayor Brown determined that he would have to get to Starvros before Dirk and the others.

"Well, what do we do, then? There is nowhere to go but up, Dirk. I hate to think of those girls climbing this mountain in the dark. I could not forgive Starvros or myself if something happened to one of those girls," the Mayor said.

"I could not forgive either, Mayor Brown, and Starvros will pay dearly for this escapade," Dirk reiterated.

"Are we going to break camp and follow suit by traveling all night to catch them?

Mayor Brown asked, moving the subject away from Starvros.

"I would love to camp here for the night, Mayor Brown. This might be the last good campsite on the mountain, but I think we shall do as they did. If they can travel in the dark so can we," said Dirk, decisively.

Dirk began to bark orders to the men. No one grumbled about breaking camp and continuing up the stark mountain in the dark.

Mayor Brown looked up at the formidable mountain and frowned.

'His coming along was not a good idea, but he knew he had to be there. Only he could keep Dirk and the men from mob violence against the lad. He was not, prepared to climb a mountain either and he did not want to spare men to take him back down the mountain.

They did not know what dangers they were facing in the territory of the Snow Monster. His snarls, heard earlier convinced Mayor Brown that the Snow Monster knew they were on the mountain and in a face-to-face encounter with the elusive monster, they would need every available man.

Dirk saw Mayor Brown's hesitation and came over to him.

"Mayor Brown, you will be tied to Gustavo and me. I will climb first, and then you, Mayor Brown and Gustavo will bring up the rear. He will help you with your footing and show you where to place your hands and feet. He will be beside you the whole time we are on the face of the mountain. Gustavo is a very good climber. Everyone else will pair together, tied to each other as we are. Look after your fellow climber and we will climb steadily throughout the night, Dirk said raising his voice so the other men could hear his instructions. Whoever reaches a campsite first will signal the others. We will rest there and continue later in the day. The day's snow fall will have slowed them down, too." Dirk continued.

Mayor Brown's relief was all too evident as he allowed Gustavo to tie the rope to him, to Dirk, and to himself.

"Get your axe out and hack places in the rock to put your hands and feet and pull yourself up the mountain with the loose end of your rope. Use the places where your hands were, for your footing," said Gustavo handing Mayor Brown an axe.

"Let's go men, we are wasting time, said Dirk as the blood rushed to his face and his swarthy complexion blushed red from the anger that fueled him onward. Dirk muttered and climbed throughout the night.

"Starvros will pay dearly for this! I will kill the upstart! This is the last time he will take what is mine! I dare not speak her name! Abbey Laurel...I mean Tika! I mean Tika, yes Tika!" Dirk said, shaking his head to free the cobwebs of anger from his mind.

Mayor Brown was having a hard time keeping pace with Dirk. Laboring for breath as they continued up the mountain façade, he was finding it more difficult to find crevices for his hands, or places to tie his rope onto in the mountain wall. His weight seemed heavier with each rise, each pull and every inch he crawled up the mountain. His feet slipped more often and many times Gustavo had to help him up the face of the mountain.

Mayor Brown and Gustavo grunted and strained in their effort to keep up the pace with Dirk. Many of the villagers lagged behind and Dirk beckoned at them to keep up. Some of them found the steps carved in the walls that the trio used to climb up the mountain wall and found the going easier, quicker for them.

By morning, they had reached the flat place in the mountain where Starvros and the girls had stopped briefly in their flight up the mountain. Dirk barked orders to the villagers to rest for an hour and then they would continue on their journey.

"They are breaking the trail for us. They are making the journey easier for us. We will only stop to eat and then we will continue our journey. If we keep this pace we will soon overtake them," Dirk said.

Mayor Brown collapsed on a huge snow covered boulder in the clearing, visibly winded, tired, and shaken by the ordeal of climbing up the mountain wall, he breathed heavily, sucking in great gulps of air.

"Slow down Dirk, he gasped. We need to do more than stop to eat. We need more than an hour's rest. You have kept a grueling pace all night. We need sleep!" Mayor Brown said, panting for breath.

"I hate to pull rank on you, but it is mid-morning. Why don't we stay here the rest of the day and start again tonight?" Mayor Brown said pleadingly.

The men looked from Mayor Brown to Dirk. Dirk's thick eyebrows drew together across his brow obliterating the frown, the men saw on his face. The men moved uneasily away from Dirk and Mayor Brown. They knew what that frown meant. Dirk was furiously angry. The men were well acquainted with Dirk's tirades. The men began to look for other things to do. Bobbo began to look for firewood and Gustavo offered to help him.

Clyde, George and Josef set about making camp with the help of the other men.

Dirk clenched his fists and placed them on his waist to control himself and still he shook with rage.

"Mayor Brown did I hear you clearly?" he bellowed. Snow fell from the trees rooted nearby.

"You want to stay here! What fool would do a thing like that? We must continue until we overtake that upstart and destroy him! We are hard on Starvros' trail. I do not want to lose him when the upper plateau levels off before the peak of the mountain. He could disappear in these mountains and I would never find his trail. You are a weak, tired old man who should have stayed in the village with the women and children," Dirk said vehemently.

"Dirk! Mayor Brown said in a commanding tone, as he lifted his brow and looked fully at him. "I am still the Mayor of Circle Valley. I called this assembly of men together to look for my niece, Moira and Starvros, because they are citizens of Circle Valley. They are my responsibility wherever they may be. I may be tired, and old, but I am the only authority here according to the laws of our village. You have forgotten yourself and I will overlook it this time because you are so emotionally involved. We can all use your experience on this journey, but do not presume you are in charge of anything. I have allowed you to lead us through the mountains. You do not lead because you have power and authority in Circle Valley or anywhere else. As I said before we will wait until nightfall to continue our journey, Dirk. I was asking for your opinion! Now I am telling you what we will do!" Mayor Brown said in a cold, calm, voice, without anger.

Dirk stared hard at Mayor Brown, breathing loud and heavy, and the Mayor returned his stare. Dirk dropped his eyes before the mayor and turned to the men standing nervously by observing the scene.

"We will make camp here men and resume our trek up the mountain at dusk. Continue what you were doing," Dirk stated flatly.

The men let out a sigh of relief and nervous chatter continued until tiredness and sleep claimed them all.

Dirk awoke still seething over Mayor Brown pulling rank on him in front of the men. He could not understand why Mayor Brown wanted to protect Starvros.

"Anyone that helps that young upstart is my enemy!" Dirk stated to the wind that had left a fresh batch of snow and was moving away to the east.

'It looks as if the wind is going the same way we are,' Dirk thought. He shook himself and aroused the camp. He appointed Gustavo to continue to look after Mayor Brown in light of the earlier events. He wanted to limit his contact with Mayor Brown. He wanted nothing to distract him from his main target- finding Starvros and destroying him. He specifically told Gustavo to keep Mayor Brown busy when they found Starvros and the girls.

Mayor Brown awoke with a sense of unease. He went over the previous day's events in his mind. He did not like the way Dirk saw their journey as a way to destroy Starvros.

"He did not even mention Tika or Moira last night," Mayor Brown said as he realized there was something not quite right with Dirk's feelings toward the boy. I wish I knew what was disturbing Dirk. I have never seen him so agitated before. He could be dangerous, possibly more dangerous than the Snow Monster," said Mayor Brown into the swirling east wind. In his musings, he did not realize he had walked to the edge of the precipice.

Gustavo came behind him, "Who is more dangerous than the Snow Monster?" he spoke loud into Mayor Brown's ear.

The Mayor jumped and spun around. His foot slipped on the frozen tundra and he teetered on the edge of the cliff. Gustavo reached for him and Mayor Brown's heavy bulk caused Gustavo to slip and fall. Gustavo called for help as he sensed more than saw that he and Mayor Brown were about to plunge over the edge, into nothingness. The men looked up when they heard Gustavo's cry of alarm, everyone dropped what they were doing when they saw the two men struggling to keep from falling off the cliff. Several of the men who reached them first, grabbed the rope tied to Gustavo, and it went taut in their hands as Gustavo and Mayor Brown went over the side of the mountain. Gustavo and Mayor Brown slammed against the side of the mountain, evoking a moan from Mayor Brown who hit the wall first. The sudden stop in mid air almost jerked Mayor Brown from Gustavo's arms. Mayor Brown held onto Gustavo fiercely, afraid he would plunge to his death below.

"Do not let go of me, Mayor Brown," said Gustavo through gritted teeth.

"I will not," mumbled Mayor Brown through his pain.

"I am going to tie this loose end of the rope around you so that they can pull the both of us up the mountain, said Gustavo through gritted teeth. It took all his strength to hold on to Mayor Brown. He worked the rope around Mayor Brown with a little help from him.

Gustavo knew Mayor Brown was hurt, but he did not know how bad his injuries were. The villagers held tightly to the rope as others came to help hold on to the duo. The villagers shouted to Gustavo to see if they were all right. Gustavo managed to call for help. After securing the rope around Mayor Brown and himself Gustavo tugged the rope for the villagers to pull them up the mountain, hoping the rope would hold their double weight. Dirk went to the front of the rope and began to pull the pair up the mountain in unison with the rest of the villagers. Through their combined effort, Mayor Brown and Gustavo were lifted back onto the top of the mountain, into the clearing, well away from the edge of the cliff.

Once back on top of the mountain Mayor Brown lashed out at Gustavo through his pain.

"Do not ever walk upon me like that! Gustavo," Mayor Brown said sharply speaking through his pain.

Dirk hushed Mayor Brown. "It is not Gustavo's fault, Mayor Brown. What were you doing at the edge of the cliff? Never mind, let me check you over for any injuries,"

Dirk said, as he checked Mayor Brown thoroughly.

"Bobbo you check Gustavo over, too. We need every able bodied man if we are to continue this journey.

While Dirk was attending to Mayor, Brown Gustavo spoke.

"Mayor Brown I only came to tie the rope on you so we could climb the mountain like Dirk told me to do." said Gustavo, stung by the tongue-lashing from Mayor Brown.

"I- I am sorry Gustavo. I -I really should be grateful. You did save my life. Thank you," the Mayor said grabbing and shaking Gustavo's hand with his pudgy, sweaty hands.

Dirk completed his inspection of Mayor Brown. "You will live Mayor Brown, but you will have severe bruising and some pain with it. Bobbo, is Gustavo all right?"

"Yes, Dirk he is good. He will have bruising and pain, too," said Bobbo.

"We will deal with all of this later. Right now, we must move on. We still have much to do to catch up with Starvros and the girls. We cannot stop. We have seen firsthand the dangers in this mountain. We do not know the dangers we will face at the hands of the Snow Monster. So, be extra careful, men. Watch yourself, each other and your surroundings. We are on unfamiliar terrain, go slowly and make each footfall sure. We do not need any more unforeseen accidents," Dirk stated to the men. If you do not have a staff, I urge you to get one and strap it to your back with your spear. You will need it in the higher elevations and the increased snows we will encounter." Dirk averred.

The villagers continued to congratulate Gustavo as they prepared to make their ascent up the mountain. Gustavo retied Mayor Brown's ropes using more rope than he used in the past. He alone knew Mayor Brown's weight could pull him and Dirk down the mountain if he slipped again. Gustavo broke into a cold sweat as the incident with Mayor Brown replayed in his mind.

'I will not let that fat, pudgy, old man kill me. I do not like the fact that Dirk has put him off on me. I will keep my knife handy and if that tired old man slips again, I will cut the rope.' he thought. Gustavo tied the knife in its sheath high under his vest where he could reach it in a hurry. There is no need for both of us to die, and I will kill Dirk if he has anything to say about it. He is the one who is in love with Mayor Brown's niece. She has her hooks into him. That is the only reason I can see that he wants to kill the boy. He must feel the boy is a threat to his getting the girl. He is old enough to be her father. To be fair though, that is the way of the village. My own wife was a young maiden when I wed her,' Gustavo thought.

Gustavo pulled his mind away from his thoughts as Dirk yelled for them to start up the mountain. They took the lead again. Dirk began the ascent, then Mayor Brown, followed by Gustavo. The other villagers did not spread out over the face of the mountain as before but stayed in a tight formation as they continued their trek up the mountain.

Mayor Brown was still very upset. He guessed that Dirk told the men to stay close in case he slipped again. Mayor Brown reviewed the day's events and concluded it was not his fault. He fell over the cliff because Gustavo came up behind him and startled him. Anyone who climbed mountains knew you did not walk up behind a person standing on the edge of a cliff. Mayor Brown did own secretly that in his musings about Dirk, he did not remember walking to the edge of the cliff. Who knows if he may not have walked off that cliff by himself, into oblivion? He was ashamed of his tirade against Gustavo. The man may have saved his life, twice! Mayor Brown thought, reluctantly. He did not want to be a burden to the villagers. He was a somewhat healthy man, even a little wide in the belly. However, he could hold his own with the best of them. He sputtered at the thought of Dirk calling him a tired, old man! He did not go on the hunts because as leader he needed to remain in the village and take charge of things. He was not as poor because of a stocked pantry, meat stored in the smoke house, and more farm animals. He could not help it if his ancestors prepared for the future that left him better off than some of his neighbors. Some people were born to rule and some were born to be ruled. Every king must have subjects. However, his was a poor kingdom, and it was getting poorer by the day, with the daily offering to the Snow Monster, added to their needs. His stores were dwindling as well as the community storehouse's supplies, getting lower by the day. Hunting parties yielded very little to restock. the storehouse. He could understand the underlying desperation of the villagers. He could understand Starvros' reasoning as the poorest citizen of Circle Valley. He was beginning to see the boy's idea of finding the Snow Monster and destroying him, as the only way to end the curse on their village. He would benefit most from the reversal of the curse as leader of the village. All of the villagers would gain more from the death of the Snow Monster. Surly Dirk and the others will come to realize this. So, why did Dirk want to kill the boy? Ah, it will resolve itself when we find Starvros and the girls, he thought.

The villagers continued climbing the mountain well into the next day. When they reached the clearing hoping to find Starvros and the girls they were surprised they did not find them sleeping.

"Where are they?" many of the villagers asked, wearied by the final trek up the mountain.

"I cannot tell anything from these tracks. It looks as if someone, something or maybe that wind from the west has wiped their tracks away. There are no tracks leading out of this clearing in any direction. It seems as if they vanished leaving no trace. Some of you men spread out in every direction and see if you can pick up a trail. A few of you set up camp. We will stay here until we pick up a trail, eat and get some rest. I will check Mayor Brown and Gustavo out fully and tend to their bruises, said Dirk. Some of the men fanned out in four different directions within the confines of the clearing, searching for a trail and clues to the trio's direction. A few stayed behind and set about making camp, setting out a meager meal, and a guard.

Mayor Brown raised an eyebrow at Dirk.

"Why do we need a guard, Dirk?" he said.

"We are further in the mountains than we have ever been, Mayor Brown. We do not know if wild beasts are in these mountains and we do not know a thing about the Snow Monster, and what he may have at his disposal," Dirk said.

"Maybe he needed our food to feed more than himself. Maybe there are more of those monsters in this mountain than we know. I do not know, Mayor Brown. What I am sure of is that we are in his territory and we should be taking care from this point on," Dirk stated.

"Besides, Starvros and the girls have disappeared without a trace. Whether by the hand of the Snow Monster or something else I cannot tell you. I have a sensed a foreboding presence since we reached the higher elevations in this mountain, all is not what it seems to be," Dirk stated with emphasis.

"I too, sense something sinister Dirk, and that thick cloud of fog rolling toward us from the west will not help our cause. We should not be camping out here in the open. I would feel better in that stand of trees or with the mountain at my back," stated Mayor Brown.

Dirk turned at the Mayor Brown's words and saw the dark, angry-looking. black clouds coming toward them with a dense menacing fog rolling, and tumbling at a fast pace. It was not like any fog bank or cloud cover he had ever seen before. The clouds tumbled, rolled and roared as if it were alive and was moving with speed and purpose toward them as they sat defenseless in the open clearing.

Dirk, amazed further by the fierce wind that blew the fog along had never seen fog driven by the wind. Fog usually drifted in a slow manner. Dirk rose and called the men to return to camp immediately, by blowing the horn of danger. It was not the same horn used by Mayor Brown, but a smaller one they took on hunting trips to signal the capture of prey or danger. The men came running from all directions, wondering what alarmed Dirk that he would use the horn of danger, again. "Look," Dirk shouted as they assembled before him. Everyone turned toward the rolling, tumbling, cloudbank.

"What is it?" some of the villagers asked.

Some began gathering their gear They stood stark in the clearing against the coming fog, unable to move, as the evil storm approached them.

"Do not stand there gawking, you fools! Run for the forest, hide in the trees and take your gear and your bedding. Tie yourself to a tree in pairs and cover yourself from head to toe. Get moving! said Mayor Brown as he grabbed much of his gear and began to run for his life.

His words reached the others and they paired up heading for the forest after Mayor Brown, amazed that he could move so fast. They moved as a unit, as their fathers had trained them so many years ago. It was a ritual, old and almost forgotten. The rhythm of their movements eased the fear from their minds and they moved into the trees with one purpose, and that was to come out of the storm, alive. Silently they worked together against an enemy that threatened them all. They lashed themselves to the trees as the Mayor had instructed them, picking trees big enough to hold two men. Dirk grabbed the Mayor and lashed him to a tree by himself. Mayor Brown grabbed Dirk's hand, 'Why are you tying me to a tree by myself, Dirk?" the Mayor asked softly.

"The rope will not hold you and another man securely, Mayor," said Dirk.

"Oh, it is because of my girth, eh Dirk?" The Mayor asked, chuckling out of nervous fear.

"You will be all right Mayor Brown. I will come for you after the storm is over and I will be tied to the tree across from you." Dirk stated through gritted teeth.

Already he could feel the cold icy wind and the dankness of the fog as it stung his nostrils. He covered Mayor Brown from head to toe with his bedding and then checked to see if all the men were secured and covered before making his way to the tree he had picked out across from the Mayor Brown. Dirk shivered so much he had a hard time lashing himself to the tree. His fingers barely tied the ropes securely. He was wet from the fog. Finally he was able to secure himself before the terrible onslaught of the storm.

It penetrated the thick animal hides of their outer garments. It penetrated the coarse fur lined boots. It was as wet as rain, without rain. It was cold as ice, without ice. It pinned them to the trees, tearing at their bedding with icy fingers of wind, daring them to reveal themselves to its fury. Each man prayed in his own way to live through the deadly fog.

The storm did not move away as quickly as it came upon them, but stayed and tormented the men with its icy fingers, tempting them to remove their bedding from their faces and stare into its chilling depths. The wind tore at their clothing, as if to unclothe them to its tortuous onslaught. It tried to freeze the bedding to their faces to snuff all life from their bodies. The thick blankets held against the wind and the men were thankful for their womenfolk who painstakingly wove the blankets from the fur of the llamas they kept in the community pen. Thus, they stayed throughout the night tormented by the thick menacing fog. Men cried out in fear as the wind and fog raged at them like something alive. Throughout the night, it fought them, beat them and bruised them with debris from the forest floor. Limbs from dead trees pelted them. Leaves pasted to their bodies by the icy fog caused them to look like grotesque monsters. Their bedcovering resembled burial shrouds, thick with ice as the wet, cold wind matted the bed covering to their bodies and molded it to their faces like icy masks.

Mayor Brown heard the keening wind moving away from them after a long time, while lashed to the tree. He could not tell if it were day or night. The storm was diminishing. Mayor Brown feared for Tika and the others. He feared for the villagers and for himself. He damned Starvros for bringing them from their safe village into these mountains on his silly quest. "Terrible Mountain," an apt name for the events taking place since they reached the last plateau before the peak of the mountain. Something or someone did not want them to reach the peak of the mountain. For the first time the Mayor was beginning to believe that whatever or whoever it was, it was more afraid of their presence in the mountains. However, Mayor Brown had never encountered this evil before. He did not think they would survive the evil storm, but they did. Mayor Brown had forgotten about the Snow Monster, but he sensed something more dangerous than a monster was behind the storm. Mayor Brown hoped they would not regret coming after the trio.'

Mayor Brown came out of his reverie and tried calling the men to see if they were all right but could not open his mouth through the icy matted bed coverings.

Mayor Brown panicked. He began clawing at the bed covers to free his mouth and nose however, his pudgy hands only met thick, cold ice. He pulled at the covers, gasping for breath, and they were wet, icy and heavy on his face. Mayor Brown tried to turn toward the tree so that he could dislodge the ice from his face by banging his head against the tree trunk, but he could not turn his head. Terror mounted, he felt lightheaded from lack of air. He had no air left in his lungs.

Suddenly, he felt someone scraping at the icy shroud that covered his mouth. He heard Dirk shouting at him to remain calm. His breathing, coming shallower, Mayor Brown fought to calm himself and wait for Dirk to free him. Soon the coverings fell from his face and Mayor Brown collapsed in Dirk's arms, taking great gulps of air into his lungs, his chest heaving with the effort. He tasted the bitterness in his mouth, felt his stomach lurch. Mayor Brown struggled to gain control of his body. He did not want Dirk to see how sick with terror he had been beneath the shroud.

"You are okay now, Mayor Brown," said Dirk standing before him looking unscathed from the terrible storm.

"Gustavo, free Mayor Brown from the tree while I see to the other villagers," said Dirk Gustavo stepped forward and began to loosen the ropes from Mayor Brown, mumbling beneath his breath, "Why is he pushing Mayor Brown off on me? I do not want to marry his niece."

"Did you say something Gustavo?" Mayor Brown asked.

"No! No! I was talking to myself," Gustavo said, staring crossly at Mayor Brown.

"Why are you looking at me like that Gustavo?" Mayor Brown asked.

"Since you asked, I will tell you. Dirk keeps putting you off on me. You are not my responsibility. I do not want to marry your niece. He saved your life because of Tika.

If it were not for Tika, he would not help you! When he does not want to be bothered, he calls Gustavo to do the things he does not wish to do! I am tired of it! I have a mind to climb back down this awful mountain and leave all of you here," Gustavo said with anger.

Mayor Brown truly looked at Gustavo for the first time. He was a big man, too, but not as big and stocky as Dirk. His hair was as dark as Starvros' and he was pale in places where the summer color was fading on his face. He squinted from small, beady, black eyes. He had a long, narrow nose that made him resemble one of the birds of prey, a hawk or an owl, Mayor Brown thought. He tried to reassure Gustavo that he was a burden to no one, not Dirk or Gustavo.

"I am my own man, Gustavo. I will take the lead in whatever happens from this point on so that neither you nor Dirk will be confused about who leads this expedition. I can see I was mistaken in giving that lead to someone else. I will correct that error this instant," said Mayor Brown as he turned and stumbled and slipped on the icy ground toward Dirk and the rest of the men.

'The man must be harboring some resentment toward Dirk. I must warn Dirk to be careful. Yet I must take over this expedition or none of the men will respect me as Mayor of Circle Valley. No one is going to usurp my position as Mayor.

Dirk must understand that I could have chosen any man in the village for Tika to marry,'

Mayor Brown thought.

Mayor Brown reached Dirk and the others with much effort. Stopping to catch his breath, he held his hands up to get the men's attention.

"Men, as Mayor of Circle Valley I am going to take the lead in this expedition. I have allowed others to lead and it has caused some confusion. Tika is my niece and Moira and Starvros are citizens of Circle Valley. I am taking full responsibility for their return," Mayor Brown stated firmly.

"Every one appears to be safe and unharmed by the storm so we will camp here, eat, warm ourselves and get a good rest before we begin again. I am sure the storm waylaid our adventurous trio, also," said the Mayor, firmly. Dirk approached to voice his disapproval. The Mayor Brown turned toward Dirk, looked at him squarely in the eyes, and said,

"Dirk we will not discuss this. I need you to trust me. I know what I am doing."

Dirk backed away from Mayor Brown. In that moment, he understood the power of authority. He was Dirk the blacksmith. He was not a man of power and authority like Mayor Brown or the Shaman. The kind of power they had was an inheritance from father to son. The blood of ruler ship, is not acquired, it is inbred. Sure the men in the village respected him, even followed him, but he did not have power over them. Dirk's eyes narrowed as he thought.

'What has happened, Mayor Brown was content to let me lead the men when we started on this journey. He was talking to Gustavo. I wonder what Gustavo said to him. I will find out from Gustavo!' Dirk said, his anger mounting at the thought of following Mayor Brown's commands for the rest of the journey. The man could not lead his own household. We would not be here if he had tamed that wild niece of his a long time ago,' Dirk thought as he waddled on the slippery ground and stood behind Gustavo.

Gustavo jumped when Dirk called his name. Gustavo could tell he was angry. He turned slowly and faced Dirk.

"Gustavo, what did you say to Mayor Brown," Dirk said in a quiet, but firm voice.

"Nothing Dirk, Why do you think I said something to Mayor Brown?" Gustavo stammered in a voice pitched high from the fear rising in his chest.

"He is taking over the expedition, that's why, stormed Dirk. "If I find out you had something to do with this..."

"Do not threaten me Dirk. I am as much man as you are, maybe more. I have a

family, a wife. I am not running around in this mountain chasing a young girl who most likely ran away to keep from marrying me!…

Before Gustavo could say any more, Dirk struck him in the face knocking Gustavo to the ground. He slid away from Dirk on the frozen, icy ground.

The villagers turned at the sound of raised voices to see Gustavo slide on the ground to stop at the base of a huge tree. His head hit the tree with a sickening thud and Gustavo's body went limp. The men rushed to him but he was lifeless!

Mayor Brown turned to Dirk.

"What have you done, Dirk?" Mayor Brown asked.

"He said some things I did not like and I struck him. I-I did not mean to hit him. I am Dirk. I am the strongest, bravest man in Circle Valley. He had no right to talk to me like that! Is he dead? Are you sure he is dead?" Dirk asked.

"Yes, Dirk, he is dead! said the Mayor Brown.

The villagers looked from Mayor Brown to Dirk and to Gustavo, puzzlement on their faces. There was something going on they did not understand. An evil seemed to be invading the expedition. They never thought Dirk would hurt, Gustavo.

"Men, take Gustavo's body and cover it with large stones. Gather his belongings to take back to his family. Dirk, the laws of our village is clear. Since you admitted to striking Gustavo and causing hid death you will be responsible for the family of the man's life you have taken. As long as Gustavo's women and children are alive, you will take care of them. You will not marry anyone else until Gustavo's last heir is an adult member of the village or you die whichever comes first. In addition, you will be branded an outlaw to all in the village, after the manner of our laws. While we are on the expedition the branding will have to wait until we return to Circle Valley, Mayor Brown spoke quietly, but firmly.

Dirk could not believe what he was hearing.

"No, No, No! I will not wear a brand and be an outcast in the village. I am Dirk! I am the blacksmith! I am stronger, braver and better than all of you!" Dirk shouted.

'Branding was an old custom of the village. If a man caused the death of another villager, accidental or intentional, branding was one of the punishments handed out

immediately. Taken into the woods away from the women and children, and seared on the back of his scalp with a hot iron, leaving a visible scar rendered the person an outcast and an outlaw among the villagers. No one spoke or interacted with the branded person. No one had ever been branded in the village during his life span or to his knowledge. It was a good way to deter violence in the village,' Dirk thought and he would be the first person branded in the village in his lifetime. Dirk was not about to submit to such a thing willingly. Mayor Brown must be mad!

Dirk pulled his long hunting knife from its sheath beneath his leather tunic.

"You are not going to brand me! Do not move any of you! I have already killed one man; it does not make a difference how many more of you I kill! However, one thing I know, you will not brand me! I am taking my gear and I will leave all of you in these mountains. See how you make it without Dirk!" he shouted.

The Mayor and the villagers turned to each other, mouths agape, watching as Dirk disappeared from their sight into the woods. Murmurs began as soon as he was out of sight. Mayor Brown spoke brusquely to the men and held up his hand for silence.

"It would have been foolhardy for anyone to try and stop Dirk. We have one dead man. We do not want anymore. I am sure Dirk would kill more of us if we attempted to stop him. It is best to let him go. These mountains have a way of meting out its brand of justice. Dirk is right. He will not live as a branded man. He has chosen his own way," Mayor Brown stated.

The incident with Dirk left Mayor Brown with an increased sense of unease. He shook himself to free his thoughts.

"It is unfortunate that things have taken a twist. We will not be going after Dirk. Our first priority is to find Starvros and the girls. We must find them soon and I want to get started right away. We have wasted much time and daylight. I do not want to be caught on the face of the mountain again at night. Let us hope we can make it to the last plateau. Josef and Clyde, since you are the next best climbers, you will be tied to me and help me up the mountain. The sooner we get started the sooner we get off this accursed mountain," Mayor Brown said issuing orders, briskly.

CHAPTER 6

TIKA IS CAPTURED

Tika continued with the duo, but her heart was no longer in the quest. She had shied away from the revelation earlier. The night in the trees waiting for death at the hands of a herd of reindeer made her see that what she was running away from, she ran right into like a stonewall.

She knew that Dirk would protect her with his life if he had to but Tika saw the curse of the Snow monster as a deterrent to anyone's happiness in Circle Valley. No one in the village could really live a meaningful and happy life as long as they were chained to that blasted curse. Starvros was the only person in the village who revealed the true state of their lives.

'I must find Dirk as soon as I can. I will leave Starvros and Tika and go back down the mountain to Dirk. Together we will free ourselves from the curse of the Snow Monster. Our happiness depends on it!' Tika's thoughts raced as a plan formed in her mind.

Tika slowed her steps. Starvros and Moira moved purposely onward, getting further ahead of Tika unaware she was not keeping up with them. Tika lagged behind them until the rope was almost taut. She untied herself and began the trek back over the ground they had walked.

'I must find Dirk! I must find Dirk!' The refrain kept swirling around in her mind as she trekked back in the deep matted snow. She was oblivious to everything around her. Dirk filled her mind. She could see him clearly. He was calling her name. There was a sense of urgency that she get to Dirk!

Suddenly, the air rent with a loud snarl, then a low guttural growl, almost in Tika's ear, She stopped in her tracks. Her tongue cleaved to her mouth and the scream choked off, as a foul stench and a blast of warm, wet air, hit her in the face. Tika's knees bowed and she fell over in the snow, face first, in a dead faint.

At the sound of the Snow Monster, Starvros and Moira stopped. They both turned in fear looking for the Snow Monster to see Tika far away in the distance, fall flat on her face in the snow. Starvros looked at Moira. "How did she get there?" asked Starvros. She was tied to you, Moira. She was your responsibility!" he continued, his voice rising. He could taste the salty saliva backing into his throat.

"That's not fair! Starvros, I have stuck by your side through this entire quest, and as soon as your girl friend does something foolish, you blame me. Tika is not my responsibility. Since you care for her so much why did you place her at the end of the line? Next to you is where she you could check on her? You know as well as I do that she has been a problem since we started this trek in the mountains," Moira said.

"I-I am sorry, Moira I am upset, Starvros apologized.

"Is she hurt?" asked Moira.

"I do not know," said Starvros. We had better go get her. She has fallen face first in the snow. She is not moving. She will suffocate if we do not get her out of the snow, soon."

Moira pulled the rope that was tied to Tika. "The rope was not cut or broken Starvros. She untied herself." Moira shouted, puzzled.

"Not now Moira! Starvros said, running past her as fast as he could. "She will die if we do not get to her. Hurry Moira!" Starvros' boots felt heavy as he closed the distance between him and the fallen Tika. He forgot the snarls of the Snow Monster, he forgot Moira. He only saw Tika in the distance and hoped he was not too late to save her life. Starvros reached Tika first and struggled to turn her over in the deep snow. She was in a dead faint. Her face was pale with light tinges of blue around the lips. Moira came up behind him as he pulled Tika to him and buried his face in her arms.

97

"She's not dead is she?" Moira asked, fear making her voice sound high pitched and thin, as she bent over near him, gasping for breath.

"I do not think she is dead Moira, but I think she has fainted and she needs some air. I think she will come around as soon as she gets air," Starvros responded. Starvros sat in the snow with Tika in his lap, calling her name repeatedly.

"She can't get air bundled up in your arms, Starvros," said Moira.

"Wipe her face with some of the snow, Starvros. The cold wet snow will bring her around."

"Not at this time Moira. I think we should carry her to safety first. We do not know what happened to her and we do not know if we are safe out here, either. The Snow Monster could still be in the area. We will find a place to shelter, we can revive her and find out what this is all about," Starvros said.

"Why would she run away from me? What was she doing out here alone? Was she going back to Circle Valley?" Starvros asked with anguish in his eyes; bewilderment making his brows furrow until they met in the center of his forehead.

"I do not know, Starvros, but we need to get moving. Tika needs a warm fire, a hot meal is needed by us all and we need to rest. We have set a grueling pace trying to stay ahead of the villagers and yet, face the unknown entity of the Snow Monster, and with the thinner air in the mountain we are experiencing the effects of the weather, on our minds, as well.

When Tika has had some hot food and rested, maybe then she will enlighten us as to why she was running away from us. We must stick together, more now than when we first began this quest. I know Tika and I joined you for our own reasons, but your reason for this quest is the main thing that must guide the choices we make that will affect us all. We are beginning to know our enemy because he is slowly revealing himself.

I know from the previous warnings in the cave, the unnatural storms and now this, that whoever or whatever is in this mountain has become a formidable enemy and has made every effort to impress us to give up the quest and leave this mountain.

Someone or something is afraid of what we will uncover on this quest. Starvros we will have to discover the answer soon or we will perish in this mountain. I, for one, would like to know her reason for putting us all in danger, and another thing Starvros; it seems the Snow Monster is stalking us, instead of us stalking it!" Moira stated as she bent to help Starvros lift the helpless Tika to safety.

"We cannot carry Tika and our gear too, Moira. We will leave them, come back after them later, after we find shelter and start a good campfire. I do not care who sees our fire now. All of what you said is true; Moira and we will ponder it all later. For now, we have our hands full with Tika," said Starvros as they pulled and half carried the unconscious Tika to safety.

Starvros and Moira carried and dragged Tika to a small stand of trees in the clearing close to the mountain wall, which made a nice secluded campsite; they could see anything that approached their site.

"You stay here with Tika, Moira and I will go back and get our gear," said Starvros to Moira.

"I am afraid to stay here alone Starvros!" Moira wailed.

"Not you too! Moira. I thought you were braver than Tika," Starvros chided her.

"It is not that, Starvros, it is just that the Snow Monster is trying to divide and conquer us one by one. If we are always together we are stronger than he is," said Moira.

"We can wait until Tika comes around and then we will all go and retrieve our gear. We will be able to find out what she knows about who is out there and make our plans then," Moira continued.

"Aye! You are right again, Moira. Aye, let us wake this sleeping beauty. Get some snow Moira and wipe her face," Starvros concluded.

"Me!" shouted Moira.

"Yes, you!" Starvros said laughing at her expression. Just in case she comes to swinging at the Snow Monster, after all it was your idea to stay and revive her, so be my guest." he chuckled.

"I will get you for that Starvros Gunther," Moira said playfully.

'This was the way they always acted toward each other in the past,' Moira thought, wistfully as she gathered a hand full of snow and wiped Tika's face.

Tika came to sputtering and swinging her arms wildly. When she opened her eyes and saw that it was Moira, she grabbed the girl and hugged her tightly.

"Let me go Tika. What is the matter with you?" Moira said, pulling out of Tika's grasp.

"I am so glad it is you and not that horrible Snow Monster," Tika said looking around to see if she was safe.

"You saw the Snow Monster!" Starvros and Moira said together, startled by her words.

"Well… I did not actually see him, but I smelled him. He blew a blast of his awful breath in my face and he growled at me, and snarled in my ear. It was as if he was standing right in front of me, but I could not see him. I-I g-guess I-I fainted after that because I do not remember walking here. Oh! it was awful! I am so glad you and Moira found me! I could be a prisoner of the snow Monster or dead! What was I thinking?" Tika wailed.

"Yes, what were you thinking? Tika, and where were you going? It looked as if you were heading back down the mountain to me," said Moira standing over the distraught girl with her hands folded.

I-I do not know what I was thinking Moira, Tika said. It was a moment of panic, I guess. "Help me up Starvros," she said to divert any more questions from Moira. She may be able to fool Starvros, but not Moira. Tika did not realize until this quest that there was more depth to Moira than anyone knew. She had an innate way of figuring out the most complex situations. Most of the situations they found themselves in because of the Snow Monster, Moira knew before Starvros.

"We have to go back and get our gear now, Tika. Are you going to stay with us and not run away?" Starvros said the anguish in his eyes, lost on Tika.

"I promise I will not run away again, Starvros. I was silly. I know that, now.

This mountain is too dangerous for one person to run willy-nilly around in it. It is too dangerous for the three of us. Are you sure you would not rather wait here for Dirk and the villagers to come and rescue us?" Tika asked timidly.

"No, Moira said firmly. "I am not returning to Circle Valley. I do not know what changed your mind, Tika, but my mind is made up, I will go on with Starvros You can stay here and wait for the villagers," Moira said looking at Tika contemptuously.

"I cannot wait here alone!

What if the Snow Monster comes back, Moira? If you are that set against going back to Circle Valley, then I guess we will have to go on." Tika sighed.

"Now that the issue is settled we will go get our gear," said Starvros.

'Starvros was learning to stay out of their controversies. They will disagree and they will make up. It is the way of women, he was finding out. The more he got involved the worse it got between them. It was better to allow them to figure it out,' Starvros thought.

The air was cold and mist hung in the air like sheer fabric. Ice clung to everything turning all they saw into icy sculptures.. The moist air stung the lungs with every breath they took. The trio retraced their tracks back along the frozen matted ground to the clearing. Moira looked back at the tall looming trees. It was strange to see a stand of trees and no birds. Not one bird filled the darkening sky.

"Do you know that I have not seen one bird since we reached this plateau? Yet, I feel as if many eyes are watching me. It is an uncanny, feeling," Moira said wonderingly.

I felt the same way before I fainted in the snow, now that you mention it Moira," said Tika.

"Come on girls, stop dallying. I want to get out of here quickly," Starvros said quickening the pace. He sensed more than saw that something was not right in the clearing. Some how he felt vulnerable, like an animal caught in a trap.

They found their gear where they left them, but a keening sound reached their ears and it was coming toward them. "What is that sound?" asked the girls in unison.

Starvros hunched his shoulders afraid to speak. In his mind he screamed, 'What now!' Starvros tilted his head back and looked up at the evening skyline. No stars were visible, the moon was not out, and off to the west he could see the thick rolling, black clouds headed their way, driven by a fierce wind. Starvros saw the rolling fog falling toward them with speed he had never seen before.

Starvros turned to Moira and Tika.

"Run!" he said shouting above the keening wind.

"Run back to the trees girls, as fast as you can. He grabbed them both and pulled them along as fast as he could.

"Do not struggle with me! Do as I say! Run, for your very lives depend on it!" Starvros shouted, trying to keep the panic from the girls. Reaching the forest Starvros tied each of the girls to a tree explaining to them as fast as he could to follow his instructions. He covered them pulling their bedding from their packs and tied the bedding and their packs to them with the rope. He covered them from head to toe. Starvros' panic made them submissive to his will. Neither one of the girls questioned what he was doing, but obeyed him completely. Starvros told them not to remove the covering from their face and to wait out the storm. He would get to them when the storm was over. If any of them survived the terrible storm approaching them.

Starvros tied himself to a nearby tree as securely as he could. He covered himself with his bedding and shouted one last time for the girls to keep their faces covered no matter what happened.

"You are frightening us Starvros," said Tika above the wind.

"Remain calm, Tika. We have to get through this storm! Remember, I am nearby, Starvros said to the frightened girl. He did not know how much more Tika could take before she fell apart completely.

"Starvros do you think the Snow Monster sent the storm to destroy us?" Tika shouted above the keening wind, louder now as the fingers of fog rushed toward them.

"Do not talk Tika. We have to wait out the storm. There is nothing else we can do! We have to survive. Stay covered up and pray," said Starvros as he covered his face with his bedding and secured it in place. Starvros struggled to get his hands beneath the ropes he had used to bind himself to the tree.

Starvros felt helpless tied to the tree while the storm moved in, pelting them with debris flying before the wind, tormenting them throughout the night. He shouted several times to Moira and Tika to try to calm them, but did not think they heard him over the roaring of the wind. Starvros felt the cold seep through his clothing and he shivered violently, as the warmth seeped from his body, replaced by a cold that bit hard into his bones. He heard his teeth chattering and clenched his jaws tight afraid he would bite his tongue off.

What kind of evil is this? We have encountered one problem after another since we came on this quest. Is there no end to the malevolence of his enemy? What more can he do to us? Why is he doing this to us? Will we make it out alive? Will we discover the secret of the Snow Monster? Will we end the curse on Circle Valley? What price will we have to pay to uncover the truth of the Snow Monster? All the questions he had no answers to surged through Starvros' mind as the storm raged against him. All the words of glory, the feelings of triumph left with the ravaging wind and the dank wet fog.

Starvros berated himself for allowing the girls to continue the dangerous quest. It was one thing to put self in harm's way, but not Tika and Moira. He had no right to endanger their lives. Starvros felt the weight of what he had done. He did not think things through carefully before starting on this silly quest. Dirk was right. He should have left the hunt for the Snow Monster in the hands of the men from the village. Starvros was not sure if they would survive this storm, he was frightened about things they did not know, things he did not understand, things Starvros should have left to the men It was certain they did not know these mountains or its inhabitants. For safety the Mayor had decreed that no one would trek any higher than the first plateau when hunting for food in the mountains.

Starvros took a long look at his motive for coming on this quest. He did not think his motive was very noble. The more he thought about it, Starvros felt shame run through his body and felt his face flush. Pride!" Starvros whispered, "I wanted to show the men of the village that I was better than they were. I wanted to do something to make them like and respect me. I have put everyone in the village in danger. Oh no! Oh no! I thought I did not need them to help me make my living. I thought that made me a better person than they were. We could all die out here and never find the Snow Monster. The storms alone, are so dangerous. We could die out here and no one will ever find us. They never found my father and they never found Mayor Brown's father or others who thought they could find and destroy the Snow Monster.

If the Snow Monster is behind this storm, it is an evil storm. Could it be another warning from the apparition in the cave? Starvros' thoughts swirled a round and round in his brain much like the wind swirling around them in the storm. The storm was brutal as it pelted them throughout the night. Debris, ice and snow as wet as rain water soaked the trio through completely.

Starvros finally heard the wind moving away from them, when he heard a scream.

"Tika! Moira!" Starvros shouted, trying to free the ropes that were tighter from the wet ice and cold wind. He heard Tika scream again, and he heard Moira calling his name. He pulled and tugged at the ropes with hands numb from the cold, ice storm, to freedom and stumbled on the icy ground toward Moira. When he touched her, she screamed again.

"It's me, Moira. It is Starvros. What has happened?" He said, pulling the covers from Moira's face.

"I do not know Starvros. I heard Tika scream. I heard sounds, but I could not get the covers off my face to see anything or anyone. Is she all right Starvros?" Moira asked. Her eyes, opened wide, engulfed her entire face.

"Do not get the hysterics, Moira. I came to you because you were closer and the ground is very slippery," responded Starvros.

"Hold still while I untie you and we will see about Tika. The storm may have frightened her." Starvros said, his teeth chattering from the cold.

"Stop wiggling Moira, you are making the wet ropes tighter." Starvros said.

"I-I a-am not w-wiggling Starvros, I-I a-am s-s-s-shivering. I- I a-am so-o-o-o c-cold, Starvros," said Moira.

Freeing Moira at last, Starvros grabbed her by the hand and they stumbled and slid on the slippery ground to find Tika.

The pair stopped in their tracks, focusing through the last of the fog as it moved away. The tree stood alone. Starvros turned to look at another tree, then another. He turned and looked around the forest.

The trees stood in their ice-clad coats shimmering against the moonlight appearing over the horizon as the storm moved away in the distance. The area gleamed from the light of the full moon. Ice glistened as droplets of water dripped onto the frozen tundra. The ground resembled a frozen lake, which the icy wind and the cold wet fog had polished until it shone like frozen metal.

He saw the trees, but...

"Where is Tika?" Moira asked before Starvros could say anything further.

"Get your things Moira," he spoke brusquely to Moira.

"Gather your things Moira," he said again.

"Where is she Starvros? Where is Tika?" Moira asked.

"I am not budging from this spot!" Moira said tears streaming down her face.

Starvros turned back toward Moira, grabbed her by the hand and jerked her roughly, propelling her forward.

"Starvros, Starvros! Moira shouted, jerking away from him.

"Stop it now, Starvros and tell me where Tika is or I will never move from this spot!" Moira shouted.

"Moira! I do not have time for any more drama. I am sick and tired of something bad happening every time I make a move. I feel like one of the puppets my mother used to make to entertain me when I was younger. I feel as if someone else has control of my life and is pulling all the strings. I do not have any say in it, and am jumping around like a trained dog," Starvros shouted back at Moira.

"I said, let's move, and that is what I meant, Moira. We must move quickly. Tika is in danger and I do not have time for explanations. You must trust me! I know what I am doing! Where is that girl who said I needed to follow my instincts on this quest and at the first sign of trouble, what do you do? I am ashamed of you Moira. I thought you had more backbone. Let me do this, Moira. I must trust my training and my instincts to find Tika. I am as anxious as you are, but that will not help us find Tika. We must keep our heads and do what we set out to do; hunt for the Snow Monster. If we find him, we will find Tika!" Starvros said.

Silently Moira moved forward with Starvros guiding her by the wrist. He walked as swiftly as he could on the slippery ground, stopping only to gather their belongings and move toward the forests. Still moving cautiously on the ice, Starvros pulled his pack onto his shoulders slipping his arms into the ends where he had sewn makeshift straps.

Starvros pulled Moira to his side and adjusted the pack on her back. Together they walked from the clearing into the forest heading toward the face of the mountain. Starvros searched the ground, his brow wrinkled in concentration as he looked for signs of bent twigs, footprints or disturbed debris to give him a clue to Tika's disappearance.

'Agh, Agh! Nothing! Nothing! I do not see a trace of evidence to show which way Tika went." Starvros stated.

Moira jumped at the sound of his voice. Moira turned toward Starvros and said,

"Remember Starvros, the Snow Monster left no trail when he left Circle Valley either.

The ground is so matted from the reindeer herd, I do not believe Tika walked out of these woods. It is some kind of enchantment or something. Didn't you sense that about the storm, Starvros?" Moira concluded.

"Yes! I did, Moira. I guess I lost my head when Tika disappeared. Was I rude to you, Moira? If I treated you bad, I am sorry. I just feel so responsible for anything that happens to you girls," Starvros said.

"You don't have to feel guilty about us Starvros. Tika and I came on this quest for our own reasons. You did not ask us to join you. If we did not think of all the dangers, neither did you. It is not your responsibility to keep us safe. I am sorry we put you in a place where you feel you have to look after Tika and me, Starvros." Moira said as they continued trekking through the forest.

"Starvros do you think Tika's disappearance has something to do with the warnings from the apparition in the cave?" asked Moira.

"Yes, I think the apparition in the cave has everything to do with everything that has happened to us since we started this quest, said Starvros. We have stirred up a sleeping monster," he stated flatly.

The duo came out of the forest onto a broad plateau that slanted upward toward the peak of the mountain.

"This must be the last level before we reach the peak Moira," said Starvros.

"Use your staff to test for cracks and crevices, Moira," Starvros said.

Moira laughed, "I was just about to tell you the same thing Starvros," she said.

The going was slow and arduous over the frozen tundra. About midday, they stopped for a brief rest and a quick meal of the suet made by Starvros' father.

"It will keep up our strength Moira.

"It does not taste too bad Starvros, but I am really beginning to miss those meager meals we had at home. It is not that I want to go back to Circle Valley or anything like that, but it is funny what you can get used to, and what you miss when you don't have it any more, isn't it Starvros?" asked Moira.

"I guess I miss my mother and father most of all Moira. Those other things that people miss, I never had them, to miss them," Starvros said.

"I am sorry, Starvros," Moira said.

"You do not have to be sorry for me. I will play the hand life has dealt me, but I will also hold those accountable who shirk the responsibilities life gave them. It is the shirkers in life who make it harder for everyone else," Starvros said passionately. Soon they stopped to rest again. The going was slower and each footfall felt as if they had stones in their boots. Tiredness overtook Starvros after their small meal and Starvros fell into a fitful sleep.

Moira let him sleep. He needed the rest. 'Everyone was on edge, and the thinner air in the higher elevations added to their emotional state,' Moira considered as she waited to wake Starvros from his nap. She kept guard with the large knife she kept in a sheath beneath her slips. She saw no need to let Starvros know she carried the weapon.

Starvros tossed about, calling Tika's name several times. His dreams were filled with ghostly snow monsters that chained a frightened Tika to them and taunted him to find her. Tika was calling his name. "Tika, Tika where are you?" he called.

"She is not here Starvros, wake up. You are dreaming, said Moira softly. Get up it is time to get back on the trail and find Tika," she continued.

By evening, the setting sun played tag along the tundra, glistening in the trees, running along the frozen ground sending prismatic lights into the atmosphere. The birds Moira did not see before the storm, swooped and frolicked in the bright sunshine. Moira and Starvros rounded an outcropping of rock and stood before a huge cavernous grotto hewn into the mountain. To the left a stand of fir trees glistened in multicolored hues

from the rays of the setting sun bouncing along ice formations on the branches and limbs from the previous day's storm. They stood as centuries old sentinels against the cavernous grotto.

"Oh!" said Moira

"Wow!" I did not know ice could look so beautiful," said Starvros as he surveyed the wonder before him.

The bright sunlight with its red hues flickered on the ice covered walls of the grotto sending deep colored red tinged light dancing up and down the ice-crusted walls,

and stalactites, which littered the cavern, floor and hung from the ceiling in varying sizes and shapes. The sunlight created a wavy pattern like a waterfall of purplish colors cascading down the grotto walls. The grotto floor, with its massive columns of stalagmites pointed like huge fingers toward the grotto roof.

The centuries of melting snow had produced differing shades of crusted ice in the formations. All the colors of life presented itself in the structure before them. Deep blues, blacks, browns, reds, yellows, orange, violets, crimson and greens of every hue, radiated inside the cavernous grotto. Moira and Starvros gaped at the stunning light show. It was a sharp contrast to the starkness of the blindingly white, snow-covered countryside.

"Isn't it beautiful Starvros?" Moira whispered.

"Yes, but do not be fooled by its beauty, Moira. We must search the grotto thoroughly because I believe it will lead us to Tika." Starvros said as they continued toward the grotto with the last of the rays from the setting sun. They were engulfed in light that cast their shadows onto the grotto wall like grotesque giants.

Moira grabbed Starvros' hand as they continued cautiously toward the grotto, as the light show included them in its dance along the walls and columns of ice within the grotto.

Starvros turned and looked at Moira, shocked by the charge that moved through his body at her touch. He grabbed her hand firmly and smiled at her. He looked into her frightened eyes and tried to reassure her with his eyes. Moira returned his smile as the pair walked toward the rear of the grotto.

Light did not penetrate far back into the grotto because of its size. Starvros stopped, let go of Moira's hand and searched the ground. When he was near she was not aware of the cold, but when he moved away from her, she felt as if she lost something very important to her. Moira was puzzled by her reactions.

"What are you looking for Starvros?" Moira asked, shivering from the cold.

"I am looking for a stick to make a torch. I will wrap rags around it so that we can see," Starvros said

"We will light a fire first, we will eat and then we will explore the grotto. We will be

looking for a way into the Snow Monster's castle. I am sure this is the back entrance. I think most old castles have a cave like entrance like this grotto at the rear of them or through the dungeons. The torch will help us see much better." Starvros said excitedly.

"Yes, you may be right Starvros. I will help look for a good stick for the torch,"

Moira said as she moved away from Starvros.

"Wait, Moira. We will search together. I do not want you to disappear, also. We are too close to discovering the Snow Monster. I believe that is why he took Tika. He is trying to frighten us into leaving this mountain and forget the quest. He wants us to admit defeat. However, I will not leave now. I am angry. He has Tika! I want to find the Snow Monster and free Tika. I want to free our village from that blasted curse more than anything else. We have suffered so long and have lost much. It is time we recovered our losses. It is time for him to pay!" Starvros said.

"Wow, what a mouthful Starvros, I did not know you were such a passionate person," Moira said.

"Huh? Are you teasing me Moira?" Starvros asked.

"Why, no sir, I am not teasing you!" Moira said laughing.

"Oh, there is a stick for the torch," Moira said before Starvros could respond to her teasing. She bent over and retrieved a stick from the debris-covered floor. She brushed away the debris and handed the stick to Starvros.

"Hurry Starvros, it's getting darker in here and I am wet, cold and hungry!" Moira continued.

"Good find, Moira," Starvros said. He pulled off his pack and searched through it feeling for the cloth to wrap around the stick to make a torch. Starvros tore one of his bed covers into rags for the torch. Starvros gathered debris from the grotto floor to wrap in the cloths to make them burn steady. He added some of the suet made by his father to give it the oil base needed to keep the torch burning.

"All I need is a place to make a fire," said Starvros.

"There! Look Starvros! It looks like a ledge or natural shelf in the mountain wall!

"We can make a fire there," said Moira running to the shelf ahead of Starvros.

Starvros came behind Moira and lifted her onto the shelf. He swung himself onto the ledge, picked up the torch and surveyed their surroundings. The ledge, hollowed into the mountain wall by water dripping down through the mountain from melting snows was soft beneath their feet from years of debris. Pine needles, leaves and moss made a soft cushion beneath their steps as they made their way further along the ledge.

It was damp but not wet or soggy. Huge boulders lay haphazardly around the ledge as if the mountain was falling apart inside. The stalactites suspended from the grotto roof to the floor of the ledge were not as big as the ones in the cavern.

"Be careful, Moira. We do not know if there are falling rocks in this grotto. These huge boulders had to come from somewhere. I do not want any falling on our heads,"

"This is a good place to light the torch, Moira. As you say, we are wet, cold and hungry, We will make camp here for the night and search for Tika at first light," said Starvros.

"You are right Starvros this place will make a good camp site. We will be able to see anything that approaches us, too. said Moira looking around at the darkened gloom of the cavern.

"We can settle down for the rest of the day and get started early in the morning with our search for Tika. I do not think the Snow Monster will harm her. He has his reasons for taking her, whether it is to frighten us or conquer us one by one. However, I hope she is not so afraid wherever she is," Starvros exclaimed.

"I do not think the Snow Monster knows what he is in for Starvros. He will have his hands full with Tika," Moira said laughing at the image in her mind. Where ever she is I am sure Tika is giving the Snow Monster a good tongue lashing, or she is unconscious in a dead faint," Moira said wryly.

"You said a mouth full, Moira," Starvros said laughing.

"Yet, this is a serious situation and we must not forget that, Moira." Starvros said stifling the laughter.

"I know, Starvros," Moira said as the laughter died at his words.

Starvros and Moira set about making camp. Starvros soon had a huge fire going which started the light show going again in the grotto; only it was more subdued in the dim light of the campfire. They used the many boulders and stones found in the grotto to enclose the fire and make seats for them to sit on. Moira set their food out on a few of the boulders she and Starvros pushed and dragged around the fire. She then went to their packs to set out their bedding for the night.

"Oh Starvros, our coverings are still wet from the storm! I am tired and cold and I want to go to bed! I feel the cold and dampness seeping into my bones. I do not think I will ever be warm," Moira moaned.

"Moira, you sound like Tika," Starvros said, laughing.

"That is not funny, Starvros. I do not sound like Tika. How are we going to sleep tonight with wet covers?" Moira asked.

"We can lay the covers on ropes tied to the ice columns here on the ledge. They are not as big as the columns in the cavern. The heat from the fire will dry them and until they dry, we can go to the forest beyond the grotto and cut branches to lie on and cover up with by the fire. Does that sound like a good solution to the problem, Moira?" Starvros asked.

Starvros put action to his words and soon had the covers strung up around the ledge to dry.

"Do you want to wait here by the fire Moira while I go and cut branches for us to sleep on?" Starvros asked.

"No, I will go with you. Although, the covers hide us from prying eyes, natural or unnatural, I do not want to be alone after what happened to Tika. Come on, Starvros, the sooner we leave, the sooner we get back." Moira said.

"Do not remind me of that, Moira. We will go together to get the material for our beds and return here to eat and sleep. Things will look better in the morning. Do not forget your staff, Moira." Starvros said as he helped her down from the ledge to the grotto floor.

Hand in hand they walked toward the forest, their feet crunching loud on the ice covered tundra. Starvros cut several low hanging branches to make their beds on the moss-covered ledge. He cut more to cover the two of them and still more for kindling, while Moira gathered firewood and dried pinecones underneath the thick trees. Starvros stuffed as much as he could into their packs and with their arms loaded, they headed back to the cavern at Moira's urging.

"Let us go back to the grotto Starvros, I really am tired and cold!" She pleaded.

"Yes Moira, Let us go back to our roaring fire," Starvros said smiling.

Moira gasped. 'She liked his smile which included you and warmed you inside at the same time. Why did she feel weak when he looked at her?' Moira thought as she looked at Starvros wistfully.

"What?" said Starvros.

"Nothing," said Moira quietly.

"Come on, then, back to our campsite." Starvros said, looking puzzled at Moira who hung her head and looked away from him, her cheeks flaming pink at his puzzled gaze. Tears stung Moira's eyes.

'Oh no! I love Starvros and he loves Tika. How could this happen? We have been childhood friends since I can remember. In fact, I was his only friend. At first I befriended him out of pity, but now...What a mess this quest has become,' Moira thought as they made their way to the campsite with their arms and packs full of bed making material.

"At this rate Moira it is going to take us a while to make it back to the cavern, so move slow but steady and we will get there without being too tired." Starvros said.

"I know Starvros, but I am very tired. I will be glad to see our campfire and I hope it is still lit and burning steady. I am ready for bed," Moira said.

"I too, am ready to lie down for the night. I do not think I will eat a meal, Moira.

If it is all right with you, we will make a huge bed with these branches and lie down together to warm each other until the morning.

"Y-Yes t-that is a-all r-right," Moira stammered.

'What will I do, lying so close to him?" My hands are sweaty and my stomach is jumping like frogs on a lily pad! Why did this have to happen now! I cannot be in love with Starvros!' Moira thought.

Moira's thoughts kept going round and round in her head so that she did not notice the

distance they traveled.

"Moira" our campsite is around the next bend, said Starvros, startling Moira out of her reverie.

"I am so glad Starvros, for I am really tired and ready for sleep, Moira mumbled.

"What did you say Moira?" Starvros said as he bent his head near her face to hear her words.

Chapter 7

Surprises for Tika

Tika awoke to dizziness and feelings of dread. Her mind felt fuzzy like she had slept too long or too hard. She shook her head to clear her thoughts and the cobwebs that lingered.

"W-Where am I?" Tika asked.

Tika tried to focus in the pitch darkness.

"Maybe if I stand up I can figure out where I am," Tika said to herself.

Tika sat up as more dizziness assailed her. She paused, put her arms out to her sides and steadied herself as she continued to rise to her feet. Tika stood up completely and inched forward slowly using her feet as a guide to search the area around her.

Tika began to talk to ease the fear that gripped tightly in the pit of her stomach as she searched her surroundings.

"I remember the terrible icy fog, and wind storm. I remember Starvros tying me to the tree and covering my face and body with my coverings I remember being pelted by the icy cold wind and debris, but I remember something else in the storm…SOMETHING TOUCHED ME!" The fear rose to her throat as she realized something came to her in the storm.

It was different from the debris, which pelted her. It was different than the icy cold wind. It was not the cold moist fog.

"I remember! I screamed and screamed for Starvros and Moira and when neither Starvros nor Moira heard my cries, I-I fainted. I think I fainted. I-I could not have walked here, could I?" Tika said. Oh no not again!" Tika wailed as she realized- I have been captured by the Snow Monster."

Tika took great gulps of air to slow her breathing. She gagged from the sour contents that rose in her throat. Tika placed her hands on her stomach and pressed firmly to keep the spasms from overtaking her. She spat the salty taste of fear onto the floor. "A floor!" Tears stung her eyes as Tika realized she was not out on the cold, snowy tundra.

Tika continued to inch forward until her hands touched a cold stone wall'

"A wall!" Tika said.

Tika laughed. The tears streamed down Tika's face. Relief flowed where fear and bitterness languished briefly.

"I am inside! I am not abandoned out in the cold to die alone! I am not out in this terrible mountain lost to my family forever," Tika said as relief poured through her like a waterfall releasing some of her fears!

"Hoo, hoo," she uttered joyously.

"I was captured!" Tika said.

"The snow monster has captured me!"

"I have got to find out where I am," Tika continued.

"Is Starvros and Moira here, too?" Tika said excitedly losing the fear in a moment as she thought of her comrades.

"Are we all prisoners here?" Tika questioned.

Tika continued to inch her way around and found herself in a small room as her eyes adjusted to the gross darkness. Her mind reeled as the word "dungeon," flew into her mind.

"No, I can't be a prisoner in a dungeon!" Tika said as she bowed her head into her hands and began to cry again.

"Why me? Who is doing this to me? Something evil is going on. I felt it since we began this quest. Oh Dirk, if only I had stayed in Circle Valley and married you, I would not be in this dungeon now, captured by the Snow Monster." Tika mumbled through her tears.

Tika cried harder than ever when she thought about Dirk. She did not think of Starvros, but of Dirk.

"I ran away from him only to become captive of the love hiding in my heart." Tika said.

"I do love Dirk!" Tika whispered. 'He would protect me even from my own impetuosity, which caused me to follow Starvros on this foolish quest,' Tika thought as the revelation of her love for Dirk swirled in her brain.

Tika lifted her head and shook her long raven locks.

"I will find a way out of here, I do not need anyone's help. I grew up in this terrible mountain. I come from a long line of mountain women. Hunters are my heritage. These people made their living in the worst part of the world while living in the shadow of the curse of the Snow Monster. It has made us stronger. Only we do not know it because we cower in fear from his posturing and roaring in our mountains. Who could endure under the terrible conditions forced upon them by the curse and still manage to eke out a living for hundreds of years. I am not sorry I came on this quest. We still have our mission. We have to find out what the curse is and how to destroy it and the Snow Monster. If he has brought me to his lair, then he has made a fatal mistake. I can help Starvros from the inside. We will be victorious yet! All I have got to do is keep my head, wait for my chance and try to out maneuver the Snow Monster," Tika panted.

Renewed confidence flooded Tika's mind.

"My view is clearer, now. I do not love Starvros. I wanted to love him because I rejected Dirk. Dirk will move heaven and earth to rescue me and I must be ready to do my part. So come on Snow Monster, show yourself," Tika challenged loudly in the darkness.

Tika moved around in what she discovered was a small dungeon-like room. She found a small cot and sat upon it. Tiredness swooped upon her. Her tirade seemed to have drained the last of her energy. There was a thin ragged blanket. Tika pulled the blanket around her, gathered her feet upon the cot and was soon asleep.

Tika did not see or hear the heavy slit in the door slide into place. The figure looking through the door sighed in relief.

She will sleep from the sleeping powder I cast into the room. I do not need a screaming girl on my hands. I have enough trouble trying to figure out what to do about the lad and the other girl as well as a whole village of men traipsing about in my mountains. The girls and the villagers mean nothing to me, but the lad…

I am aware of the prophecy concerning a lad…

After many centuries of peaceful existence the Snow Monster now faced ruin at the hands of a small lad. The lad must never discover the truth of the curse. It would be his end as the Snow Monster. He did not like his lot in life but he did not like death as an option either. He was as trapped now as he was centuries ago when all this began. However, a plan was forming. He could use the lad to free himself from the curse.

His mind unwittingly went to that night.

"No, not now," The Snow Monster said loudly.

"I will not revisit that night again. It is torture. If I could undo the past I would.

"My powers are limited by the curse, but…"

The Snow Monster shook himself free of past memories and spoke brusquely into the air,

"Bring her to me when the sleeping potion wears off." he disappeared from the doorway and the figure standing beside him melted away into the darkness, having no need to speak because they always obeyed his commands.

Tika woke to the sound of a door opening. Light from the doorway streamed across her face. Tika blinked her eyes rapidly to adjust to the light, raising her hand to shield them.

"W-who is t-there?" Tika called.

"W-who are you? W-why am I here? Answer me!" Tika called loudly, frustration building because no one answered her questions. Tika could feel the fear and anger fighting for expression in her mind.

"Say something whoever you are," Tika said crossly. Anger moved the other emotions out as her appeals were met with silence.

"I said, who is there? What do you want with me?" Tika said, rising and stomping toward the open doorway.

There was no one there! Tika peered out the door as her eyes grew accustomed to the light. She was not in a dungeon! Relief flowed and the anger and fear dissipated leaving her limp as a rag doll leaning against the doorjamb. Tika stepped gingerly into the hallway. She stood in a long narrow hall with doors flanking both sides. Tika's eyes widened as she realized she was in some sort of edifice. Torches, perched high on the walls added what light there was along the hall. She counted five torches including the one outside her door that had awakened her. Tika looked behind her to discover she was in the last room along the hall. There were three doors on the same side as the room she had vacated, and as she traversed the hall she tried each door to find them locked tight. She knocked and called Starvros and Moira's name but got no response. Tika's spirits dropped when she got no response from the last door. Her comrades had not been captured with her. She was alone! Tika continued down the dimly lit hall and stood before a huge thick door, larger than the other doors, it filled the hallway opening.

"No one can hear anything through that door, Tika said as she reached out to grab the latchet. The door swung open and Tika screamed. The occupant on the other side of the door yelled in a loud raspy voice.

Tika stood face to face with a shrunken little man of indeterminate age. He stood straight and erect which made him appear taller. He had a long neck and a beaklike nose over huge black eyes, which snapped angrily at her, under gray, bushy brows. His stringy gray hair was long and sparse in places that was not covered by a green and yellow cap sitting slightly on the back of his head. His arms were long and thin which did not agree with the rest of his physique. His legs were short and bowed. He looked like a rat on two legs. He wore a gray tunic over a brown woven sweater and baggy gray trousers were stuffed into thick deerskin boots, well worn over the years but, they looked well made. Tika could tell they were lined inside with fur.

'No wonder she could not hear him come and go,' Tika thought.

They stood in the doorway looking at each other. Both, breathing quickly after being startled by the other, tried to speak but no sound came as they both opened and closed their mouths.

The silence was broken as the man who stood before her found his voice first.

"You are awake!' I was coming back to get you, but since you are awake, come along!" He reached a long narrow hand and grabbed Tika's wrist propelling her through the huge door into a huge room.

"Do not touch me! Let me go! I did not give you permission to touch me!" Tika yelled, twisting and wrenching free of his hand.

"Help me, someone help me!" Tika continued.

The little man stuck his face so close to Tika's face she could smell the putrid odor from a mouth filled with rotting teeth and spittle drooled from the corners of his mouth. The eyes were dead as he spoke in a quiet raspy monotone that arrested her attention, more than any threat of violence could do.

"Listen, Missy, I am Bartoll! You come with me and be quick about it or I will have to call for more help to handle you. You hear me missy! You don't want Bartoll to have to call for more help do you?" said Bartoll menacingly.

"No, I do not want you to get more help," said Tika rubbing her wrists. He was strong! Tika already saw bruising where she had wrenched away from Bartoll.

Bartoll looked at Tika and said, "Come along missy, do not stand there gabbing.

We do not want to keep my master waiting for long."

"Your master, is he the Snow Monster?" Tika said, her fear forgotten in the light of this new revelation. She was finally going to meet the elusive Snow Monster. Tika felt lightheaded at the thought. 10

"Ha! I will meet him before Starvros or Moira. Seems like Starvros' quest has become my quest, Tika said shaking her raven locks.

"You keep your questions to yourself, Missy. You will find out only what my master wants you to know, shortly," said Bartoll as he nudged Tika to walk before him.

'You do not know me very well. I will find out the truth about your master,' Tika thought.

Tika shrugged away from Bartoll. She did not want the little man to touch her again. She walked in the direction he pointed. Tika walked slowly through the rooms as Bartoll indicated which way she was to go. Tika tried to remember her way through the maze of rooms for an escape route, but Bartoll sensing her design, grabbed her by the elbow and propelled her speedily through the rooms. Tika felt he was going around in circles purposely to confuse her.

Tika recognized the obvious signs of wealth. She had never seen wealth like this in Circle Valley, except for the Shamans' and her own house, but they paled in comparison to the wealth she saw unfolding before her very eyes. Tika saw shrouded furniture in rooms as well as furniture with ornate carvings and cabinets with painted drawings, tapestries with ancient scenes, animal hides of animals she had never seen before covered the bare floors. Tika noticed the furniture became more opulent and decorative as they moved through the rooms. The furniture went from plain wooden furniture to furniture with scrollwork and intricate designs. The floors went from a dirt floor in the kitchen area to bare wood floors, and finally intricately carved wood floors, and inlaid rock and pebble floors.

Soon they reached a big ornate carved door. It took all of Bartoll's strength to open the stout door. Once inside he grabbed Tika by the wrist, stood perfectly still, and erect. Tika was about to object to the way she was being treated, but looking around the room she was stunned into silence.

Tika's eyes widened as she saw gold and black veined drapes at the long paned windows flanking a huge, black, marble fireplace. Massive chairs arranged before the fireplace. She counted six of them. The floor, thickly covered gave soundlessness to their footfalls as Bartoll pulled Tika to the center of the room. He seemed uncertain about what to do with her. Tapestries depicting hunting scenes hung on most of the walls that was not covered with pictures of people Tika did not know. Elegant tables stood in front of the windows covered with artifacts and trinkets Tika had never seen before glittered in the candlelight, reflected by the prisms of a gigantic candle-lit chandelier above a giant table in the center of the room. Next to it was an even bigger chair, intricately carved and covered in deerskin.

"It looks like a throne," Tika said.

A stone bench graced a corner, carved with an elaborate base with rounded feet resembling animal paws. Next to the bench was a table filled with food on gold plates with gold chargers, gold cutlery and gold trimmed goblets, which caught Tika's eye and she heard her stomach rumble and her mouth watered when she realized the food was real. Tika dashed past Bartoll and fell upon the food, stuffing her mouth before the old man could react.

Bartoll was upon her, "Missy, you are not to do that! You must wait on Bartoll to present you to my master!" he said, shocked at what she had done.

"But, I am hungry! I have not eaten since before that blasted storm," Tika wailed her mouth full of delicious tasting food.

"Put the food down, Missy. You will be fed in a more dignified manner than manhandling the food like that," said Bartoll. The King demands his subjects act with decorum," Bartoll continued.

"King, did you say King? I thought I was going to meet the Snow Monster! Who is this king?" Tika asked, as food tumbled from her mouth onto the thick carpet.

"Oh you are a troublesome girl!" Bartoll said, as he led Tika to the stone bench.

"Sit down here until the master arrives. I will present you to him and he will decide what to do with you." Bartoll said.

"But I am so-o-o hungry!" ...What do you mean by" what will be done with me?" Tika asked. "I hope he has the decency to feed me before he does anything with me," Tika said smartly.

"You will see, now calm down and wait here for the master. You will not try to run away will you? There are those who watch for the ones that run away and they bring them back to my master, and I never see them again. Missy, you take heed to what Bartoll says and you will be okay, but if you try to run away the watchers will find you. You hear me Missy! Stay here and wait for my master. I must go and replace the food you have eaten or my master will be angry with me," Bartoll said, backing away from Tika to another smaller door in the big room. Bartoll went through the door and Tika was left with more questions than she knew.

Now there was a King, and watchers to deal with on this quest!

Things are getting more complicated. What have we gotten ourselves into?" Tika questioned. Tika sat down on the bench. It was too much to take in. Tika was numb from more than the cold of the storm.

"I have been captured, but by whom?" Tika asked aloud.

"And you are a very pretty captive, too my dear," said a voice from the big ornate doorway.

Tika turned toward the door and leaped up from the bench.

"Why you are prettier than Starvros," Tika said.

"I-I mean handsomer than Starvros," Tika stuttered.

Tika saw a tall, broad man with dark curly hair matted thick to his head with locks framing his face. He had long side burns and a thin mustache over full sensual lips.

A square jaw line defined a strong chin with just the hint of a dimple in his cheeks when he talked. She could not determine the color of his eyes from the distance between them.

He moved with grace for a big man and he oozed an animal like musky odor which set Tika's nerve tingling as he neared Tika and took her hand. Tika did not snatch her hand away as she had done with Bartoll. Tika's gaze held captive by eyes that were not eyes, that reflected the room, her and the candlelight, and there was no warmth in those eyes.

"I have never been called pretty before, my dear. Allow me to present myself I am King Hector!

"King Hector! I have never heard of you! Where is the Snow Monster? Who are You? Where are my friends? Why was I captured?" Tika rushed the questions forming in her mind at the man standing before her. He was so handsome, Tika admitted, but she did not trust him. There was something dangerous lurking beneath the surface of the charm he was throwing her way.

"I am the King of Circle Valley," King Hector said, matter-of-factly.

"Circle Valley does not have a king, you liar," Tika shouted.

"You do not need to shout, my girl, but yes, I am the King of Circle Valley. I have been King of Circle Valley for over 500 years. I rule this castle and this terrible mountain- Mount Ra-Ninjitsi," the King said bitterly.

"I do not rule the people of Circle Valley, I have a…

"Well, there is no need to go into that,

Tika interrupted him.

"Who are you really?" Tika asked, looking at him deeply, trying to see past the façade he was presenting to her.

'There is something deeper here. Something more sinister," Tika thought as she gazed wonderingly at the well-dressed man before her.

"I told you who I am, and I am not used to people doubting my word, young lass," King Hector said, pompously.

"Isn't that right, Bartoll," the king said as Bartoll reentered the room through the small door with a tray full of food. The aroma sent Tika's stomach flipping and jumping and a loud roar emanated from her stomach..

"Okay, okay, but can we finish this while we eat, Tika said following Bartoll to the table.

Bartoll turned after laying the tray on the table and spoke in his quiet raspy voice,

"My master does not lie, missy and I do not know anyone who has called him such and lived, watch your tongue and your manners when you are in the presence of the King."

"Why am I here, then?" Tika asked.

"All will be told to you in good time, lass, for now consider yourself a guest of King Hector. Once a person enters the castle, they cannot leave it. It is enchanted. I brought you here for myself. If you try to escape, the watchers will capture you and return you to the dungeons. It is up to you lass. Will you be a guest by invitation or by force," King Hector stated quietly.

Tika looked at him, gauging whether he spoke truthfully or not. Tika could not tell, she only knew she had to gain time until Starvros, Tika or Dirk and the villagers came to her rescue.

'They will find me eventually,' Tika thought. Tika curtsied to the King.

"I will be a guest of peace, King Hector, even if I was brought here by force," Tika said.

"A good choice, lass, now, why don't we eat some of this food your stomach was growling for," King Hector said.

Tika rushed to the table not waiting for King Hector and began to laden her plate with the food.

"You need to learn good manners young lady." King Hector said.

"I have manners," Tika retorted. "I am hungry!"

I hope you are not harboring the foolish notion that your friends will rescue you. I have already set in motion directives for their capture. Everyone running around in my mountain will be my captives, King Hector said as his voice deepened to a guttural snarl and his visage changed. He grew larger and larger. His pretty hair grew until it covered his entire body, the clothes he wore fell as rags to the floor. His face was completely covered. His teeth elongated becoming fangs in his mouth and his tongue hung from his hairy face. His body covered in tangled masses of black flowing hair, loomed above Tika. Claws curved toward her face on hands bigger than her entire face.

Tika screamed and fainted, falling to the thick pelt covered floor. The creature turned when the transformation was complete, Stepped over the girl on the floor and left the room not seeing her or Bartoll. He was following a long-standing directive.

Bartoll stooped and picked the unconscious girl up in his arms. She was slight and easy to carry. Bartoll used the door he had used before only this time it swung open effortlessly. He carried the unconscious Tika back to the room she was in earlier.

He laid her carefully on the bed. Bartoll forced a few drops of a potion between her lips. This will help her to forget what she saw. No one must know that King Hector and the Snow Monster are the same. Bartoll did not question the age-old directive. He only obeyed his Masters' directives. Bartoll sighed deeply. He hated that the girl saw the change. He still could not get used to the sight of King Hector changing into that awful creature. Bartoll backed out of the room and stood in the opening, looking at the beautiful girl lying on the bed. He only wanted someone for himself. Bartoll knew of the loneliness that ate away at him. The intense longing for the family he lost, but some things were best, not tampered with. Bartoll could sense a change coming about because of the things already set in motion. The girl and her two friends, the villagers and now this…Bartoll closed the door and went to wait for his Master's return.

Tika awoke to much confusion. Where am I? How did I get here? What is this place? Ouch, my head hurts! Where are Moira and Starvros? Tika stood up and reeled like a drunken man. What is this? What is happening? Tika sat down on the small cot, holding her head in her hands. Waves of nausea flowed through her body. She felt lightheaded. Her brain felt like it was full of sheep's wool. Soon the symptoms passed and Tika was able to stand. She walked slowly to the door of the small room she found herself in and tried the door, and to her surprise, it opened. Tika poked her head through the door peering out to see it there was anyone beyond the door. There was a long hallway with torches high on the walls of hewn stone. As Tika turned to look up and down the hallway, she saw she was in the last room at the end of the hall. As Tika tried the doors to the other rooms, she found them locked. When she reached the last room, she stood before a huge stone door with a heavy latch. Tika had the queer feeling she had seen that door before. When ever, if she tried to remember her head hurt terribly. Tika grabbed the latch with both hands and pulled. The door looked heavy and she pulled with all her strength. The door moved slowly a few inches. Tika continued to pull on the huge door until the opening was wide enough for her to get through. Tika squeezed through the door and found herself in a large kitchen with a huge fireplace, lots of pots, cutlery, plates and cups. Tika passed through the kitchen into another room. She traversed many rooms and saw no one. Tika knew that she had to keep moving until she could know where she was, how she got there and why she was here. Tika went up several stone steps at different levels. She finally came to an opulent level. The floors were thick with animal pelts. Tapestries covered the walls; ornate tables situated in the area with various items, covered in thick dust filled the rooms. At the end of the hall was a closed door. Tika did not want to retreat so she opened the door and entered the room. Once her eyes adjusted to the darkness of the room, Tika immediately saw a huge tapestry on the wall above a large stone fireplace. It was a woman. The tapestry was hand stitched and depicted a woman with flowing blonde hair over a high forehead with a long narrow aquiline nose sitting above a thin shapely mouth. A heart shaped chin looked out of place. The thick flowing hair covered large ears with tiny pearl earrings, the eyes were the bluest, blue Tika had ever seen. She had a long neck and soft white shoulders showing through a sheer fabric blouse with a blue jumper the same color as her eyes. As Tika continued to stare at the image, wondering whom the woman was she had the strangest feeling she had seen the face before. Where could she have seen that face? There was no one in Circle Valley who looked like that; Tika knew this for sure. If there were someone in Circle Valley, then she would have a comely competitor! No, No, Tika, how could you have seen this woman before? Obviously, she lived long ago. Tika could tell by the condition of the tapestry and the dust, which dulled the image, but those piercing blue eyes seemed to follow her everywhere, as if condemning her for invading her sanctuary. Tika could tell from the feminine touches in the room that it was her room.

Tika shook her head to clear her thoughts and the cobwebs that fogged her brain as she continued to investigate the room.

Suddenly the door she had so quietly closed flung open and Bartoll stood in the entrance, breathing heavy.

"Missy, what are you doing in this room? You are trouble, nothing but trouble! How did you get in here? No one is allowed in here!" hissed Bartoll in his raspy voice.

You must leave at once! Bartoll continued, before my Master finds us both in here, walking toward Tika.

Tika looked at Bartoll with wide fearful eyes. Memory returned in a flash and Tika screamed as the visage of the Snow Monster loomed in her memory and she fainted.

CHAPTER 8

MAYOR BROWN LEADS HIS TROOPS

"How are we going to find Starvros and the girls, Mayor? Asked Jorge, since Dirk and Gustavo are gone, we have lost our two best trackers," he continued.

"Jorge, I am not a bad tracker myself. Our ancestors have trained us all. We know the ways of the hunter. Because I choose to stay in Circle Valley does not mean I cannot lead nor am I a coward. I say to you that I can lead you men as well as Dirk or Gustavo," the mayor stated, unused to having his orders second-guessed.

"Aye, but when was the last time you went on a hunt? This is not a trek in the woods, Mayor Brown," said Josef.

"If Starvros can do it so can I, the Mayor stated as he moved away from Jorge as if to

dismiss his doubts.

"Let's get to it, men. We are wasting time! Break camp and prepare to climb. There is very little chance to rest until we reach the last plateau before the summit!" restated the Mayor excitement in his voice, mingled with fear.

Everyone pitched in and soon they all had assembled before the Mayor with their gear all packed, waiting for further instructions.

"Men, the Mayor stated as he cleared his throat, we will continue to look for a trail left by Starvros and the girls. I am sure that evil storm has set them back a day and we will be able to catch up to them on the morrow." The men trekked in pairs up the mountain throughout the rest of the day and well into the evening. They reached the third level of the mountain, before the peak and continued to span out on the flat expanse of land looking for signs of the trio. We are onto them, Men. Look for any signs or tracks that will lead us to Starvros and the girls. I believe we are also close to the Snow Monster's lair, so keep a sharp lookout for anything unusual and warn everyone. Do not make too much noise, and use your staff to check for fissures, crevices and ravines beneath the snow. The ice storm has frozen everything making the going more dangerous. Do not yell or make any loud noises. We do not want to start an avalanche, nor do we want to separate from each other and get lost out here or fall into hidden crevices or canyons. I want every man here to make it back to Circle Valley alive and well. Be very careful from this point on, we have many unforeseen dangers on this journey. I will assume Dirk's responsibilities for Gustavo's family, now that he is gone," said the Mayor issuing orders to the men as they began their final ascent to the mountain peak. Everyone fell silent as they concentrated on getting up the face of the mountain safely; the mayor assigned himself to Jorge and Josef to insure his safety the rest of the way up the mountain.

Upon reaching the flat plateau, they quickly set up camp to rest. After a brief rest, they continued on their way, thrilled to find evidence of the trio's site.

Mayor Brown rubbed his hands together from the cold air in delight that they finally found signs of the trio. It meant they were still alive and moving toward their final destination-The Snow Monster's lair! The villagers traveled onward following the trail left by Starvros and Moira.

Though the sun was not visible because of the clouds that seemed to settle permanently on the peak, the snow glistened like tiny prisms. The threat of more snowfall hung over the villagers like the misty fog. It made the men eager to get off the mountain. They pushed forward with lips pressed together, eyes focused on the trail ahead. There was almost no conversation except to give directions or warnings when a crevice or fissure or sharp rocks under the deep snow was visible or found, with their staffs which they poked through the snow; gauging the deepness of the snow or if they were on solid ground. The air was colder than it was in the lower elevations. Any moisture froze to your face and many of the men with beards wore thick scarves around their faces, thanking their wives for their skills on the looms, weaving the thick clothes from plant and animal fibers.

The villagers traveled for most of the day as the men found a pattern to work through without Dirk or Gustavo. They moved slower because of Mayor Brown but they moved steadily. Snow fell randomly throughout their trek up the mountain.

"Be careful men; use your staff to test for crevices and fissures underneath the snow…!"

"Yowl!"

"What has happened, now," the Mayor yelled as the sound of a terrified yell reached his ears.

"It is Clauder," Clyde said running toward the Mayor. He -he f-fell into a crevice. The snow moved beneath his staff and he fell in. I can see him! We need to help him, Mayor," Clyde stated, breathing heavily from fear and the exertion of running in the deep snow. Mayor Brown and the villagers moved slowly toward Clauder as Clyde led the way back toward him.

"Use your staff, man!" the Mayor hissed. We do not want anyone else falling into a crevice. Obviously, the ground is softer around here! You three walk around behind the fissure so that you are behind Clauder. Clauder are you able to move, asked Dirk. Are you all right? Hold on we will get you out of there," said the Mayor.

"Aye, hurry Mayor! Clauder called. I cannot hold on much longer!"

He had fallen into a crevice that had a protruding ledge. It slanted slightly upward which prevented Clauder from falling into the crevice completely. Covered in snow, Clauder moved slightly.

"Bobbo, you and Karlief and Rafello tie ropes to each other. Leave a long piece in front of the lead man, which will be Bobbo. Inch your way to the edge of the crevice and throw your end of the rope to Clauder so that he can secure himself. The rest of us will hold on to the end of the rope tied to you three and pull you back and eventually pull Clauder out of the crevice.

The three men moved slowly toward the edge of the crevice stopping often to check for cracks and crevices. Sweat poured from their faces. It flowed into their eyes, but each man refused to stop and wipe the sweat away. Their eyes focused on their footfalls, as each man made sure he stepped on solid ground. Eventually they were close enough to throw a rope to Clauder. Bobbo talked to Clauder giving him instructions. Clauder moved slowly as he tied the rope and looped it around his upper body. When secured, he gave a tug on the rope and the villagers began to pull in concert with each other. It was a rhythm as ancient as Circle Valley. Clauder, pulled back onto solid ground and checked for injuries stood, with tears of gratitude in his eyes for his comrades, who would not leave him to die, but risked their lives to save his. He thanked the men and turned to thank Mayor Brown.

"It is not necessary to thank me, Clauder. You are a citizen of Circle Valley and your well-being is important to me. Let us get moving, men! I meant it when I said be careful! We do not know this terrain! Pair up, and tie yourselves together, then tie your rope to the pair behind you. The last pair will tie their rope to the pair before them, thus we will all be linked together like a chain," said Mayor Brown. The villagers traveled onward with no further incidents, well into the evening, rounding an outcropping of rock to see the huge cavernous grotto glowing red in the darkened sky.

"What is this?" the Mayor spoke as he observed the scene before him.

"Is it the great deep-the place for evil souls?" whispered Clyde.

Others said, "Where are we?" "What is this place?" "Why is it glowing red?" "It is evil!" "We must leave this place!"

"Nonsense, men, let us go and see what this place is about," Mayor Brown sputtered. The men gathered around the Mayor as they moved as one unit toward the cavernous grotto. "Slowly, men, said the Mayor. There is no need to hurry. We must be careful. Keep a watchful eye for the unexpected."

Soon the villagers reached the grotto and saw the fire burning brightly on the ledge almost like a welcoming beacon, which gave the cavern the red glow they saw when they rounded the rocky outcropping.

"What does this mean, Mayor?" asked Karlief.

"It is eerie!" There is no one here, but the fire beckons like someone or something was waiting for us," Bobbo said speaking into the Mayor's ear.

"I don't like it," Bobbo continued.

"Maybe we should move on, further away from this place," Josef stated, feeling the eeriness of the place and the hairs on his head began to move as fear spread along his torso.

"No, Men. It is obvious the children made the fire! See their bedding spread out to dry further along the ledge." the Mayor spoke, his eyes darting about, never resting long in one place. The torch on the ground over there is more proof that they were here. We have caught them at last!" The Mayor said gleefully.

"Where are the children now, Mayor?" Rafello asked.

"This is their campsite, men and we will settle down here to wait for their return It is late this will make a good campsite and if they do not return, this will be a good base to set out to look for them when morning comes. We have had a grueling trek this day and I believe it is time for a good night's rest before we face Starvros and the girls or the Snow Monster, whichever appears first. We will need our strength to handle it. Make camp and let's eat a good meal before we face the morrow," the Mayor stated emphatically. There is plenty of room on the ledge for all of us. We will set a guard. Bobbo you take the first watch. We will have our captives by morning and we can get off this terrible mountain and return the children to the safety of Circle Valley. Things are turning out better than I thought," stated the Mayor.

"Help me onto the ledge men!" Mayor Brown commanded. He found a huge boulder before the fire Starvros and Moira started and ensconced upon it to await their return. Mayor Brown sat and ruminated about the events that took place since Dirk left them to fend for themselves. Mayor Brown congratulated himself on having led the men to this successful part of the journey. The end was almost in sight, all he had to do was wait for the children to return to their campsite, take them as prisoners and return to Circle Valley. He was glad Dirk left. Mayor Brown saw that he leaned on Dirk like the other men. He did not expect Dirk to be the first to crumble under the burden of their undertaking to find the girls and Starvros. Dirk was the strongest, bravest man in the village, or so they all thought he was until he killed Gustavo. Mayor Brown realized that leadership was more than a title, more than a right of birth and more than what you think it is. Leadership is experienced in the trenches, gained through working together in the hardships of life and figuring out how to solve those hard times with courage, foresight and humility. Mayor Brown failed to develop his relationship with the men of the village until now. Starvros' quest helped him to see that life was more than accepting what came your way. Life is what you make of it. The villagers accepted the curse on Circle Valley and lived under its precepts without question. They only complained and fought among themselves over their lot in life, blaming everything on the Snow Monster, and that blasted curse. Mayor Brown's reflections interrupted when he heard Bobbo shout, "Halt! Who goes there?"

CHAPTER 8

DIRK'S ESCAPES TO MOUNT RaNanjitsi

Dirk slowly backed away from the Mayor and the villagers and walked quickly as he could on the slippery, frozen tundra, and disappeared into the woods leaving the stunned villagers behind. Dirk walked back the way they had come over the plateau to the forest. Dirk was determined to make his escape as quickly as he could. He knew there was no hope for him and Tika. I have lost another love through no fault of my own. Dirk continued onward, stopping shortly, listening to see if the villagers were following him. Dirk meant it when he said he would kill them if they tried to brand him.

"I am Dirk! I will wear no one's brand! I did not mean to kill Gustavo. It was an accident. Gustavo was my friend. I do not know what happened to change him, but I do know that I could not let him talk to me like that. The other men would not respect Dirk if I let Gustavo off without a warning. Mayor Brown was being unreasonable, throwing his authority around and treating Dirk like an outlaw. I am Dirk, the best hunter, tracker and the bravest man in Circle Valley! I have no choice but to leave Circle Valley. This is all Starvros' fault. His silly quest has caused Dirk to lose everything. I must find a way off this terrible mountain. I will try the back side of the mountain away from the villagers," Dirk said as he fumbled his way through the tough terrain looking for a way off the mountain, away from Tika, Starvros and Circle Valley. As Dirk bent his head into the wind, he vowed silently that if he ever saw Starvros Gunther he would kill the boy with gladness. Dirk traveled far into the evening.

'This is not the way we came, so I am sure I have left the villagers far behind me.' Dirk thought.

Dirk continued his journey far into the day, traveling away from the villagers toward the backside of Mount RaNinjitsi. The terrain was wider on the backside of the mountain. It was less mountainous and had more ground cover. Dirk was careful to use his staff as much as possible on the unfamiliar terrain. Dirk kept moving well into the night purposing to put much distance between him and the villagers. By early morning, Dirk surmised he was well on the other side of the mountain and the villagers were not in pursuit. Dirk slowed his steps and looked for a place to stop and regroup, and plan his next step. Dirk was a seasoned hunter and he knew he could not travel in these mountains without a plan. Dirk knew he needed to replenish his supplies. He did not know when he started the journey that he would not be returning to Circle Valley. Fear of the unknown tried to assail him but Dirk pushed the fear away.

"Dirk will find a way! First I must rest and clear my head," Dirk said.

Dirk traveled on looking for a place to camp and soon came upon a small stand of trees with craggy rocks and boulders strewn around like children's toys. It was a pristine landscape. No footprints but his. Dirk did not see one animals' footfall in the clearing. The air was moist and mist hung heavy beneath dark looming clouds.

'This side of the mountain is as gloomy as the other side of Mount RaNinjitsi, but this will be a good place to rest and regroup,' Dirk thought and set about making camp for the rest of the morning.

Dirk lay upon fresh branches he cut from the stand of trees. He was eager to rest and be on his way. A sense of freedom gripped Dirk.

'He would be free from the curse of the Snow Monster once he found a way off Mount RaNinjitsi. It was a strange feeling,' Dirk thought as sleep claimed him, quickly.

Dirk awoke hours later well rested. He prepared a meal and sat on a boulder surveying his surroundings. Dirk noticed random stacks of snow covered mounds in the snow toward the edge of the clearing. They were spaced evenly apart.

'What is this?' Dirk thought. Dirk gathered his belongings after his meal and went to investigate the mysterious snow mounds. Dirk reached the first snow mound and brushed away the snow and debris to uncover boulders stacked atop each other.

'This is odd? How did this get here? Who did this?' Dirk pondered in his mind. He went to the next snow mound and uncovered a similar stack of boulders.

"It looks like a marker for a trail! I will follow the trail and see where it leads. Maybe it is a way off this terrible mountain." Dirk said. Putting action to his words Dirk walked from one snow mound to another uncovering it so that if he had to retrace his steps he would not make a misstep, but could follow the pillars of boulders back the way he had come. Dirk walked on following the snow mounds where they led and soon found that he standing before a great yawning ravine. Dirk walked quickly from the ravine. He did like the way it made him feel. It was as if he wanted to throw himself over the side of the ravine into the nothingness, which presented itself before him.

"What is this? Ugh! It is always one obstacle after another with this terrible mountain!"

How do I cross that ravine? What is on the other side? Who is on the other side? What is this awful place? Dirk uttered.

Questions he had no answers to tumbled around in his mind. Fear gripped his heart!

"No! I will not be afraid. I am Dirk! I am the bravest man in Circle Valley! I will not let this mountain defeat me! It is evil!" Dirk said. Dirk began to walk alongside the ravine far enough away to keep from leaping over the side. Dirk used his staff as usual searching for cracks and crevices beneath the snow.

"I will rest again and search the area for another trail off this mountain. I feel I am close, but the mountain seems to fight back at every turn. There must be a trail across that ravine!" Dirk averred'

Dirk crawled into his bedding and slept fitfully with dreams of chasing Starvros, Tika, the Snow Monster, and ended with him falling into the ravine, where a ghostlike Abbey- laurel held out hands for him to come to her. Dirk awoke with a start. Sweat poured from him. He breathed deeply of the fresh morning air to free the cobwebs of his nightmare from his mind. Dirk rose and rekindled the dying fire, warmed himself and ate a small breakfast. Dirk knew he would have to ration his supplies until he found a way off the mountain.

The sky was thick with grayish- black rolling clouds. Dirk saw the cold wind blowing up from the ravine and the snow scampered before it across the snow-covered terrain a myriad of glistening particles, resembling a dust storm. The particles of snow blew toward him like a thing alive and covered him causing him to shiver with cold.

"Hurry up fire. I need to pack and get out of here. I do not like this place!" Dirk said as he gathered his gear while trying to warm himself. Dirk stretched his cramped muscles and decided to follow the ravine well enough away from the edge until he found a trail that connected the ravine to whatever was on the other side of it that would lead him off Mount RaNinjitsi. There was something sinister about the backside of Mount RaNinjitsi. Dirk could feel it.

Dirk was facing the mountain he had come down. There were meager forests interspersed with huge boulders that looked as if they had fallen from the mountain peak itself. Dirk turned toward the ravine and gasped. Thick clouds, black with snow, hung heavy, hugging the ground in the distance, making it appear as if the ravine had disappeared.

"It is there! I know the ravine is there! What kind of sorcery is this?" Dirk said.

Dirk gathered his pack and flung it over his shoulder. There was no more time for speculations. It was time for action.

"I will never get off this mountain if I think too much." Dirk said, as he walked purposely toward the ravine he knew was there; but kept a respectable distance until he saw the yawning cavity that was the ravine itself. Dirk traveled parallel to the ravine keeping it in sight as he searched for a trail. The snow began to fall as Dirk made his way alongside the ravine. They were huge flakes of snow, filled with moisture.

'There must be a river at the bottom of the ravine. The snow is wet and heavy and it is freezing on my face,' thought Dirk.

Dirk stopped and searched his pack for the heavy woolen scarves the women in Circle Valley wove every season for the men of the village. Dirk wrapped the scarf around his face to ward off the snow and the wind swirling up from the ravine.

'No wonder this is a pristine place. Nothing could live on this side of the mountain and have warm blood in its veins,' Dirk thought.

Dirk could not see beyond the thick heavy clouds and the snow, which rushed to cover everything in sight. Dirk soon saw the pillars of stones, but they were higher than those that led him to the edge of the ravine and placed systematically beside the ravine close to the edge. Dirk stopped before one of the pillars and touched the stone and caked debris.

"It is manmade! It is a trail marker of some sort! It is like the others, yet not like the others.

'If I continued to follow the other pillars I would have walked off the mountain into the ravine,' Dirk thought to himself.

"Maybe it is the trail I have been looking for!" Dirk said. "I will follow them. They are sure to lead me off this mountain. The snow mounds I followed earlier was a trap to lead the unsuspecting to their death. This is the true trail!" Dirk continued.

Dirk followed the stone sentinels; sure, they led to the true trail off Mount RaNinjitsi.

"Nothing stops a failure, but a try," Dirk said, as he launched into the deepening snow with renewed gusto. By early evening, Dirk was completely on the eastern side of Mount RaNinjitsi. Dirk was pleased with his progress and grateful for the stone sentinels leading him from the villagers and Circle Valley. Dirk bent his head and continued onward through the heavy falling snow.

When Dirk stopped to assess his movements, he stared at the ravine willing it to share its secrets with him. At that moment, the thick clouds parted and great stone pillars stood on either side of a massive bridge, yawing into space. Dirk's mouth gaped open. He opened his eyes wide and blinked several times to see if the massive structure would disappear before his eyes.

"Is it really a bridge? Am I seeing things?" Dirk stated, excitedly. He walked briskly as he could to the massive structure and touched the stone pillar nearest him.

"It is real!" Dirk laughed aloud. He felt lightheaded and giddy.

"At last I have found the trail off this terrible mountain, yet it is no trail, but a bridge. "Where does it lead? I wonder! I have to find out!" Dirk shouted to the howling wind and the flying snow. Dirk danced and pranced before the stone sentinels. Dirk finally came to his senses.

"I will rest and then investigate this bridge to see where it will lead Dirk," he said as he found a boulder to sit upon and gaze at the massive structure before him.

There were two gigantic stone pillars, one on each side of the bridge roped between them. They were moss covered and ice crusted, filled in places with all kinds of debris from the trees, including bits of rocks from the mountain itself. The bridge itself, thickly roped to the massive pillars and planks, no not planks but trees formed the base of the bridge, latched together as they stretched into nothingness. They were not hewn planks, but actual trees from the forests.

'How old is this bridge? How long has it been here? Who built it?' Questions with no answers flooded Dirk's brain until he was dizzy.

Years of moss and debris formed over the planks weather beaten surfaces worn smooth by wind, rain and snow. The bark, stripped off long ago, and new moss grew in areas long worn smooth and shiny with icy particles and dead vegetation, crusted here and there. The pillars were ice encrusted from the misty wind blowing up from the ravine. It looked formidable and dangerous. Dirk could not see the end of the bridge, and neither could he see the other side of the ravine. Therein lay the mystery and the challenge.

"I will need a good night's rest before I tackle that massive bridge. But, tackle it I will!" Dirk vowed.

Dirk found a campsite between some fallen boulders near the wall of the mountain. He was still close enough to the stone pillars to spot any danger coming his way. Dirk believed from his inspection of the bridge that no man had traveled that bridge for some time.

'How odd this is!' Dirk thought as he settled in his camp for the rest he needed before the onslaught of the bridge while waiting out the heavy snow fall, was a good idea, too. Dirk slept before the small fire he built and woke to the cold morning air. Dirk pulled himself from his bedding and shook like a great dog, the sleep from his body. Excitement visited as soon as memory of his discovery flooded his mind. The bridge! It was like an entity in his mind. Dirk walked to the bridge and stood before it. Its destination hid by thick dark, gloomy clouds in shades of blue, purple, black with tinges of white, red and yellow peeping through. Dirk felt he could reach out and touch the clouds with his bare hands. They looked substantial from his vantage point. Suddenly the clouds parted as if revealing an intimate secret to him like someone pulling hangings back from a window. Dirk expected to see the sun shining through the clouds, so he unprepared for what his eyes glimpsed through the clouds.

"A castle on a mountain peak, who built the castle and does someone live there? What mountain is that? Does the bridge lead to that mountain?" Dirk spoke aloud and jumped at his own words. As soon as he spoke, the clouds closed upon the vision, leaving Dirk with doubts about what he saw.

"This mountain is playing tricks with my mind! Did I really see a castle on a mountain peak across the ravine," Dirk sputtered.

Dirk waited to see if the clouds would reveal its secret again. His mind reeled with questions. This quest seems to come up with more questions than answers, said Dirk as he waited. No one ever mentioned a castle on top of a mountain as long as he lived in Circle Valley, but then no one in Circle Valley has ever ventured this far in the mountains before, either. Dirk thought about how limited their lives were by the curse of the Snow Monster.

"I wonder who lives there. It must be atop the twin peak to Mount RaNinjitsi!" Whoever lives atop Mount RaNanjitsi may know how to get off this mountain, but then I will be off this terrible mountain once I cross that bridge won't I?" Dirk answered his own question. No one in Circle Valley talked about the other mountain- the twin peak to Mt Ra Ninjitsi. It was taboo! Now, here he stood before the mountain that could possibly be his salvation, his answer to getting off Mount Ra Ninjitsi.

'The way out of here is through that mountain, It has always been there for us to discover but because no one ventured far from Circle valley we would never have found our way out of that cursed valley. The way out has remained a secret to this day! Ha! I have discovered one of the secrets of the snow monster. He has kept us chained to Circle Valley in fear so no one would find the way out. Maybe that is the reason no one returned to Circle Valley. Maybe they found this route and made their way off the mountain.' Dirks thoughts continued.

"I will find out! No mountain will defeat Dirk. I am the bravest man in Circle Valley. I am the village black smith. I am the best hunter and the best tracker. No one or thing gets the best of Dirk!" he said. Dirk pulled a rope from his pack and tied one end to one of the formidable pillars as tightly as he could. The other end he tied to himself.

"If I fall through the bridge, the rope will keep me from falling to oblivion!" Dirk stated as he put one foot in front of the other and started across the bridge without a backward glance. Dirk walked slow and sure, making each footfall count as he moved across the bridge uncoiling the rope as he went. The clouds engulfed him and the updraft winds tore at him, trying to push him back with every foot forward he made. It was as if his intrusion upon the bridge maddened the wind. The tiny particles of ice, snow and debris found their way into every loop in his clothing woven by the Clauder's wife in Circle Valley. Dirk thought he knew what it was like to be cold, but he had never experienced a cold like this. He felt like a living ice sculpture. Dirk bent into the wind, lowered his big head and pushed on across the ravine. Dirk dared not look over the side into the nothingness. He watched only each sure footfall. Progress was slow, but Dirk was determined to cross as much of the bridge as he was able before nightfall caught him out on the bridge. Dirk traveled for most of the morning and stopped to eat and rest before proceeding across the bridge. He sat and looked back at the way he had come and fear leaped upon him as he realized he was hanging out in space with nothing beneath him but the wood beneath his feet. His breathing came in gulps as panic tried to steal the air from his lungs. He tasted the salty taste of fear. He could see nothing, not the pillars, not the mountain behind him or the mountain before him, or the chasm beneath him. Dirk turned back toward his destination, struggled to his feet and began to move forward.

"I must keep going. I cannot go back. I cannot let fear and panic destroy me. I will reach the end of this bridge. I will once again place my feet on solid ground. This bridge does lead somewhere. I am sure of it. I know what I saw. I saw a castle atop a mountain peak," Dirk said. He began to repeat the refrain like a mantra to keep his mind focused on reaching the end of the bridge and stepping his feet on the slopes of Mount RaNanjitsi.

By late evening Dirk felt, he was most of the way across the bridge. Sweat poured from him in his effort to reach the other side of the bridge as quickly and safely as he could.

"I am Dirk! I am the bravest man in Circle Valley! I will not let this bridge defeat me! I will conquer it! I will find a way off this terrible mountain! I will leave Circle Valley behind forever!" Dirk repeated the refrain as he continued across the ravine.

The weather was taking their toll on Dirk. He spoke his mantra through red, raw and swollen lips. His cheeks burned a bright red from the wind that ravaged him like a thing alive. Ice crusted on his nose where it ran in protest against the wind and debris assaulting it. His eyebrows were thick with snow and ice. The dampness coming with the wind seeped through his clothing into his bones making every step an ordeal.

I believe I will make it across before nightfall, but who could have made a bridge such as this. It is not natural. The ravine seems too wide to support a bridge of this kind without evil or sorcery or magic. It is as if some kind of enchantment is supporting the bridge. I hope I don't find something or someone more menacing than the Snow Monster on Mount RaNanjitsi.' Dirk thought as he pulled his clothes tighter and checked that the rope was still intact that he had tied to the pillar. It seemed a lifetime ago that he had stepped out onto the bridge. Dirk made progress as he pulled and tugged the rope after him, but nightfall caught him out on the bridge. Dirk groaned. He was in total darkness. Dirk felt suspended in space.

"What an eerie feeling," Dirk mumbled as he slowed his progress to feel each footfall before making a step. Dirk kept going. The clouds were thick and black and looked strange from the absence of light.

"I must stop and rest. I cannot make a fire. I am cold, so cold. I did not come this far to die on a bridge!" said Dirk.

Dirk continued his journey moving quicker, willing the end of the monstrous bridge to appear in front of him. He traveled throughout the night moving steadily. By early morning, the time between night and day the clouds began to lighten. Dirk was so happy to see the rays from the morning sun stream through the thick, black clouds stabbing the darkness with millions of daggers of light which pierced the clouds and hitch hiked on the droplets of moisture floating up from the ravine and rode them down into the ravine until they disappeared in the darkness below.

'I believe I have come most of the way across the ravine. I should be placing my feet on solid ground, soon,' Dirk thought.

The wind subsided with the morning light. The thick clouds thinned as if the sun melted them from the sky. Dirk sat and ate a small meal before resuming his journey. He was encouraged by the meal and the weather and looked forward to the journeys end. Soon Dirk saw stone pillars looming in the distance like the ones on the opposite side of the ravine. They stood against the clouds like stone, ice- shrouded trees.

"I will be glad to get off this bridge," Dirk stated as he neared the end of the massive bridge. I will soon be off this terrible mountain and I will be free of Circle Valley, the villagers, Mayor Brown and his laws. The loss of Tika is unfortunate, but after the death of Gustavo, she was no longer mine to claim. If it must be, it must be. Events have stolen her from me. I cannot turn back now. My destiny has changed with my own actions. There are consequences to every choice we make in life. I see that now. I would love to continue to blame Starvros for all this, but we are the masters of our own destiny, by action or inaction; there is still an outcome to be perceived and understood," Dirk spoke his thoughts aloud as he stepped onto solid ground between the twin pillars on either side of the bridge.

"It took a day and a night to cross that massive bridge. It must be enchanted because I know of a certainty no humans forged that bridge across that great ravine. The ravine must be what separates the two twin mountain peaks. The snow monster is on Mount RaNinjitsi, and controls the elements and the citizens of Circle Valley; I wonder what entity controls Mt. RaNanjitsi and its elements. Dirk will soon find out because I am going to find a way into that castle and force whoever is there to lead me off the mountain and as far away from Circle Valley as I can get. There must be people and lands besides Circle Valley and these accursed mountains. Whatever is there, Dirk will find it." Dirk stated firmly.

Dirk let out a long sigh of relief. He grinned broadly. He jumped up and down, moving well away from the edge of the ravine.

"I will make camp and since it is late in the day I will rest and explore what is in my view before I venture any further," Dirk said.

Dirk soon found a place close to the mountain wall in a boulder-strewn area.

"This will do nicely for a campsite. With my back to the mountain, I will be able to see anything approaching my camp. Dirk felt like this had happened to him before, and then he remembered he had camped at a place like this on Mt. Ra Ninjitsi before he walked onto the bridge. How strange is that,' he thought to himself. The site was well enough away from the ravine and added protection from the strong winds blowing up from the ravine.

"I will explore this twin mountain, and then I will look for the castle I glimpsed through the clouds. I must be careful. I do not know what is in this mountain, or who inhabits the castle. I do not want them to find me before I find them." Dirk stated.

Dirk surveyed the small area where he built his campsite. It was not a large area but it was big enough for a small stand of trees, a grassy area interspersed with boulders of various sizes and a small stream, which surprised Dirk. Dirk stood looking up at the mountain wall and the dark clouds, which hugged its rugged façade. Dirk saw the crevices in the mountain wall and wondered how he would reach the top of that monstrous peak.

"That will have to wait. I will rest. Tomorrow is a good time to explore the way into the castle," Dirk stated.

Dirk sat on a boulder at his campsite, ate a small meal, climbed onto the bedding cut from some of the trees and was soon asleep. Dirk awoke, well rested and ready for the day's events.

"I will find a way off this mountain today! I am sure of it, said Dirk as he broke camp after a light meal. As he stood gathering his thoughts, the clouds parted and he could see the castle atop the peak of the mountain, again. Dirk moved toward the mountain wall his eyes riveted on the castle he could plainly see from his vantage point. Dirk saw the stark, gloomy castle sitting atop the peak of the mountain. It was a huge slate-colored castle, almost black in color from years of weathering. It looked as if it was hewn from the mountain itself. Dirk saw the many towers, turrets and slits in the stone used as windows. No light emanated from the structure and there was no sign of human activity. It resembled a huge, ugly bird waiting to swoop off and consume its prey. The clouds closed on the view of the castle and Dirk shuddered.

"Who can live in a place like that? I will find out. Dirk is afraid of no one. I am Dirk the blacksmith. I am the bravest, strongest man in Circle Valley. I am the best hunter, the best tracker. Dirk will find a way into that castle. I will force whoever lives there to tell me how to get off this mountain. I have no choice! They will have to contend with Dirk!" Dirk stated.

As Dirk started to ascend the mountain the clouds grew darker and descended lower as if they wanted to hide the ugly castle, shielding it from his intrusion.

'The wind howls louder than the snow monster growls.' thought Dirk.

There was no sign of life in the castle. No animals slithered about. No birds flittered around its huge façade. There were no trees, just the rugged mountain peak and the castle that towered on top of the world, as he knew it. Its sheer isolation made it more menacing as Dirk drew closer on his assent up to the mountain peak.

Dirk reached the peak by mid morning. Dirk stopped and panted heavily, looked around and surveyed the area. It was larger than he thought. There were trees off in the distance wearing thick coats of ice and snow, some trees sported burns from snow lightening, indicating the ravages of severe storms and winter's havoc on the area. There were sharp slate-colored, jagged rocks sticking up through the snow-covered terrain. Dirk saw that his tracks marred a pristine landscape. Dirk realized he still had a slight incline to travel to reach the castle sitting high on its solid rock formation. Dirk was right to think the castle was hewn from the mountain. He saw no seam separating the castle from the mountain. Dirk smiled as he considered that there might be a tunnel in the mountain leading to the inside of the castle.

'All I have to do is find the tunnel entrance which probably has not been used for some time. I see no evidence that the landscape has been disturbed by humans,' Dirk continued his thoughts as he surveyed the castle.

"I am weary of climbing mountains! I must find the way into that castle. However, that will have to happen later in the day. I must get some rest. It has been grueling crossing that bridge and climbing up to the peak of the mountain. I do not know how many days I have been at this since I left the villagers and Mayor Brown behind. I have lost track of time. I did not know getting off Mt RaNinjitsi would be so difficult. I hope that it will not be as difficult to get off Mt RaNanjitsi. It will be all over when I find out who lives in that castle and force them to show me the way out of here. I must do what I must do," Dirk stated as he found a campsite on the slight assent up to the castle.

Dirk went about setting up camp and prepared a light meal, ate silently engulfed in his thoughts. He then crawled atop the bedding he cut from the trees hugging the mountain wall and was soon asleep.

Dirk awoke feeling cold and wet, with a feeling of heaviness all around him. Dirk tried to move and found himself pinned to the ground. Dirk opened his eyes and they filled with heavy wet snow. Dirk tried to speak and snow filled his mouth. Dirk sputtered and spat trying to free himself of the wet snow.

'What is this? I am buried under the snow. There must have been a heavy snowfall while I slept. I will be buried alive if I do not get out from under all this snow,' Dirk thought.

Dirk began to wiggle and writhe to free his arms from the heavy snow. They were so cold. He could feel the numbness spreading in his body. Soon he was able to lift his head as he continued to wiggle and writhe beneath the snow that covered him completely. He could move his legs and at the same time, he moved his head back and forward to keep the snow smooth so that he had enough space to breathe in small shallow gulps. The snow was heavy upon his chest. He could not take great gulps of air. Dirk could feel the pounding of his heart, the burning in his lungs, the sweat that poured from his brow as he managed to free one of his arms. Dirk hurried to free his other arm and began working at the snow that covered his chest and body. Soon he was able to breathe deeper than before. Dirk kept moving, wiggling and writhing beneath the snow, trying desperately to free his body from the massive amount of snow that clung to him like a living beast. After much effort Dirk was able to pull has legs free of the snow. He then maneuvered his body until he was able to flip over on his stomach, and used his muscular legs to push through the heavy snow until he lifted his head to see the evening sky, strewn with myriad of stars and a big white moon, full and bright. Dirk stood to his full height and shook the snow from him like a great dog, breathing greedily of the cold tingling air that filled his burning lungs as if his life force depended on that one breath. Dirk swayed from the affects of that deep breath. He followed with smaller, quick breaths, breathing in and out in shallow breaths until he cleared his head of the dizziness that assaulted him. Dirk stood in the evening light and looked around to survey his surroundings. He remembered going to sleep after the exhausting trek over the great bridge, his ascent up to the peak and making camp. It obviously snowed while he slept. He knew there were storms in this area and lots of snow, but he was shocked about the amount of snow that fell while he slept. It was up to his waist, now.

Dirk breathed heavily of the cold wet air as he realized that if he had not woke up he would have died beneath the snow.

"Dirk, you fool! I will never sleep out in the open again, in these mountains. I know better. There should be some caves around here. Better than that, there is a castle! Why should I die out here/ I will make my way to that castle and find out what I must find out. Dirk sputtered as he dusted the clinging snow from his clothes. He dug beneath the snow for his belongings, got his bearings.

Dirk set off in the direction of the castle and used his staff to test for hidden fissures and crevices hiding beneath the deep, snow -covered tundra. As he jammed his staff into the snow in order to reach through the deep cover, his staff kept going, pulling him off balance before Dirk could react, he fell head long into a hole. Dirk yelled in surprise as he continued to fall until he hit the ground with a loud thud, and passed out from the force that knocked the wind from his lungs. Debris and snow fell atop Dirk, but he did not feel it.

Dirk came to roaring to his feet until he felt the aches in his body.

"What the... Where am I? What happened?" Dirk said loudly. What is this place? Dirk said, questions flooding his mind.

"Where am I now? I must have fallen through a tunnel or something." Dirk said as he brushed the debris from his hair and clothing. Dirk felt around for his cap. It was very dark in the tunnel. A small amount of light filtered down into the tunnel from the hole he left when he fell through the tunnel from the evening sky.

'The entrance must have yielded to the weight of the heavy snow fall.' thought Dirk.

Dirk took a few steps and laughed as he realized he had found the entrance into the castle. He stood on solid ground, not ice- encrusted tundra.

Dirk stood quietly for several minutes waiting to hear any other sounds other than his own breathing and the loud thumping of his heart in his breast. There was only silence. Dirk looked around trying to gauge his surroundings. Dirk stretched out his arms and moved forward to see what was in front of him by the meager evening light coming through the hole he left when he fell into the tunnel. He touched the cold wet wall of the tunnel and followed the wall where it led him, stepping carefully in the darkness, stepping gingerly, and placing one foot in front of the other. Soon his foot hit a stone step and he almost fell forward because the wall was suddenly gone. As he investigated, he found that he was standing before some steps that led upward. Dirk took one-step at a time, stopping on each step to get his bearings. Dirk knew he was in a tunnel leading into the castle. He continued up the steps as they wound and twisted going upward inside the mountain. Soon Dirk reached a flat place much like the one at the bottom of the tunnel. Dirk felt for a wooden door. There was no door. Dirk panicked.

'Was this the end of the tunnel? Did he come all this way to die at the top of the tunnel? There was no reason there should not have been a door at the top of the tunnel!' thought Dirk.

Dirk started banging on the wall and calling,

"Let me out of here, Let me out of here! Someone help!"

Dirk banged on the door until his knuckles were raw and bleeding. No one came. No one responded to his cries for help. It was dark in the tunnel as night came. Dirk sat down on the top step and pulled his pack from his back. He rumbled through it until he found the salve he used on the few farm animals they were able to breed in Circle Valley. He rubbed his raw knuckles with the salve.

"Ouch! Ouch! that stings, said Dirk.

Dirk continued rummaging through his pack until he felt the flint and rock he used to make fires. He gathered debris from the few steps he could reach in the darkness and set about to make a small fire on the landing. Soon he had a small fire going. Dirk needed to look around and get his bearings before the fire died out in the small space. Dirk added more debris to the fire that flickered briefly and then began to burn steady. There is air feeding the fire Dirk said as he saw the flames turn red. Dirk leaped back up to the landing, leaned his shoulder against the wall and pushed with all his strength. years of working the anvil as a blacksmith came to bear and the wall began to move under his strength. Dirk kept pushing as the wall continued to move inward. Dirk heard it scrape against the stone floor. Dirk pushed harder and it soon gave way as it cleared the debris-strewn floor. A large hewn stone had been lodged into the opening to the tunnel.

Dirk continued to push and it moved further into the room behind it. Dirk peeped around the opening and saw a hallway. He was inside the castle!

"I have found a way into the castle," Dirk whispered, giddy with the thought that his journey was almost over.

"All I have to do is find the person or persons who live here and force them to lead me off this mountain," Dirk continued.

The embers from the fire were dying as Dirk decided to move the stone back in its place.

"I do not want the villagers to find their way into the castle if they are still pursuing me. It would be easy to follow my trail since I seem to be the only thing moving around this mountain," said Dirk.

Putting words into action Dirk pushed the stone back in place after clearing the debris away from the bottom of the stone. It moves much easier from this side than it did from the other side. Soon the hewn stone was back in place and Dirk turned to survey his surroundings. Dirk hoped the noise did not disturb anyone in the house and he waited to see if anyone alerted to his presence before moving any farther into the castle. Dirk waited for what seemed like a long time. No one came. Dirk knew he was in a hallway but, now that the stone was back in place, he was still in darkness. Dirk put out his arms until he touched both walls, they were cold and damp to his touch. There were no doors or entrances along the narrow hall. It curved several times, but he encountered no one.

'This must still be part of the tunnel,' thought Dirk. He continued until he came to a huge, thick, wooden door at the end of the hall.

CHAPTER 9

GIZELLA STEPS IN

"Starvros," Moira said sharply as a figure he did not see stepped from behind an outcropping of rock in front of the cavern.

"Halt!" Who goes there? Identify yourself or be run through with my spear!" the voice said as the figure loomed out of the darkness toward them with spear drawn.

Moira screamed as Starvros thrust her behind him to face the menacing figure coming at them with its spear raised to thrust through them.

"Halt, I said, who are you?" the figure said again in a low guttural growl.

"Why, I know that voice," said Moira as she regained her footing, her senses and her voice.

"It is Bobbo, from the village!" Moira said.

"Is that you Moira? The voice said in surprise.

"It is I, Bobbo, Moira said, the fright leaving her as quickly as it had come. This was someone she knew. She also, knew Bobbo was no threat to her. He would not hurt anyone.

"Is that really you, Moira?" Bobbo asked again, hardly believing his ears.

"Yes Bobbo, I am Moira." H-How? …

"Yes, cut in Starvros,

"How did you get here and where are the other villagers," he said sternly.

"Hey you, you keep quiet. You are in a whole lot of trouble!" said Bobbo.

Starvros bristled at Bobbo's tone of voice and before anything else Starvros leaped at Bobbo. His hands grasped Bobbo's neck trying to choke the words from his mouth. All his raged surged to the surface. At that moment, all of Starvros' anger toward the villagers centered in Bobbo.

All of his frustrations since beginning the quest found expression in his attack on Bobbo.

"Stop! Starvros! Stop!" said a surprised Moira. "Please stop!

Starvros!" Moira said as

Tears flowed down her cheeks. Please do not kill him Starvros!" Moira grabbed Starvros' shoulders and pulled with all her strength. At last, she was able to pull the distraught Starvros from Bobbo.

"What are you doing Starvros?" She asked, panting heavily.

Starvros fell to his knees, moaning. Bobbo fell to the ground, eyes bulging as he rubbed his throat, red with the imprint of Starvros' hands. Bobbo gasped as he spoke.

"You are going to be sorry you did that Starvros. I am not going to be killed in these mountains like Gustavo. You are as crazy as Dirk" Bobbo retrieved his spear before Starvros could react and pointed the spear at Starvros.

"Getup! You are my prisoner. You will be taken back to Circle Valley to answer for your wrong doing!" Bobbo continued in a whisper.

Moira helped Starvros to his feet and moved ahead of Bobbo to their campsite.

"What did you mean about Gustavo?" Starvros asked Bobbo, as he understood Bobbo's words.

"You will find out soon enough. It is not for me to say. The Mayor will have plenty to say to the both of you!" Bobbo said curtly.

"The Mayor?" Starvros and Moira spoke together.

Rounding the bedding hanging over several fires to dry, Starvros and Moira came face to face with Mayor Brown, seated upon a huge boulder before their fire on the ledge. He resembled a king sitting on his throne before his subjects, and his shadow cast on the grotto wall flickered and gyrated as if mocking them. Moira held Starvros' hand tighter.

"Well! Well! Well! Who is this? It is our little kidnapper-Starvros! The Mayor said slowly. You, young man have set in motion events that will leave Circle Valley forever changed. You have hurt and affected us all. Your pride and stubbornness caused you to undertake things you neither know nor understand. You have involved the whole of our village in your scheme as well as Moira and Tika," stormed the Mayor.

"Two? Two? Two? W-w he…

Before the Mayor could say another word Moira stomped her feet on the frozen ground trying to circulate her blood to get warm and spoke loud,

"Mayor Brown, you have no right to speak to Starvros like that. Sitting at our fire warming at our expense. I am cold! I am hungry! I am tired! Starvros did not kidnap anyone! Tika and I joined him on his quest for our own reasons. Mine are not your business and I cannot speak for Tika!" Moira said, blinking and wiping tears from her eyes as her chest heaved with anger. Her face flushed and her eyes flashed angrily at Mayor Brown.

Mayor Brown ignored Moira's tirade and stared straight at Starvros.

"Starvros! Where is my niece? She was not with you and Moira! Where is my niece?" the Mayor said quietly.

Starvros and Moira turned and stared at each other, then at the Mayor. Each took a big gulp of air and dropped their gaze before the Mayor.

Both spoke in unison.

"We do not know where Tika is!"

Mayor Brown struggled up from the massive boulder to stand over the pair like a huge bird of prey.

"You do not know where Tika is?" thundered Mayor Brown. Debris, ice and snow from columns suspended in the grotto roof, fell to the grotto floor at his words.

"No! We do not know where Tika is," stated Starvros. His tone flat.

"Tika disappeared without a trace during that fierce, fog and ice storm. We looked for signs, but we could not pick up her trail. The only thing we could do was to keep to our course. We believe Tika has been captured by the Snow Monster, Mayor Brown."

Starvros said, finding his voice after the Mayor's tongue-lashing.

"Captured by the Snow Monster? Nevertheless, you do not know this for sure do you Starvros. Just as you started this quest without knowing what you were doing, or knowing anything about the beast you wanted to hunt, you have endangered Tika's life and everyone in Circle Valley. Tika's disappearance could be in retaliation because you are in the Snow Monster's territory. You Starvros will pay dearly if anything happens to Tika. This quest has already claimed one man's life, I am not about to lose another citizen! Do you hear me Starvros?" The Mayor sputtered and spit at Starvros.

Starvros bristled like a big angry dog. Starvros tilted his head back to look Mayor Brown in the face as he loomed over him on the ledge.

"I have already paid dearly for Circle Valley, Mayor Brown. My ignorance is due to you and the other villagers. So do not threaten me! I did not force Tika to come with me. I was as unaware of her plans as you were. I tried several times to send her and Moira back home. They would not go back to Circle Valley. I tried to keep them as safely as I could. I tied Tika to a tree during the storm. I tied Moira to a tree during the storm and I tied myself to a tree during the storm. When the storm was over, Moira was tied to her tree. I was still tied to my tree, but Tika was gone along with her bedding. The best we could do was to continue the quest. I believe the Snow Monster has taken Tika for his own reasons. If we find him and destroy the curse we will save us all!" Starvros squared his shoulders and stared steadily at the Mayor without flinching.

Mayor brown squinted at the lad who stood before him. Gone was the timid, hesitant lad who broke in on their meeting only a few days ago. Much has happened on this quest and the Mayor sensed there was much more for them to experience. Mayor Brown shook his head. It seemed as if they had been in the mountains a lifetime.

"We will deal with you both when we get back to Circle Valley. I agree with you that we have to find Tika, but you will do so as my prisoner, Starvros. Moreover, you, Moira will be returned to the home you left so unceremoniously, the Mayor stated.

While the Mayor talked, Starvros surveyed the villagers milling around. Someone was missing. Starvros turned back to stare at the Mayor and cut in,

"Where is Dirk, Mayor Brown? I would have thought he would lead the expedition to find me, as well as Tika!" Starvros continued talking, his forehead furrowed in puzzlement.

"I remember Bobbo saying something about Dirk. What has happened? Where is Dirk? He also mentioned Gustavo, and I do not see Gustavo among the men. Where are they?" Starvros asked the Mayor.

"Dirk is no longer leading this journey, I am!" the Mayor stated sternly.

"You are!" said Moira and Starvros in unison.

"Yes I am! reiterated the Mayor. We had some problems along the way and Dirk chose to leave us and go on alone! Details of Gustavo and Dirk are none of your business Starvros! The only thing that concerns you right now is that you are our prisoner! We will bind the both of you between two of the villagers until we can descend this blasted mountain and return to Circle Valley, after we find Tika, of course! It seems as if you have gotten your wish Starvros. Your quest for the Snow Monster has become our quest. If we are to make it back to Circle Valley alive, I am afraid we will have to hunt and kill the Snow Monster. There is some merit to your quest. After much thought, I find the village will do better if the curse and the Snow Monster were destroyed!" Mayor Brown stated.

"Do you think Dirk had something to do with Tika's disappearance, Mayor Brown?" Starvros asked, realizing Dirk had left the villagers.

"Dirk had nothing to do with Tika's disappearance, he was caught in the storm, too," cut in Josef the butcher.

Josef had a muscular frame and broad shoulders. He was wide-backed with a thick waist. His black eyes set in a reddish, hairy face, with a short, stubby nose over full weather-chapped lips, filled his face. His hair was red also, and matted to his head like a fur pelted cap. He had short arms ending in big meaty hands. He stood on firm muscled thighs supported by short legs and small booted feet. He looked as if he would topple over onto his face.

Josef was quick to defend his friend Dirk.

'I do not know what happened between Dirk, the Mayor and Gustavo, but me and the other men felt that branding Dirk was too harsh even if it was a law in our village. The law was ancient and had never been used before. All the men felt that losing Tika and having to take care of Gustavo's wife and children was punishment enough for their friend,' thought Josef as he realized he spoke out of turn.

The Mayor frowned at Josef's intrusion. Josef melted into the background away from the Mayor and began doing chores for the camp.

"We will use a little more wisdom than you did Starvros. We will camp here for the night and resume search for Tika at first light. The first one to wake will awaken the others. Continue, as you were men. Let us finish our preparations and get some well-needed food and rest. Two of you will take the prisoners and tie them between you. See that they eat and are warmed. The rest of you spread out and gather bedding for everyone. We must get some sleep. The morning will bring more developments, and we will need our rest to deal with them." The Mayor said, as he sat on the boulder before Starvros and Moira's fire. The men gathered the duo and tied them to themselves with sturdy ropes and knots.

Moira leaned toward Starvros and whispered,

"I am not going back to Circle Valley, Starvros!"

"Silence girl! I will have the men build a cage for you and transport you down the mountain in it. We are all tired, cold, hungry, angry and frustrated. Get them out of my sight!" the mayor stated angrily, dismissing everyone as if he were a king with a kingdom.

Clyde and Josef nudged Starvros and Moira forward toward their camp further along the ledge. Their shadows danced and gyrated on the cavern walls as light and shadow interplayed in the darkened grotto. Bobbo went back to his sentry duties and the camp settled down for the night after eating a meal.

Starvros was silent, but his resolve was set in the squaring of his jaw as a muscle twitched and his nostrils flared from the acrid smoke of the campfires. Starvros knew it was useless to fight at this point. What he did know, was that his escape would come at the first opportunity that presented itself to him. He also knew that he would have to leave Moira and Tika behind. This was his quest. This was his mission. Starvros knew he had to finish what he had started. He could not go back to Circle Valley a failure, no matter what Mayor Brown said, and after this day's events, he felt it was better if Moira and Tika returned to Circle Valley. After all his intent was not to leave Circle Valley. His intent was to destroy the curse of the Snow Monster so that he could live in Circle Valley free from the power of another entity to control what he did with the life that belonged to him. Starvros sensed that maturing and learning was a solitary process. If he was to be a man in Circle Valley, then this quest had to be his rite of passage. Some things needed doing alone. Starvros' heart was set upon finding the Snow Monster and destroying the curse more as a part of his destiny and freedom from death and destruction. His thoughts swirled around in his brain as the turn of events thwarted him again in his search for the ever-elusive Snow Monster.

Steam rose from the wet bed coverings hanging in various places in the cavern to dry mingled with the acrid smell of many campfires, which provided a cozy backdrop as the villagers settled down for the night. However, they were oblivious to the cozy atmosphere. Each man looked around, eyes darting here and there searching the shadows in the large cavern, uneasy, waiting for what; they did not know. Frown lines furrowed their brows as the men sat uneasily beside their campfires. Their muscles stood out, firm with the tension of the moment. There was a sense of expectation, or rather a knowing ingrained from years of training that something momentous was about to happen. Each man checked and rechecked, positioned and repositioned his weapons and kept them near at all times.

The villagers had prepared for an early wake up by drinking much water before settling down to sleep. It was a surefire morning wakeup call usually reserved for hunting parties. Sleep eluded them as they settled into fitful rest. Something in the dark cloudy sky, the starless night, the silent night, the cold, moist air that did not allow warmth to seep into their bones, that spoke of something momentous, something expectant. They waited.

Starvros and Moira lay between two of the villagers and warned not to talk to each other. Mayor Brown did not want the couple running off again on a wild chase to find the Snow Monster. Mayor Brown wanted to find Tika and get off this terrible mountain as soon as possible. The Mayor knew this, but the unexpected things happening to them since they reach the higher peaks of the mountain caused him to fidget with nervousness. The Mayor thought about the difficulties they faced getting to this point. He thought about his near fall off the edge of the cliff, the icy fog-like storm, the fall into the frozen lake, the fall into the ravine, the raging storms, and the deep snow covered tundra and now this. He sensed an eerie, evil eminence and he wanted off the mountain as soon as possible. Sleep did not come easy to the Mayor that night, but it came. Soon, the Mayor and the villagers dropped off to sleep.

Bobbo, on duty as sentry was to awaken the camp when morning came. Bobbo found a comfortable spot for lookout and nodded on and off throughout the night. Bobbo was half sleep and half awake. Bobbo tensed. The hairs on his arms stood up. Chills ran through his entire body. His nostrils flared as a rancid odor reached him. Bobbo slowly opened his eyes as his hand clutched the knife beneath his tunic, at his waist. Bobbo looked up and saw the horrible creature as it approached him and lost all speech. His mouth opened but no sound came out. He could not talk, he could not scream, he could not yell. His eyes bulged in their sockets. All color drained from his weathered face, leaving red streaks where the deep crevices lined his cheeks. Bobbo could only stare at the huge creature as it reached for him and he fell before it, unconscious. The Snow Monster moved on, not looking back, knowing that his watchers would gather that one up and take him back to the dungeon.

The Snow Monster approached the cavern and waited for the watchers to join him and surround the villagers. Without their sentry, they were his to capture at his will. When all was set in motion, the Snow Monster let out a loud, snarling roar.

He threw back his huge head and …

"G-R-O-O-O-W-L! S-N-A-A-A-R-L!"

The villagers awoke as a unit when the sound of the Snow Monster's roars penetrated their uneasy sleep. Every man leapt to his feet, knife unsheathed, to face the unknown enemy. They peered into the darkness, seeing nothing, only sensing the danger, full-blown, tingling every sense in their body. The men stood to attention, waiting for their attackers to show themselves. They would fight to the death. It was their training. Something ancient and noble awoke in their breasts. They could feel the influence of ancient warriors flow through their veins. They stood, ready!

"Ouch! Ouch!" said Starvros and Moira, as the ropes that bound them to their two captors jerked them around. They both stood still as the Snow Monster rent the air with another piercing growl. The villagers crouched low turning toward the sound, knives held closely to their chests. Starvros drew his knife and was surprised when Moira bent over, lifted her skirts and drew a huge blade attached to her thigh by a leather strap. Moira twinkled at Starvros before crouching as the villagers, holding the huge knife before her in the hunter's crouch. Starvros followed suit and prepared for the battle with an awesome foe he had seen only once before. Starvros did not know if he was ready for the battle, but he would fight for everything he held dear. In that moment he knew it was Circle Valley, the villagers, Moira, Tika and even Mayor Brown that meant something to him. His love for Circle Valley drove him to take on a quest he knew nothing about. Starvros knew he loved it enough, to face the Snow Monster to free it from the horrible curse.

The Snow Monster snarled again. G-r-o-w-l-l-l! S-n-a-r-l!

Starvros turned toward the sound, trying to pierce the darkness, trying to gauge the direction the attacker would come. Turning toward the cavern wall, Starvros saw the hideous shadow of the Snow Monster cast upon the cavern wall by their campfires. Still there was not enough light to see the face of the enemy. Starvros saw other shadows moving against the cavern wall.

"The Snow Monster is not alone!" Starvros whispered.

The men backed toward each other placing Starvros, Moira and Mayor Brown in the center amid much protest from Starvros and Moira, as a knife slashed the ropes from their wrists. They formed a circle around the trio and crouched with a knife in one hand and a spear in the other hand, facing the threat before them.

The villagers crouched even lower, knives and spears ready for the onslaught. They saw the figures emerge from the darkness coming toward them. They were ready. They would fight the enemy who had tormented their lives, their families, their very life style, and in that instant they all united in a common cause and that was to destroy and free themselves from the curse of the Snow Monster. In that moment, the villagers saw the clarity of Starvros' vision. They would never have a normal existence as long as they were willing to live under the tyranny of another. They afforded him a better life style than any person or thing had a right to expect in this life. The greed of the Snow Monster had forced them to live an abnormal existence and they determined they no longer wanted to live that way. The villagers posed in battle stance, hardened with purpose, born out of adversity. Their visage was fierce as they waited to defend their very lives from their centuries-long oppressor. The death of the Snow Monster was their only road to freedom. Determination lined every face in the circle of villagers surrounding Starvros, Mayor Brown and Moira. Starvros looked from one to the other of the men who came looking for a boy and found unity of purpose.

Rafello, Clyde, Jorge, Josef, Ferdo, and Portor, Karlief, Clauder, and others. Men forever changed by the events taking place this day. They were certainly a motley crew, but they meant something to Starvros in that instant. Joined by a legacy he had to buy into, Starvros realized he spent so much time blaming the villagers for his ills, instead of taking the time to pursue his legacy with them. He isolated himself from them. He determined he did not need them and he severed himself from the community. The fault did not lie with them, but within him. They became only what he made them in his own mind. He gave them the power to take what was rightfully his. They treated him as he expected to be treated. He set the parameters in his life. He summed up every occurrence and gave it meaning in his life. Not once did he attempt to cultivate a relationship with the villagers. He only waited for them to do what he expected of them. He never looked inside himself to see what was expected of him." Starvros' thoughts startled him.

Starvros turned as the Snow Monster snarled and growled again.

"He's ready to attack men! Mayor Brown shouted. "Hold steady, steady…

Suddenly a bolt of light penetrated the darkness of the cavern and the villagers fell as if dead. Moira and Starvros fell, also. The dark figures ran toward the darkness, afraid of the light.

The light dimmed and Gizella, the wicked Fairy Queen stood in the midst of the cavern.

The Snow Monster roared and growled before her, but she held her ground, not flinching or cowing before his wrath. The only sign of emotion in her cold facade was the up and down movement of her chest as she breathe heavily in the moment.

Gizella was tall and lean. Her face was long, ending in a pointy chin. A long aquiline nose covered thin lips, which formed a straight line in her narrow face. High cheekbones held small beady eyes that were a startling, icy-blue color. The pale eyebrows and no lashes gave her an even colder, menacing visage. It was a contrast to the platinum colored hair piled high above a protruding forehead. Large ears stood away from her face as if flapping in the wind, with pointed tips, that spoke of her heritage as the reigning Snow Fairy Queen. She wore an ice blue cape and matching gown. Ermine fur lined the cape and the hood, which sat on the back of her thin shoulders. Boots peered beneath the gown made of fur pelts lined in the ermine fur. She had fur-lined gloves to match her cape. It was all for show. As the Snow Fairy Queen, she ruled over the elements in the mountains. She was no stranger to icy storms and raging snows. If she blinked, ice would form. If she waved her hand, storms would brew. When she waved her arms, winds blew fiercely. She could freeze water with a look and a glare meant trouble for an entire region. The weather in the mountains reflected her moods. She was something to deal with and she spoke plainly and wasted no actions.

The Snow Monster continued to roar and snarl at Gizella's interference.

Catching her breath, Gizella took a menacing step toward the Snow Monster. No sign of fear marred her spectacular face, only fierce anger registered as she spoke in her high pitched, raspy voice.

"What have you done? What are you doing? How dare you?" she sputtered at the Snow Monster.

"It's a good thing I saw what you were doing through the orb on Mount RaNanjitsi. You have put us both in danger with your meddling! You were to keep these people out of the mountains, and out of my hair! You were to keep them busy with the food offerings. I warned you about the prophecy! I have kept these people out of my mountains since the days of your foolishness. I hate humans! Now because of you, there is a whole village full of humans running around in the mountains! Not since that night, many centuries ago, have there been so many people in these mountains. You are a disappointment. If I did not know better I would think you orchestrated all of this! Call your minions and take them to the castle! Lock them in the dungeons until I decide what to do with them and you take extra care with the boy, he is dangerous! Put him in a room by himself, take the other girl and put her with the others. These will sleep a while because of the sleeping potion I cast upon them.

I thought the apparition in the cave, the ice storm, and the other goodies I sent their way would send them scurrying back down the mountain to continue the bleak existence I set before them, but they continue to defy me, invading my mountains, disturbing my peace...the prophecy! "AGH!" I cannot worry about that now!

Do as I say! I will talk to you later, at the castle! I must return to my castle and study how to rid myself of these humans! I hate humans!

Go; do as I say, now! They will keep very well in the dungeons!" having said all that Gizella spoke four words, "Abau -Vabau -tarbau -rabau," and vanished from the Snow Monster's sight.

The Snow Monster snarled, growled and roared as his minions reappeared in the grotto from a doorway that opened in the back of the grotto wall. The Snow Monster's minions carried their unconscious victims into the castle through the door and deposited them in the dungeons beneath the castle, which sat atop the peak of Mount Ra Ninjitsi. They returned for the villagers' belongings until there was no sign the villagers had been in the grotto, except for the dying fires of their campsite. The Snow Monster was the last to enter the doorway as the light from the dying fires cast the shadow of his monstrous frame upon the grotto wall. He waved his hand and the fires died, as total darkness closed on the formidable creature, the villagers, Mayor Brown, Starvros and Moira.

The Snow Monster's minions took the villagers to the dungeons below the castle and they melted away into other parts of the castle to their assigned spots and became as wood, statues that came alive at their master's call.

The Snow Monster made his way through the castle to the room he previously shared with Tika. He stood in the middle of the room until the change reversed itself. His fur became skin. His paws became hands. His huge feet became a man's feet. His face changed from the horrible looking monster with fangs to the face of King Hector. His body firmed into the body of a muscular man in his mid fifties. He was naked. Bartoll entered the room quietly with fresh clothing. He went about dressing the man before him without speaking a word. When he was finished, he stood before his King, no expressions visible in his wizened face. He waited for further instructions.

The King spoke harshly to Bartoll, "Take the girl and put her in the dungeon with the others, Bartoll and leave me alone. I will call you if I need you! No, wait put the girl in a room alone. I do not want her with the rest of them and put the other girl in a room alone as well, Bartoll."

"Yes, sire, as you will," said Bartoll in his raspy voice. He bowed to his King and backed out of the room to do his bidding.

King Hector sat down as soon as the door closed drained of his strength. The night's events left him, bereft. He did not want to think on the things that happened or the future consequences of his actions. For over five centuries, he had never deviated from the course set before him. He never took one independent thought or action from the dictates of the curse, set upon him, because of his own actions. Yet it seemed as if his actions were not his own, but a longstanding directive, out of time. He felt as if he were following a course, not of his own choosing.

"Why did I take the girl hostage? What did I hope to gain by capturing the villagers and the boy?" he asked himself. There was no answer.

King Hector moaned and covered his face. He had never seen Gizella so angry. Not since the night, this horror began, had he encountered her anger. He was afraid. He, who put fear in others, was afraid of what the Snow Fairy Queen would do to him and the villagers. He was afraid of what she would do to the girl he captured, and the boy.

"The boy!"

'She is afraid of the boy! Why? What did she say about the prophecy? Argh! I cannot remember! I must find out. I must get her to reveal more details to me.' thought King Hector.

"No! I will find out from the boy, why he is a threat to Gizella," the King stated.

"Bartoll," the King shouted loudly.

"Bartoll bring the boy to me!" the King shouted.

Meanwhile down in the dungeons, the sleeping potion was wearing off as the villagers arose with a start, remembering only the danger they were in. They crouched low in the darkened dungeon ready for the onslaught. They reached for their knives and drew empty hands in the darkness.

"Where is my knife? What is this? Where are we? Bobbo spoke first.

"Aye! what's going on?" echoed the other villagers.

"Ho! we are not in the grotto!" stated Clyde.

"Where are we then?" ventured Josef

Bobbo walked away from the group reaching out in the darkness.

"We are inside, men. We are in the dungeons, probably beneath the Snow Monsters lair," said Bobbo.

"Who all is in here? I cannot see my hand in front of my eyes," said Rafello.

"Call out your name so that we know who is in here with us. We need to know if they put us all in the same room.

"Bobbo!"

"Josef!"

"Clyde!"

"Rafello!"

Clauder

"Jorge!"

"Portor!"

"Ferdo!"

"Karlief!"

"Sumpter!"

"Demitros!"

"Thaylin!"

"Mayor Brown are you here with us?" questioned Bobbo into the darkened room.

"Aye, I am here. I feel groggy. What happened?" Mayor Brown asked as he sat on the cold ground.

"Help me up, men!" The men felt around in the darkness until they located the Mayor and struggled to help him up from the floor.

"We are in some kind of dungeon. Possibly beneath the Snow Monsters' lair." Bobbo said.

"Lairs do not have dungeons, Bobbo. We are in the dungeons of a castle. The legend of the Snow Monster is unraveling before us, Men. Starvros was right all along!" Mayor Brown stated quietly.

"He was?" Echoed all the men.

"Our presence in this mountain has unsettled the Snow Monster and he has made a fatal mistake. He has revealed himself to us and has lost his advantage. He is unnerved and is making mistakes, but most of all he has lost his mystique. As long as he remained a legend, our fear was intense, now that we know he is real, we can defeat him. We gave him power over us. We filled our lives with our imaginings of what he could do to us and that made him larger than life to us. We never imagined what we could do to him! Come men, rally round, we have plans to make," said the mayor with renewed vigor.

As the men gathered around Mayor Brown, loud shouting and banging penetrated the silence.

"Help! Is anyone there? Help! I am Tika and the Snow Monster has captured me. Answer, please, answer me! Is anyone there?" Tika sobbed.

"Tika! It is Tika!" Mayor Brown said.

"Tika. It is Uncle Brown! We found you, girl. Are you all right? Are you hurt?" Mayor Brown shouted.

"Uncle Brown, How did you get here? I am glad to hear your voice," Tika shouted back. "We are all hear, Tika. We have been captured by the Snow Monster, too!" Mayor Brown continued.

"Oh no! I thought you were here to rescue me, Where is Dirk? He will rescue me," Tika wailed.

"Dirk is not with us, Tika…

"What do you mean Dirk is not with you! He has to be with you! He has to rescue me! Tika interrupted her Uncle's speech.

"Now Tika you must calm down. Getting upset will not help us. Everyone needs to keep a clear head if we are going to defeat the Snow Monster," said Mayor Brown sternly.

"I know you are right Uncle, but your capture and Dirk's leaving has left me with more questions than answers!" Tika wailed. Oh Tika will you stop all that clamoring, you are making my head ache more, said Moira as the affects of the sleeping potion the Wicked Snow Fairy Queen used to capture the villagers.

Tika spun around from the doorway. "Moira is that you? You are in the same room with me, Moira?" Tika asked.

"Yes I seem to be in the same room with you Tika, so why don't you stop making all that noise and let's try to figure a way out of here," Moira said to the distraught girl.

"It will not do our quest to capture the Snow Monster any good with all of us captured," Tika wailed.

"Oh be quiet, Tika!" Everyone said at once.

Tika began to cry silently.

"As I was saying men, we need to figure a way to defeat the Snow Monster before he comes back. I for one am not eager to find out what he has in store for us, said Mayor Brown.

"Wait everyone I did not hear Starvros' voice," said Moira

'Starvros, Starvros are you here?" Moira yelled.

There was no answer. Only silence.

"Where is Starvros, Mayor Brown? Is he in there with you? Is he still under the influence of whatever and whoever brought us here and cannot answer me?" asked Moira, panic in her voice.

"Calm yourself Moira," said Mayor Brown

"Men check the room and see if we have overlooked Starvros," said Mayor Brown.

The men milled around in the room calling Starvros' name and feeling in the darkness for him, but Starvros was not with them.

"He is not here, Moira," shouted Mayor Brown,

"Oh no! That only means that the Snow Monster has him!" Moira wailed.

Chapter 10

Gizella on the Move

Gizella appeared in the great hall of her castle and went quickly to the secret room. She fumbled among the shelves and tables loaded with papyrus scrolls, which showed their age, manuscripts, and ancient books, looking frantically for an aged book, when the orb sitting on a gnarled tree like stand glowed red in the darkened room. Startled, Gizella turned toward the orb. Her eyes glowed as red as the orb.

"What is this? The orb has not been active for centuries," Gizella said, puzzlement in her raspy voice as she peered into the orb. Gizella saw a sight in the orb that caused her to scream loudly.

"A-a-a h-h-human! A human in my castle! I hate humans! I will destroy the interloper who dares to invade my castle!" Gizella screamed and raged.

"Guards! Guards! Oh my, I have to awaken them first!" Gizella said, frustrated by the delay.

Gizella calmed and spoke the words to awaken the guards from their spell- like state.

Gizella stood impatiently waiting for the effects of the spell to take place. The complete transformation took only a few moments, as the men like statues, trophies of long ago fairy wars, her servants, moved toward her to do her bidding.

"Guards, there is a human in the castle. Do not harm him. Bring him to me. I want to see what he is doing in my castle. Be quick about it. He is in the old quarter of the castle. He must have come through the secret tunnel. Go! Gizella commanded as she dismissed her minions.

Momentarily blinded as he exited the tunnel, Dirk sensed the danger approaching. The hairs on his head pricked and the hairs on his arms stood to attention. His nostrils flared as an unusual scent reached him. His entire body tingled and Dirk went rigid as the sense of alarm spread over him. Dirk slowly pulled the knife from his waist and waited, crouched low for the attack he sensed more than saw coming. Dirk tilted his head trying to pinpoint the direction the unknown danger would come from. dirk heard the shuffling of many feet.

"There is more than one of them. I am outnumbered, but I will not go down so easily. They will know dirk is no coward!" Dirk said.

Dirk heard the clanging of metal on metal.

What is this? Dirk said, as his eyes adjusted from the dark tunnel, he saw the huge creatures standing before him. Dirk's eyes bulged, his mouth opened and closed and all color drained from his face. Dirk dropped the knife.

"Come with us human!" Dirk heard but the creatures mouth did not move. Dirk knew he was a big man, but he had never seen a creature of such breathe and height before now.

The four guards surrounded him and repeated the command, "Come with us human!"

Dirk stood to his full height. He knew he could not defeat them, but he would not cower before them. Dirk slowly bent and retrieved his knife and fell into place between the four creatures that were over eight feet tall with thick mangled black hair under metal helmets that did not hide the huge pointed ears, or the horns protruding from either side of their massive heads. Black, beady vacant eyes under thick, bushy brows and lashes over a low, thickened forehead held no emotion but looked fierce and intimidating by the blankness of his eyes. A large mouth held fangs that fit over the thick lips, were huge and pointed. Their nose was short and flat with huge nostrils. A green tunic, underneath a metal shield strapped on from behind, covered their broad chest that led to a thick waist and thick thighs covered in black pantaloons stuffed into boots that came up to their knees. Dirk knew they were controlled by something he could not explain.

"Come with us human!" Dirk heard in his mind. "Move!"

Dirk started walking and the four creatures walked, two in front of him and two behind him. Dirk knew he had no way to escape from the creatures.

'Dirk will see where and to what these creatures are taking me. Maybe they are taking me to the owner of this castle. Dirk will live to fight another day, for now I must see where this will lead me. I was a fool to think I would not be discovered. There has been no one in that tunnel for years, maybe centuries,' Dirk thought as he moved through the castle with Gizella's minions.

Gizella watched the capture of the human through the orb.

"He is magnificent! I am impressed with his bravery. he is not afraid of the guards. I created them to put fear in who ever looked upon them. How extraordinary he is! Ah, but he is a human! I hate humans! I will talk with this human and see what he is about and how I can use him for my own ends, especially since there are more of these humans in my mountains than I can count! I hate humans!" Gizella mumbled, as she waited for the guards to bring the human to her.

"A woman, a woman has captured Dirk!" Dirk said aloud as he saw Gizella standing by the orb that had ceased glowing. She was tall for a woman, or fairy Dirk noted as he saw the pointed ears peeking from long, straight, flowing, platinum tresses. Dirk looked into the face to view the coldest blue eyes he had ever seen.

"Who are you?" Dirk asked bluntly.

"Silence human you do not speak to Gizella. You speak only when I ask you a question and you answer quickly. Gizella does not wait on humans, humans wait on Gizella, she stated matter-of-factly to Dirk.

Dirk raised his eyebrows and looked at Gizella. He was not used to being addressed in this manner by a woman.

"You should be afraid of me, human, but you are not! I have not experienced a human who does not fear me before. It is a new feeling," Gizella said to Dirk.

"Who are you that I should fear you, woman!" Dirk responded loudly.

"Oh, I forgot, your kind does not know me, but you will know me soon enough human, and you will fear Gizella! How did you get into the castle? I am assuming you came through the secret tunnel since you were found in the old quarter of the castle. Humans do not come to the castle unless I bring them. How did you get on this mountain, human? You are a trespasser and that means your death or something more, but for now, the dungeons beneath the castle will hold you until I figure out what to do with you. I have pressing things that need my attention and you are an unwelcome distraction," Gizella said in her raspy voice.

"You will find woman that Dirk does not bow down to women and Dirk does not die easily. I am the Blacksmith of Circle Valley. I am the tallest, bravest man in the valley. I am the best hunter and tracker, I do not scare so easily and I do not cower at the hands of a woman," Dirk spoke contemptuously.

"Circle Valley! Not another one, I have a dungeon full of your kind! How did you get here? Gizella asked, a frown furrowing her brow.

"Is there any more of your kind wandering in these mountains? Speak up human!" Gizella demanded.

You are under the control of the snow... Oh, that is none of your business! Guards take the human to the dungeon and secure him; I have things to do than to bother with this human," Gizella said as the guards lined up beside Dirk and commanded him to follow them.

Dirk did not move, but spoke to Gizella.

"So, it is you, who controls the snow monster, eh woman? Dirk asked.

Do not call me a woman again, human! I am no human. I am Gizella, the Snow Fairy Queen, and I have ruled these mountains and the people in it for thousands of years! Gizella said with emphasis.

"A fairy queen!" Dirk shouted and thrust back his head and laughed a full throated, hearty laugh. Ho -ho –ho, Ha-ha – ha, Hee-hee-hee!

Do not laugh at me, human! Gizella said.

Do not laugh at you! I despise you. You fairies have done nothing good for Circle Valley. We have lived a mean, cruel existence because of the fairies with all their wars and whims controlling everything we do and say. We have no hope for a better future because of you. Instead, we live according to the evil curse you forged upon us through no fault of our own. You fairies have not been kind to us. We barely exist because of your selfish desires," Dirk said harshly.

"Do what you must woman, but you will get no respect or fear from Dirk, he said as he spat on the ground at her feet.

"Get him out of here, guards! Put him in the lowest, meanest, coldest dungeon you can find. I will tend to him later," Gizella said, astonished at Dirk's brashness.

"Move human! Now!"

The command spoke forcefully to his mind, and Dirk moved with the guards as they lead him away from the Snow Fairy Queen.

"Wait!" Gizella commanded and Dirk stopped as the creatures stopped at the Queen's command. How did you get to my castle, human? The others were on Mt RaNinjitsi, how did you get here? Answer me, human! Do not lie to me. I have ways to get to the truth, Gizella said to Dirk.

"I do not have to lie to you, I have no reason to. I do not fear you, woman!" Dirk responded.

"I was with the villagers, if you must know. I led them up Mt Ra Ninjitsi because several of our citizens left circle Valley on a quest to find the Snow Monster and remove the curse on the valley and its inhabitants. We, the villagers followed because we thought the boy had kidnapped two of the village girls. Dirk paused and frowned. I found out later that the girls ran away to join the lad in his quest. It was our duty to find her; I mean them and return them to the safety of Circle Valley. Dirk breathed heavily as he thought of Tika.

"H-mm, a love interest. This is intriguing. Continue human," Gizella commanded.

"As I was saying, we were looking for the trio when we were waylaid by the ice storm. It was an evil storm of fog and wind and I surmise you sent it. One of your toys, eh woman?" said Dirk, remembering the storm that nearly took their lives.

"Yes, I sent the storm and other goodies, but it did not keep you humans out of the mountains! Go on human, you are not telling everything!" Gizella snapped.

Compelled to tell Gizella everything he knew, Dirk started his narrative where he left off.

"When the storm was over, there was a disagreement between the Mayor and I and I killed one of the villagers, I did not mean to kill him, but it was my fault. A brand meant that I could not marry Tika, so I ran away and left them in the mountains. I am Dirk. I am the bravest, tallest man in the village. I am the best hunter, the best tracker in Circle Valley. I am the blacksmith. I will not go back to Circle Valley as an outcast. I was not going to take care of Gustavo's family and never have a family of my own. I left them in the woods and tried to find a way off the mountain, so I searched the backside of Mt. Ra Ninjitsi to find a trail off the mountain and saw the pillars that led to the bridge. I crossed the bridge and saw the castle on top of the peak of this mountain. I thought someone here could tell me how to get away from Circle Valley, and these mountains," Dirk said, suddenly exhausted from his speech.

"The mayor of Circle Valley is with the villagers! Where did you leave the villagers?

Gizella asked Dirk.

"In the woods after the storm, We made it to the third plateau of the mountain before the storm stopped us," Dirk answered, puzzled by her question. "I do not think you have to worry about the villagers; they went on to find Starvros and the girls. I do not think they followed me here to Mt Ra Nanjitsi," Dirk continued.

"I have heard enough. Guards, take the prisoner to one of the rooms in the old quarter instead of the dungeon. I will deal with him when I return. Humans do not worry me," Gizella said quickly as some other thought nagged at her brain.

Gizella's minions placed Dirk in the old quarter of the castle and locked him in one of the rooms. It was sparsely furnished. Dirk fell upon the bed in the room and fell fast asleep.

As soon as Dirk left her sight, Gizella ran to a corner of the room and pulled a cord. The curtain slid open to reveal shelves lined with dusty old books and old manuscripts of potions. All sorts of jars filled with herbs, spices, and things unidentifiable, crowded the shelves of the small cupboard, built into the wall.

Gizella searched through the old books that lined the shelves.

"Aha! Here it is! Something that bumbling human said reminded me of something. I must check it out and then I will go to Mt Ra Ninjitsi to see what the snow monster has to say about his escapade, today." Gizella said as she flipped over the pages of the dusty book, reading the pages, quickly. Gizella felt a sense of time slipping away from her.

"Here it is, here it is!" Gizella slapped the book closed, her eyes glowed red in the darkened room, with anger.

No! No! No! I will not be done in by a mere slip of a boy! I must find him and destroy him before my entire existence vanishes at the innocence of a child. I must get to him before he knows what he is about to do! Gizella stormed.

I must go to mount Ra Ninjitsi, now! As she spoke, Gizella ran to the middle of the room and spoke three words.

"Akra, Macrom, Datra! She waved her arms over her head and vanished in a windstorm. Papers in the cupboard flew all over the floor and the book she was perusing fell to the floor, the pages open to where she left off reading.

Dirk slept briefly but woke after a short time. Dirk sat up on the small bed in the room the guards locked him in at the Snow Fairy Queen's instructions. There was a small candle on the table beside the bed. A table with a small bowl and ewer sat against one wall. The bed covered another wall, and a small fireplace took up another wall, but there was no warm fire burning in the room for him. There was no wood or kindling to light a fire in the room. A threadbare rag rug lay on the floor at his feet, and thick velvet curtains, dusty and moldy, covered the only window in the room. Dirk walked to the window and snatched the curtains from the window to reveal thick wooden shutters. Dirk could not see out of the shutters, he did not know if it was day or night. Dirk returned to the small cot.

What does she want? She could let me go so that I can find my way out of the region. I cannot go back to circle Valley. They will brand me for sure. I have lost Tike all ready and I do not want to marry Gustavo's wife. UGH! Dirk does not like that, so well, he continued.

"No, the only hope for me is to get off this mountain. I have to find a way out of here! Calm down, Dirk, think! Think!" Dirk uttered.

Dirk paced in the small room from one end to the other, pondering how to free himself from Gizella.

'There is nothing I can do until she returns. Maybe I can reason with her, Maybe she will make a mistake, although I cannot see that one making too many mistakes, she is formidable,' Dirk thought.

"Bah! I will not allow a woman to get the best of me. I am Dirk. I am the blacksmith. I am the biggest, bravest man in the village.

"Dirk will find a way," he said, as he lay on the bed, exhaustion and hunger claiming him, again. Dirk tucked his feet beneath him on the small bed and pulled the thin covering over him to await Gizella's return.

I am tired, I will rest. That witch will return soon, Dirk noted in a small whisper. Dirk wrapped in the thin coverlet to ward against the cold seeping through the walls of the old castle. Dirk slept fit fully, dreaming of Tika calling him for help; of Abbey laurel's face drifting above him, beckoning to him to come to her; of the Mayor and the villagers stranded in the mountains calling his name; Gustavo, Starvros the Snow Monster, the wicked snow Fairy Queen. They swirled in his dreams taunting him, grotesquely malformed images of the real people.

Dirk woke with a start to a key turning in the locked door. Gizella stood large and imposing in the doorway.

"Ah, so you could sleep in my castle, human!" Gizella said as her cold blue eyes snapped with anger.

Maybe I did not fill you with dread of the Snow Fairy Queen. You yet take the Snow Fairy Queen lightly because I am a woman! Gizella said entering the room. She stormed over to the bed and snatched Dirk before he could orient himself from the sleep that fogged his mind. Gizella grabbed him by the beard on his chin and flung him onto the floor. Dirk landed on his back with a loud thud, stunning him.

You dare to lie down in Gizella's presence. human1 You should be groveling for your life, Gizella continued, ranting loudly.

I will teach you about Gizella, you will plead to die, human! Gizella tossed the bed aside like a toy, grabbed Dirk by the wrist and flung him against the wall breaking the table with the bowl and ewer. Dirk falls to the floor among the debris, on his stomach, knocking the wind from him. Dizziness rose to claim him. Dirk fought against the dizziness. He lifted his head to focus on Gizella.

Gizella raced toward him not allowing a moment of rest, and picked the big man up over her head and threw him into the doorjamb. Dirk hit the doorjamb and fell into a heap on the floor. Dirk put up a hand to ward off another assault from the enraged Snow Fairy Queen.

"Gizella, stop, stop, Dirk shouted between gasps for air, as he struggled to his feet to stand against the wall. What have I done to you? All I want is to get off this terrible mountain," Dirk cried out.

"Argh! Argh! I hate you humans, the wicked fairy roared in her frenzy. I will teach you to trespass my domain, my mountains! Argh!" Gizella screams as she rushes toward Dirk, determined to finish with him.

Gizella runs head long toward Dirk closing the distance between them. Dirk waits until he can smell the stench of her breath coming in waves before her, and suddenly steps aside. Gizella ran into the wall at full impact and crumpled to the floor in a heap, unconscious.

Dirk breathed deep trying to recover from the onslaught of the wicked Snow Fairy Queen. Dirk taking in great gulps of air kicks the Snow Queen; he does not trust her even when she is unconscious. Cautiously he checks her, keeping an eye out for the big burly guards. Dirk inched toward the door and sighed. She was so sure she could destroy him that she came alone without summoning the guards. dirk closed the door. He wanted them to think they were still fighting. He Knocked over the other table and shouted Stop Gizella Stop! Dirk grunted loudly as he yanked the coverlet from the bed and tore it into strips with his knife. He was glad she did not search him for a weapon. he watched Gizella at the same time looking for signs of returning consciousness. Dirk tied a strip of covering around her mouth so she could not call for help. Then he picked the Snow Fairy Queen up and laid her on the bed. Dirk tied each of her limbs to a bedpost, and after having secured Gizella tightly to the bed; Dirk continued to make sounds like they were fighting. "Stop Gizella, no more please," Dirk said, stomping loud on the floor of the room.

Gizella came to in time to see Dirk going through his routine. Gizella struggled against the bindings. She mumbled at Dirk. Her eyes glowed red as her platinum hair matted to her head from the sweat pouring from her body.

"M-mmf, mmmf, brrf, brrf, brouf, broump," Gizella mumbled through the gag over her mouth.

"I cannot hear you, Gizella, you are my prisoner now and I am surely not going to let you go. As I told you all I want to do is, get off this terrible mountain. I do not know how long you will be tied up but, it might give me enough time to get off this mountain before someone of something comes to help you. Who has the upper hand now, woman? I told you, I am Dirk, the blacksmith. I am the biggest, bravest man in Circle Valley and now I have proved I am stronger than you are, Gizella. Since you are under control, I will leave you and find my way off this mountain as quickly as I can. Those guards are useless until you summon them and you cannot do that tied up, can you Gizella?" Dirk whispered,

Dirk went to the door, opened it and peered into the hall. No one was there. Dirk closed the door and walked quickly through the castle without getting lost, remembering the way the guards brought him earlier.

"I will retrieve my belongings and be on my way." Dirk said. The statues stood in the great room unmoving. Dirk walked brazenly by them and searched for his camping gear.

"Hmm. I wonder if opening the door to the outside will arouse the guards. Maybe I should go back through the tunnel; she will not think that I left the same way I came" Dirk stated.

Dirk grabbed his pack where he had left it during his first encounter with the Snow Fairy Queen. Dirk headed for the kitchen to go back through the tunnel, when he noticed the shelves full of book.

"Ho, maybe there is a map that will show the way off the mountain. I will look. If there is a way off this mountain the wicked fairy would know about it," stated Dirk. Dirk stepped over to the shelves and started pulling books and scrolls from the shelves. Dirk unrolled papyri, opened manuscripts and tossed books over his shoulders onto the floor if they were not a map. Dirk aware of the passage of time threw up his hands in defeat when a book on the floor glowed.

"What kind of enchantment is this," Dirk said as he picked the book up from the floor and opened the glowing book cautiously. "The Prophecy," the letters glowed on the inside cover.

"What is this book?" Dirk said, amazed. Dirk turned the page and the book came alive with scenery. Dirk almost dropped the book as his eyes bulged. Transported to another time by the book Dirk saw another castle, he saw people, and horses, and lights, and wealth, and food, and things, he had not seen before. Dirk snapped the book shut.

"I do not know what kind of book this is, but it might be the one to provide a way off this terrible mountain. I am wasting too much time. I must put as much distance between me, this castle and especially the Wicked Snow Fairy Queen." Dirk reiterated.

Putting words into action Dirk shoved the book into his pack and headed for the tunnel entrance. Soon he retraced his steps. It took some time to climb out of the hole he fell into, but after some searching, he found the stone steps leading to higher ground. Dirk emerged from the tunnel to a raging snowstorm. Dirk cursed the storm and then realized the storm was out of control because the Snow Fairy Queen was unable to control the storm.

"She is still bound," Dirk said gleefully.

"It will be harder for her to discover the way I went. This storm is good coverage to escape," Dirk continued, as he put the pack on his back and headed for the pillars.

'I hate that bridge, but maybe I can find new direction from there after I read the book I found on the floor. I must get somewhere safe so that I can read a little of it. It is not a book with many pages,' Dirk thought.

The fierce storm made it hard to talk because it snatched the air from the lungs. Dirk covered his mouth with the thick scarves the women wove in Circle valley. Often the young women with no husband plied him with gifts until they knew he had eyes only for Tika, as many of the men in the village, but Mayor Brown chose him as the best man for his young headstrong niece, and he was the best man. dirk thought as he continued moving toward the ravine and the bridge.

Dirk carefully placed his feet while watching the trail for dangerous crevices. Dirk did not want to fall into another hole in his flight from Gizella.

'I must get across the ravine before the wicked Snow Fairy Queen frees herself,' thought Dirk.

The traveling is slow, the storm is fierce, and the terrain is treacherous, but Dirk soon reaches the bridge. Dirk stepped gingerly onto the bridge forgetting to stop to rest, or read the book. His only thought was about distancing himself from the wickedness in the castle atop Mt. RaNanjitsi.

'I do not have time for gentleness and timidity; I am fighting for my life. I will die either from the elements or from her hand. I would prefer to die by the elements, than that horrible creature. She will certainly kill me, if she catches me,' thought Dirk

Dirk continued across the bridge moving with a wide legged stance holding on to the guide rope nearest him. Dirk walked some, rested some and kept looking behind him for the Snow Fairy's minions. Dirk began to sweat, as the fear of his pursuers loomed large in his mind. His face flushed red from the effort to cross the rickety bridge. Dirk concentrated on the task before him.

'I must not think about the Snow Fairy or I will never cross this bridge,' Dirk thought. Dirk continued along the bridge, and his thoughts turned toward his life in Circle Valley.

'I am far from my life, as I knew it in Circle Valley. As a youth, I was the better runner, hunter, swimmer and tracker. I excelled at everything. I should have been more than a blacksmith. Alas, that is what my father and his father before him were; blacksmiths. We have attained no more than working with our hands, working with fire and hot metals. I am not like the Mayor, I am not smart. I am just a big dumb brute of a man. I was foolish to think that Abbey laurel could love me. it is a wonder she chose Starvros Gunther, the village shaman. He knew things I would never know. The villagers respected him. I gave my heart to Abby laurel and she spurned it. Tika ran away to join Starvros on this silly quest and I am left with nothing. Dirk is fleeing for his life from the wicked fairy.' Dirk's thoughts move to speech as he begins to speak aloud the misery of his life.

"No one will mourn the loss of Dirk. It is all Starvros' fault. I will kill him, before the wicked fairy can find me. I will find him. Dirk vows it. No one and nothing will deter Dirk from taking Starvros Gunther's life," Dirk sputtered as he continued across the bridge repeating the mantra as a refrain in a song, as he traveled back across the bridge. I cannot remember how many days I have been in the mountains. It seems a lifetime ago,' Dirk thought.

Dirk moved steadily, determined to distance himself from the wicked Snow Queen Fairy. The snow came thick and heavy as Dirk continued across the bridge. 'The Snow Queen must still be tied up' Dirk thought. He laughed aloud as the image of Gizella tied to the bedpost entered his mind.

Suddenly Dirk stopped. He tilted his head.

"What is that? What did I hear? Someone is speaking! I hear a voice! It is faint. I can hardly hear it above the wind! The wind carries the voice away from me down into the ravine. It echoes in the ravine. What madness is this?" Dirk asks.

Dirk waits a few moments as the voice dies on the wind. He continues across the bridge moving slower. Dirk crouches lower not knowing what is at the end of the bridge. "My mind is playing tricks on me. I have been in these mountains too long. The thin air is affecting my mind." Dirk said.

"What is that?" Dirk said as he heard the voice again. "Who is there?" Dirk shouted.

"I know I heard someone on the bridge! Someone is calling. Yes, there it is again! Who is there? Who is it?" Dirk yells.

'Is this a trick by the wicked Snow Fairy Queen? Has she freed herself and is ahead on the bridge? I do not want to fight with that one again. Yet, I do not want to die by her hand either,' Dirk thought.

The voice came on the wind, nearer than before and Dirk recognized the voice!

"It is Starvros!" came the reply, borne on the wind, echoing in the ravine.

Dirk could not believe his ears.

'Starvros! He cannot be on this bridge. It is a trick of the Snow Fairy Queen,' Dirk thought.

Yet again, the voice came to him on the wind, "It is Starvros! Is anyone there?"

"Starvros! Starvros is on the bridge!" Dirk said.

All the things Dirk suffered since following Starvros and the girls into the treacherous mountains rushed through Dirk's mind. Tika, Mayor Brown, the villagers, Gustavo, Gizella, they all circled around in his mind. All the bitterness over the years, and his hatred for Starvros boiled to the surface. Dirk no longer felt the cold or the snow, His face flushed in the cold air, his eyes narrowed and his brows came together in a fierce frown, Dirk's mouth quivered and spittle dripped from the snarl he uttered.

"A-A-Argh!" Dirk growled and snarled as his pulse quickened and his breathing labored. Dirk growled again as he rushed forward on the bridge, forgetting the bridge, the storm, everything, but the voice ahead of him and what it meant to him to finally free himself of the object of his fully formed hatred. The only thought in his mind was to kill Starvros Gunther! Dirk moved quickly toward the voice on the bridge as it came on the wind.

"It is Starvros, Is anyone there?"

CHAPTER 11

THE KING'S QUEST FOR ANSWERS

S tarvros awoke to a fuddled brain.

"What is going on here?" he exclaims as he jumped to his feet to grab his knife as memories flooded his mind.

"Where are they? Where is the Snow Monster and his minions? Where am I? Ho, What kind of sorcery is this? Where is Moira and the villagers? Where is the grotto? How did I get here?" Starvros exclaimed as awareness grew that he was not where he thought he was.

"I am inside!" Starvros uttered as his brows grew together in a frown. Starvros glanced around the room. It was large room with a bed against one wall. It was made of dark wood and carved from trees. Starvros could see the knotholes in the wood. The bed covered in lavish coverlets of cream with gold thread, appeared worn and threadbare in places. pelts covered the floor and muted the footsteps. Tapestries depicting hunting scenes hung from the walls. A gargantuan fireplace filled the opposite wall, made of huge boulders with a big wide hearth. A fire burned steadily in its blackened stone interior. A carved mantle rested atop the huge boulder fireplace, carved from the same wood as the bed. Many carved and lavish artifacts covered its massive surface, reflected back into the room by a large matching, ornate mirror above it. A box filled with wood for the fireplace rested on the floor beside it. Next to the fireplace, Starvros saw the only entrance to the room, a large sturdy door.

Starvros raced to the door and pulled on it. The door did not give.

"I knew it was locked, but I had to try and see if it was open," Starvros said in disappointment.

"I have got to get out of here and find the girls and the villagers," Starvros said as he stomped his foot in frustration.

Starvros pulled at his hair and rubbed his chin.

"When did that happen," Starvros said, as he realized he had stubble on his chin. His advent into manhood went unnoticed by him.

"I guess I have been busy, lately. I do not remember how long we have been in these mountains. I have lost track of time." Starvros said.

"I have to get back on track and get back to the reason I started this quest. Obviously, I am a captive of the Snow Monster as well as Tika, Moira and the villagers," Starvros continued, as his thoughts tumbled around in his mind fighting for expression.

"They must be with Tika wherever they are. Why am I here in this room? I am puzzled. What happens next? Do I wait for something to happen or do I make something happen?" Starvros questioned.

"What will you make happen, lad?" said a voice from the doorway.

Startled, Starvros turned toward the voice expecting to see the snow monster. Stunned by what he sees, Starvros steps back toward the bed. Ho! What kind of sorcery is this?"

"W-who a-are y-you?" Starvros stammers at the sight of the man standing in the doorway.

"I am King Hector. King of Circle Valley and you are the lad who has caused a lot of trouble in my domain. I have lived for centuries in peace. Oh, there was an occasional interruption or two, but nothing I could not handle until you came along. The wicked fairy Queen is very upset about you villagers roaming around in our mountains. I have been more inconvenienced today than I have in centuries, even the nightly raid to your village has ceased and here you stand a lad, a slip of a boy who is going to ruin my way of life! Why I could eat you were I the snow monster! But, at this point I am here to get answers from you rather than the wicked Snow Fairy Queen," King Hector said.

"You are the Snow Monster, too!" Starvros said.

"I did not mean to reveal that much to you, lad. however, you can do nothing about it. You are my captive, No slip of a boy is going to get the best of me! No boy is going to destroy my world, however beastly it is! I live! I am alive and I can live forever as I am," the King stated passionately.

"Maybe you can live forever off of our blood, sweat and tears, King Hector but we cannot afford you any longer. The cost of feeding you every night, along with the horrible winters has depleted our stores, and our village; our women are mean-spirited and tired; our children live in terror and unhappiness; and the men have no purpose in life except to complain about what they give to you. You are draining the life from the inhabitants of Circle Valley. Because of you both parents are gone, shackled to a curse decreed a long time ago, which no one remembers today. There is nothing more to lose, King Hector. A way to destroy you and the curse will manifest itself," Starvros averred passionately as he stood to face the object of his quest.

"You can try Starvros, but…Oh! Oh! my head. King Hector grabbed his head. He reeled back and forth like a drunken man. King Hector grabbed the mantle of the fireplace to steady himself. He lifted his head and gazed into the distance.

Frightened, of the reeling man, Starvros exclaimed, "Ho! What kind of sorcery is this?" Starvros ran to the foot of the bed away from King Hector, and hid. King Hector continued to reel about the room, and then he stood erect. Starvros waited for the King to move and when he did not move, Starvros walked quickly toward the King and waved a hand before his face. The King did not respond. The door opened and the king left the room without a backward glance at Starvros.

Starvros waited a moment after the King walked out the door in the trance-like state. Starvros grabbed his pack he noticed on the floor at the foot of the bed. Starvros bolted out the open door into the hall not knowing who or what was beyond the door. Starvros knew this was his opportunity and he took it.

Starvros waited until his eyes adjusted to the dim light in the hall, he expected the King to call his name but he kept moving. Starvros walked quickly down the hall passing several closed doors, trying to open them to find the villagers, Moira or Tika. None opened at his touch. Starvros continued looking furtively through the castle, expecting to hear King Hector calling his name or sending someone to capture him or someone who would stop his escape. No one approached him. No sound reached his ears. The castle seemed empty. Starvros passed through rooms rich with furnishings he never saw before, objects of beauty and some that were grotesque, paintings, drawings, tapestries, animal pelt rugs and woven curtains in many colors and fabrics.

I must find Moira, Tika and the villagers, Starvros said as he came upon a cavernous kitchen. It had a huge fireplace and mantle like the one in the bedroom, only more massive. Big pots sat on an iron grate above the fire that glowed red and warmed the room with the smell of food.

"Our food," Starvros thought as he heard his stomach rumble and growl from the odors that reached him. His stomach turned in displeasure at smelling, yet not tasting the delicious food. Starvros continued past the food to one of several doors that opened into the kitchen. The first door opened onto the Pantry. Starvros was shocked to see the stores of food on the shelves.

'What does he need with our food?' Starvros thought, his brows furrowed in puzzlement.

"You are determined to find food instead of the villagers," Starvros spoke softly to his stomach as it continued to growl and lurch inside him. Starvros closed the door and moved on to the next door. He could not stop to look around or feed his growling stomach.

Starvros did not know how long the King would be in a trance. He did not know what caused the trance, but he was glad for it. He opened the door and saw steps leading downward. Starvros did not hesitate. His mind told him this was the door to the dungeons, to Moira, Tika and the villagers.

Starvros sped down the steps leading him lower and lower into the heart of the mountain itself. He knew from the cold seeping through the stone- walls that he was far beneath the castle. Starvros soon reached the bottom of the steps that opened onto a circular room. Thick doors with small slits in the center faced him. The first door he looked into was empty. Starvros sped to the next door, he turned and ran down the hall and snatched a torch from the wall, and returned to the door and waved the light in front of the slit and saw Tika and Moira huddled together on a small bed. Each had a small threadbare coverlet to ward off the cold seeping through the dungeon walls.

"Moira, Tika, get up!" Starvros said in a whisper, as he tapped on the slit in the window.

The girls screamed.

"Hush, be quiet!" Starvros said, trying to quiet the screaming girls.

"Starvros!" the girls screamed again as they recognized his voice.

"Moira, Tika, be quiet, you will wake the dead or worse! Starvros said sternly as he could in a whisper, afraid the King would hear him and send his minions to find him.

"Starvros!" the girls said as they ran toward the light emanating through the slit in the door.

"Starvros get us out of here!" said Tika.

"I will try girls. Move away from the door while I try to open the door. It does not look as if it is locked," Starvros said as he struggled with the door.

The villagers heard the girls scream and the door across from the girls' door filled with faces trying to see through the slit into the dim hall.

"Who is there?" What have you done to the girls?" demanded Mayor Brown.

"It is Starvros, Uncle! said Tika gleefully.

"Starvros is trying to get us out of here," Tika continued. Starvros is free! It is Starvros get us out of here Starvros! How did he get free? What is he doing out there? That young upstart is trying to free the girls first!" said Mayor Brown.

"Free us Starvros!" said the villagers.

"Starvros is trying to free the girls so they can get away from us and complete his silly quest," said Bobbo.

Starvros turned his back to the girls and looked toward the slit across the hall. He could barely make out the faces pressed against the small slit in the door.

"Why should I free any of you? You have never done anything for me! All I wanted was to be a part of Circle Valley, a part of the village, but you shunned me. You made a difference in the way you treated me. You treated me like an outsider. I am a citizen of Circle Valley with the same rules as you. I partake of the same things as you do, but you have denied me a life like yours. You left me a castaway to fend for myself. We all lived under the same curse, but you made my living bleaker than yours. Tell me why I should help you," Starvros spoke across the hall to the villagers. Starvros fists clenched and his faced flushed, revealing the bulging, glaring eyes across the dimly lit hall, as he panted for breath in the cold room. The villagers fell silent at his rebuke, and into the silence, the Snow Monster snarled loudly through the castle.

"Oh No The Snow Monster!" Starvros snapped from his tirade as the snarls reached him.

"King Hector has somehow changed into the Snow Monster!"

"What?" said, Moira?

"I have no time to free anyone, Moira. I must leave the castle now. I will try to return later to free you.

The Snow Monster rent the air with another snarl.

"Save yourself! Starvros, Get out of here while you can. I trust that you will come back for us, Moira stated quietly.

"Why are you telling him that, Moira? No, Starvros save us now free us first. Do not leave me here Starvros," Tika cried frantically.

"I cannot Tika, I cannot. I must go I will come back for you! I promise," said Starvros.

Dirk would not leave me here Starvros. Dirk would have moved this entire castle to rescue me. Yes! Find Dirk, Starvros. Tell him I am here. Dirk will help. Dirk loves me and I love him, too," Tika said tears flowing from her eyes.

Starvros looked at Tika as her words seared his heart. Tika loves Dirk!

Moira looked from Starvros to Tika.

"Go! Starvros, Go now, Do as Tika says. Find Dirk, Starvros. Go quickly! Starvros!" Moira said urgently.

The villagers took up the refrain, Find Dirk. Find Dirk! Find Dirk! Starvros. He will save us they cried in unison.

Starvros secured his pack on his back as he dashed from the dungeon through the last door in the circular room that opened onto the cavernous grotto that was witness to their capture hours earlier or was it days ago. He only knew that he had no sense of time and he could not remember how many days they were in these mountains. He only knew that Moira, Tika and the villagers were right. He had to find Dirk and persuade the man who wanted to kill him to join with him to save Tika, the villagers and Moira.

Coming out into the grotto, Starvros heard the snarls of the Snow Monster, but they were moving away from the castle. Starvros realized he did not have time to ponder the movements of the Snow Monster. He was glad that the Snow Monster was moving away from him, not closer. Starvros only knew he had to find Dirk and return to free Moira, Tika, and the villagers.

Starvros skirted around the edge of the grotto out into the mountain. Starvros had no idea where to find Dirk, or how he would convince him to help free Tika and the others.

'Starvros had not forgotten that something happened out there between Dirk and the villagers. Dirk would not have left Tika to him so readily unless it could not be helped,' thought Starvros.

'Dirk was hell bent on killing him for his own reasons and Starvros knew he was just as hell bent on staying alive. Starvros knew something drastic happened between Dirk and the villagers that they were willing to overlook, if he saved them from the Snow Monster. Starvros also knew that whatever happened on the mountain drove Dirk from his main purpose in following him and the girls up the mountain, and that was to kill Starvros Gunther! A Starvros moved quickly through the snowy tundra, Starvros believed Tika gave him the key to convince Dirk to save them. Starvros could see her beautiful tear-stained face as she poured out her anguish in her final plea: "Find Dirk Starvros, he will save me. Dirk loves me and I love him, too!" Starvros felt his heart lurch at the memory of the girl he thought loved him plead for another man to save her. His breath stuttered from the sharp pain flowing over him. "Tika loves Dirk!" Starvros heard his voice speak what his heart could not face. 'How am I going to convince another man to fight for the woman I love!' thought Starvros.

In that moment, Starvros felt inadequate. Here is another thing the quest for the Snow Monster has taken from him. Starvros resolved in his heart to find the Snow Monster and destroy him before another day came to Mt RaNinjitsi.

Starvros knew that Dirk's love for Tika was real. Starvros now knew he did not have her heart. All this time she was running away from Dirk, Tika was really in love with Dirk! Women! They are confusing! Starvros thought, as he rounded a large field of snow-covered boulders.

The storm was going strong when he exited the grotto, but it seemed as if the flakes were larger and wetter, covering everything in sight. Starvros could only see a few feet in front of him. When Starvros looked back, his footprints disappeared. Starvros continued moving as quickly as he could through the boulder-strewn tundra. Starvros began to see small pillars in the snow. He was curious but decided not to waste time trying to figure out what they were. Starvros knew he had to hurry if he wanted to free the villagers, Moira and Tika. The pillars grew in size as he continued walking over the snow covered ground. The going was laborious because of the storm. Starvros kept going, determination outlined in the firm set of his mouth and the jutting of his chin from a firm pressing of his lips together as he moved slowly toward something he did not know. Starvros turned around a small bend in the mountain wall and stopped in his tracks. before him stood two massive pillars holding a bridge over a gaping ravine. Starvros gasped!

What is this place? Starvros questioned. It is a bridge! Where does it lead? Starvros asked.

Suddenly Starvros heard the snarls of the Snow Monster. The Snow Monster found me! Starvros exclaimed as he hid behind the large pillar and dug into the snow forming a small hump in the snowy landscape and waited, watching through a small hole he carved with his mittened hand. He trembled with fear of discovery by the Snow Monster. the Snow Monster appeared on the bridge covering the ravine. he snarled and growled his displeasure sending echoes into the ravine.

Suddenly a light flashed and the Snow Monster disappeared as quickly as he had appeared.

"Ho! What kind of sorcery is this?" Starvros said, as he emerged from his hiding place, brushing the thick wet snow from his clothing. Starvros looked at the bridge over the ravine.

"Obviously, the ravine leads somewhere and that somewhere is where the Snow Monster has gone, I am sure of It. I will continue my quest to destroy the Snow Monster and the curse. I will surely find the Snow Monster across that bridge," Starvros said, forgetting Moira, Tika and the villagers

Starvros stepped gingerly onto the bridge.

Starvros did not know what or who waited for him on the other side of the bridge, but he was determined to find out.

The unknown leapt at him as he looked into the gaping ravine beneath him. "Whoa! slow down, this bridge is dangerous. It must be enchanted. There is no way this bridge is manmade, Starvros said as he continued to cross the bridge in the storm that swirled large wet flakes of snow at him on every side. Starvros never felt as small as he felt on the bridge or so alone. the wind whipped at the bridge, causing the wet snow to crust into ice and crunch beneath his booted feet. Starvros clung to the guide rope moving slow but purposely. Starvros huddled low to make each footfall sure on the snow-covered, ice encrusted tree planks that made the massive bridge even more treacherous. One slip and he would fall into oblivion into a ravine for which he could not see the bottom. The wind continued to howl and keen like an instrument played in the wrong key. It tore at his clothing fiercely trying to unclothe him. It drove the coldness into his body and numbed fingers holding the guide ropes It swirled and twirled the snow around him like a thing alive. The snow made the wind visible and it tore at him to dislodge him from the bridge like a wild being out of control.

Starvros hunched lower and continued to labor along the bridge, holding onto the guide ropes, fiercely.

To take his mind off the wind and the danger he faced on the bridge, Starvros thought about the events, which brought him to this point. Starvros thought about the villagers, and Mayor Brown. He thought about the way they treated him and his reaction to their treatment. Starvros thought about the Snow Monster and the curse on Circle Valley and he thought about Dirk and his hatred for Starvros. They all were events in his life that caused him to make choices. Some were good choices and some were not good choices, but Starvros realized that his reactions to the events in his life are how he ended up on a bridge over a bottomless ravine, alone.

Starvros soon heard sounds that penetrated his reverie. They were faint upon the wind, carried down into the ravine and echoed back to him. Starvros could not tell if the sounds came from behind him or in front of him!

"Ho! What kind of sorcery is this? Has the Snow Monster found me on this bridge?" Starvros said.

"Quiet Starvros, make sure you know what direction the enemy is coming from," Starvros could hear the voice of his father instructing him in his ear. Starvros calmed and waited to see if the sounds he heard were real or imagined, or fanciful. It could be the affects of the weather, or the mountain air playing tricks with his mind.

"I thought I heard a human voice ahead of me on the bridge, Who is there? Who is there?

Starvros stopped at the voice he heard very faintly on the wind. He cupped his mouth with his mittened hands and shouted, "It is Starvros! It is Starvros!" Starvros called into the wind-swirling, howling storm on a bridge across a gaping ravine. Starvros strained to hear. Am I imagining things? There! That is a human voice!" Starvros quickened his pace as much as he could.

"There is someone else on the bridge!" Starvros said, excited and fearful at the same time.

"Friend or foe, they will face the wrath of Starvros Gunther this day," Starvros said vehemently as he placed one booted foot in front of the other holding onto the guide rope with both mittened hands.

Starvros heard and felt the figure rushing at him before he saw him, as the bridge began to leap and jump. Starvros grabbed for the guide rope as a figure rushed him out of the wind –tossed, swirling snow, and hit him with such force that he fell backwards onto the bridge losing his grip on the guide rope. Both men tumbled around on the swaying bridge. One man howling in anger and another howling in fear of falling headlong into the ravine from their weight on the icy boards. The bridge jumped and swerved with the impact. Starvros, eyes bulging as he recognized Dirk tried desperately to scramble from the enraged man to grab the only lifeline they had-the guide rope.

Starvros managed to grab onto the guide rope to keep from rolling off the moving bridge into nothingness, his fear retching in his throat. It took all of Starvros' strength to strain and hold onto the guide rope on the ice-slickened bridge.

"Dirk! Dirk! Are you crazy?" Starvros panted,

"Get off me, Dirk!" Starvros shouted, trying to get through to the enraged man.

Dirk finally realized the danger they were in of careening off the bridge and grabbed the guide rope as his body slammed to a halt and rolled toward the edge of the bridge. Dirk saw his body slip over the icy planks into oblivion and made a last leap for the guide rope with his free hand. The impact caused Dirk to stop his headlong plunge, but his legs dangled over the side of the bridge as it continued to sway wildly from his onslaught on Starvros. Dirk howled again and the sound echoed throughout the ravine, his eyes bulged in their sockets and all color drained from his face. Both men clung to the bridge fighting fear and panic and pain, waiting for the swaying bridge to subside. The bridge slowly lost its momentum and returned to a calm state.

The wind and snow pelted Dirk as he clung to the side of the bridge, his legs swaying wildly as he tried to regain his footing on the icy bridge. Starvros managed to hang onto the guide rope and lay panting on the ice-encrusted planks of the bridge.

"I don't have time for this Starvros," said, his mind reeling from the impact.

"Dirk, are you all right? Why did you attack me? You do not know what you are doing. You are ill, Dirk." Starvros panted between breaths, as his fear and panic subsided.

Dirk waited until the bridge was still again, before answering Starvros. Dirk breathed the cold air in great gulps to calm himself. He tasted the saltiness of fear rising in his throat.

"Um-um-S- Starvros, S- Starvros, h -help me onto the bridge. I -I do not have the strength to pull myself back onto the bridge. Hurry Starvros, I-I do not think I-I c-can h-hold on m-much l-longer!"

Starvros rose to his feet, trying not to make the bridge sway again and moved slowly toward Dirk who was only inches from him. He could visibly see the man's strength ebbing from his body and marveled that he still clung to the guide ropes. Starvros reached Dirk and grabbed the rope he kept tied to his waist since the ice storm with Tika and Moira. He tied the rope to Dirk and around the guide ropes. Starvros then tugged and pulled the big man's torso using the rope as advantage until his legs no longer dangled over the side. Both men collapsed onto the bridge, thankful it did not start to sway again. They lay in a heap taking air in like a babe suckling its mother's teats.

Finally, Starvros lifted his head and looked at Dirk.

"Why do you hate me so, Dirk? why do you want to take my life? What have I done to you?" Starvros pleads his anguish clear in a voice that cracked and hesitated on every word.

Dirk took a deep breath and answered Starvros without looking at him. His voice low with a monotone quality, without emotion or inflection.

"Long ago before you were born, I gave my heart to a woman. She did not know of the love in my heart. A bullish man like me does not find a love like that, so I told no one but my friend of my love for her. His betrayal became evident when he married her. It broke my heart and I vowed never to love anyone else, until Tika. That woman was Abbey laurel, your mother, Starvros. The man, your father stole her from me, and I cannot blame him. She was beautiful inside and out, she was gentle, her laughter made you feel such joy inside, and when she smiled, it was as if she smiled only for you. I hated your father for taking my one true love. I have hated him since the day I discovered his betrayal. I hate you because you remind me of your father and you are the one thing in life that let me know I could never claim Abbey laurel's love. I thought I had a second chance with Abbey laurel after your father went on his quest for the Snow Monster and did not return. However, I was wrong again. She spurned me because of you and I hated you the more and I talked the villagers into spurning you every chance I got. You became my enemy in the place of your father. Now that I have killed Gustavo because of your silly quest and lost Tika due to my being outlawed and branded I vowed to kill you Starvros Gunther. When I heard your voice on the bridge, I lost control and almost killed the both of us. You are more gracious than I Starvros Gunther. You saved my life and I would have taken yours, gladly. Dirk rose to his feet with much effort on the icy bridge.

"I am going to leave you now, Starvros, on this bridge and I am going to find my way off of this terrible mountain and from the villagers, the Snow Monster and Tika, Dirk said backing away from Starvros to continue his journey.

"Wait, Dirk, please wait! Hear me! Tika sent me to find you! It is providence that we stumbled into each other. Tika loves you Dirk! Tika and the villagers are captives of the Snow Monster! I escaped from the castle. Tika sent me to find you, the villagers sent me to find you, and even Moira sent me to find you, Dirk! They all know what I refused to see. I need your help to save them from the Snow Monster. I cannot do this alone Dirk. I came on this quest out of silly pride, Dirk. I wanted to prove to you and the men of Circle Valley that I was a man, too. I wanted to be a part of Circle Valley so much that I have endangered us all. One man cannot do this alone, Dirk. Help me free the villagers so that we all can fight and free ourselves from the legend of the Snow Monster., and the curse on Circle Valley. Dirk, I know that if we stop complaining and blaming each other for our troubles, and look for a solution we can overcome the legend of the Snow Monster and the terrible curse on Circle Valley. Will you join me, Dirk? Will you help me to free the villagers, Moira and Tika from the Snow Monster and destroy the curse?" Starvros pleaded.

"Aye, I will help you Starvros for Tika's sake, if she loves me as you say! You Gunther men are smooth with your words, but I do not trust you so readily. I will go back to the dungeons to free Tika and if it is as you say, I will continue to help you destroy the Snow Monster and end the curse, but if it is not as you say, I will kill you and find my way off these twin mountains.

In addition, Starvros you have more to worry about than the Snow Monster. A wicked Snow Queen Fairy lives in a castle beyond this bridge on Mt Ra Nanjitsi. I was escaping from her when I saw you and lost my head. She controls the Snow Monster," Dirk stated.

"A wicked Snow Queen Fairy who controls the Snow Monster. Ho! What kind of sorcery is this?" Starvros exclaimed.

"It does not make sense. How will we discover legend of the Snow Monster if someone else is controlling him? How will we destroy the curse? Oh! This is getting more and more complicated, Dirk," said Starvros as his teeth began to chatter from the cold seeping into his clothing.

"I remembered something Starvros that may help us, but we cannot stay here on this bridge so exposed. The wicked Snow Queen Fairy has magical powers and when I escaped from her I found this book in the castle and when you read it the pictures move and tell a story," Dirk said excitedly.

"Moving picture?" Starvros stared at Dirk as if he really lost his mind!

"It is true, Starvros," said Dirk as he fumbled to open the book.

"I saw Circle Valley and the castle and people and horses and a forest full of animals. It is not as Circle Valley is now," Dirk said

"Dirk we cannot read the book out here," Starvros said. As I was coming toward the bridge, I saw the Snow Monster appear on the bridge and then he vanished? If it is as you say and the wicked Snow Queen Fairy controls the Snow Monster, she has somehow summoned him to her castle.

Let us find shelter and build a fire so that we can eat something to ward off the affects of the thin mountain air. I think it has more than affected our minds and emotions," Starvros continued as Dirk handed him the little book.

"Better yet Dirk, let us go back to Mt Ra Ninjitsi as quickly as we can. We can free the villagers and allow Tika, Moira and Mayor Brown to decode the book and find the answers we need to destroy the Snow Monster and the curse. I have the feeling that our hands are going to be busy fighting the Snow Monster and the wicked Snow Queen Fairy." Starvros said as he moved gingerly back the way he came.

"You are right Little One. Let us hurry, I cannot wait to free Tika," said Dirk

The pair helped each other along the bridge until they came to the two large pillars at the entrance to the bridge. They kept moving toward Mt RaNinjitsi, Starvros sure of the way back to the grotto, spoke in a whisper to Dirk

"We are near the grotto, Dirk. We must move carefully because we do not know who the snow monster has guarding the entrance to the grotto, or who is guarding the villagers."

"You are right Starvros. Let us find shelter so that we can plan what to do before we attack and free the villagers. There is a rocky outcropping among those trees near the mountain wall. It is a good location. With the mountain at our back, we can see someone approaching long before they see us," Dirk averred.

"Good thinking, Dirk, come on let us pick up the pace, we do not have much time left. Use your staff we do not want to fall into any unseen crevices or tunnels," Starvros continued

"We will figure a way to free Tika Starvros, I am sure of it," Dirk said confidently.

Starvros and Dirk hurried toward the outcropping of rocks as quickly as they could in the heavy snowstorm. Each one thinking their own thoughts that circled in their brains like a dog chasing his tail. When they reached the rocks, it looked like a natural fortress. There was plenty of shelter from the wind and snow raging beyond them. Starvros dropped his pack on the ground and found a huge boulder to collapse. Starvros looked around and surveyed the area ringed in on three sides; with huge monolithic columns much like the pillars at the bridge. Starvros saw similar structures all around them.

"What is this place, Dirk?" Starvros asked.

"How should I know Little One, it resembles some kind of religious place the way the pillars are placed. Maybe the inhabitants of Circle Valley used this place to worship the fairies; long ago. This is my first time in these mountains. However, that is not the reason we are here. Let us get busy and light a fire, eat something, and plan what to do very fast. We do not have time to waste, Starvros. The wicked Snow Fairy Queen is just as formidable as the Snow Monster. I can understand why she has ruled for so long. She is vicious, but she could not defeat Dirk. Nevertheless, I do not want to fight her again," Dirk stated, firmly.

"If we can discover the curse and destroy it, maybe it will destroy her Dirk. Is not that the way of magic? Starvros asked Dirk, as he pulled cold food from his pack he retrieved from the ground.

Let us get down to planning our rescue and our fight to the death if we encounter the Snow Monster," Dirk said.

"You are cautious, Dirk. That is good. Here is some suet, cheese and bread. I do not think we should light a fire in case we alert someone to our presence. I sense we are running out of time Dirk, and maybe this book is the key to unlocking old truths, curses and legends. We have them all on this quest," Starvros stated as he ate.

"I am cold to the bone, Starvros, I do not ever want to cross that bridge again," Dirk chattered through teeth that would not stop moving.

"Let us get on with it Dirk We will deal with things as they present themselves to us. We will freeze to death it we stay out here any longer," Starvros said.

"I do not know Little One, but nothing hurts a failure, but a try. That is all we can do. Let us get on with it," Starvros.

"Open that book and we will see what it will tell us," Dirk said brusquely.

Starvros opened the book. The letters glowed red in his hands. Starvros jumped up and almost dropped the book.

"Be careful, Starvros, we do not know what kind of magic that book contains. It may provide a way to free Tika and I will not lose her again," Dirk stated.

"Oh, quit being so pushy Dirk," Starvros said smiling at the big brutish man for the first time.

Dirk nudged Starvros on the head.

"You are alright Little One, come on read the book! You can read?" Dirk asked as he smiled sheepishly at Starvros.

"I thought you said the book does the talking Dirk, in moving pictures. It must be enchanted. Well here goes," Starvros said as he turned a page in the little book.

As before, the scene opened on a view of Circle Valley.

"I never saw Circle Valley look like that," Dirk whispered.

"Me either," Starvros whispered.

"Shush!" Dirk said as the scene changed to a room in a castle high in the mountains.

It was a large great room filled with people in lavish clothes and furniture carved of dark wood that gleamed from the lights of many candles and torches in the huge great room. Servants mingled among the people carrying platters of food. Starvros' stomach growled at the sight of so much food. The meager meal they had eaten was not enough to assuage his hunger. Dirk heard his stomach growl in displeasure.

"Starvros I am still hungry. I do not know when I have eaten food like this. Close the book. I have seen enough. I am frustrated Starvros and that blasted book has opened up wounds. I do not know what day it is, I do not really know where I am. All I know is that I hate the daytime and I dread the nights in this mountain, yet I can wait to eat. I want to find the elusive Snow Monster and find out the truth about the curse as much as you do. I did not realize how much of our lives the curse controlled until seeing Circle Valley as it once was. Comparing it to Circle Valley as it is now, I see how mean our lives are. Limited by the curse as prisoners in our own village, the Snow Monster controls what we see, hear, what we do and where we go. He even controls what we eat, Starvros! What kind of life is that? It is a wonder we have not killed each other before now. I killed Gustavo and I was ready and willing to kill you too, Starvros. We have turned our hatred of our lives inward upon ourselves because we have no outlet to grow beyond Circle Valley. Growth is a natural part of life, Starvros and Circle Valley and its people could not grow because of the curse, the legend of the snow monster, and now the wicked Snow Queen Fairy, who has used us all as pawns in her schemes. Her curse would have led to our ultimate self- destruction, Little One. We have to stop them Starvros," Dirk said passionately.

"Let us get moving then, Dirk," Starvros said meekly, quieted by Dirk's speech. Starvros saw more than a big, brutish man. 'Dirk was an eloquent man of quiet wisdom and inner strength. He could see Tika falling in love with a man like this. He will treat her well.' Starvros thought.

Snarls from the Snow Monster soon broke through Starvros' thoughts, as they rent the air.

"Dirk, it is the Snow Monster! Where is he? Has he found us? Starvros asked crouching low and peering all around the area they chose to camp.

"I do not know, Starvros, but if he freed the wicked fairy, she will know exactly where we are. She has an orb at her castle that shows her everything in the mountains," Dirk said looking around as the Snow Monster snarled again.

"How will we get away from them," asked Starvros.

"We must make a run for that grotto and hope we make it there before the Snow Monster. I am sure he is doing her bidding. He is after the book! Keep it safe Little One, it is the answer for our future!" Dirk said as he drew his knife and spear to him, while he hid his pack behind one of the stone pillars.

"Lead the way Starvros, and hurry! We are running out of time!" Dirk said falling into step beside Starvros as they moved purposely toward the grotto.

"Wait Dirk, maybe the book can show us a shorter way back to the grotto," Starvros said as he opened the book and flipped a page.

"We do not have time to ask the book for help Starvros. The Snow Monster may be getting closer. The book only has to do with the curse. We must find a way out of this for ourselves. We must depend on each other, not magic to get us out of this trouble. Magic has gotten us where we are now, running for our lives! If the people of Circle Valley depended on themselves for their living instead of waiting for the wicked Snow Queen Fairy to give them good crops and good hunting trips. If they united as a family of people in the village working together for their own good, the good of all through faith and trust in each other's abilities, magic would not be an issue today. We are hunters and gatherers; we do not need magic for that, Little One." Dirk averred

Starvros put the book in his tunic beneath other clothing and stuck it firmly in the pants at his waist.

"Dirk you are right. The skill of our ancestors' flow through our blood, and our trained instincts makes us a village. We lost that for wealth and luxury, at a great cost, Dirk and that is the true curse of Circle Valley."

Putting action to words, Starvros hid his pack beneath some debris after withdrawing his knife. A huge blade his father had made before he left him to go on his quest for the Snow Monster.

Dirk eyed the blade. "I remember when I made that blade for your father, Starvros. It is one of my best works. It is strong and steady. Use it well Little One. We are going to need every weapon we have to defeat the Snow Monster, the wicked Snow Queen Fairy and their minions," Dirk iterated.

Starvros crouched low and began to move from the shelter out into the snow-covered terrain, keeping close to the mountain wall for shelter and vantage, so no one could sneak up on them. If an attack came at all, A frontal attack was the only way the enemy could subdue them. Dirk followed hard on Starvros' trail, stopping periodically to look behind him to protect their rear flank. When they ran out of mountain wall, Starvros led Dirk around the few cluster of trees on the pristine landscape, moving uphill toward the grotto entrance to the castle from which he had made his earlier escape.

Starvros whispered to Dirk to lay low to see if any guards were left behind to guard the entrance to the grotto. Starvros then scouted around and leaped quietly onto the grotto ledge, crouching low behind the gigantic ice columns suspended from the ceiling that produced the light show he and Moira viewed when they first approached the cavernous grotto. There was no light show to greet him today. The snow fell all around him in huge wet flakes as if winter had gone mad. The wind that accompanied the storm blew the snow into drifts, like clouds of fog. The snow clung to them and they resembled the snow creatures the children fashioned in Circle Valley after a snowfall.

Starvros scouted to the back of the grotto keeping close to the wall. He signaled to Dirk to follow him. Dirk leapt onto the grotto ledge and Starvros marveled at the agility of the big man. Dirk soon joined Starvros as he sat crouching in the darkened grotto, watching the entrance to the castle. They saw two watchers at the entrance to the castle. Starvros and Dirk moved quietly and quickly toward the two sentries.

Starvros could sense his father's presence in the training that came to him as he moved toward his foe. Dirk followed hard on his heels. Both men leaped in unison onto the sentries and plunged their knives into their brains. Starvros sensed that the only way to destroy them was to destroy the control the Wicked Snow Queen Fairy and the Snow Monster had on their minds.

The sentries toppled over onto the grotto floor as Starvros and Dirk spun away from them. They did not look back. Starvros and Dirk continued into the castle and Starvros led the way to the dungeons to free the villagers,

Tika and Moira. Starvros pointed out the room to Dirk to set the villagers free.

Once free and quieted the villagers and Mayor Brown turned to Starvros.

"You did not have to come back for us, lad. We have treated you shamefully and for that, we are sorry," said Mayor Brown.

Mayor Brown then turned to Dirk and said, "I do not know how Starvros found you Dirk, but I am glad he did. You did not have to come back for us Mayor Brown! Starvros interrupted, "We do not have time for this the Snow Monster is on our trail. They will be here soon!"

"They?" questioned Mayor Brown.

"The Snow Monster, the wicked Snow Queen Fairy and their minions are almost here. Men gather your weapons and prepare your minds for the fight of your lives," Starvros stated.

"The wicked Snow Queen Fairy has a castle on Mt RaNanjitsi; she controls the Snow Monster," She also has an orb that can tell her exactly where we are, but I overcame her once and I can do it again with your help!" said Dirk.

"The wicked fairy! Yes, I remember stories of a fairy queen, but I assumed it was fables made up to scare us children," said Mayor Brown.

"You knew! Is there anything more you want to tell us, Mayor Brown?" Starvros and Dirk said in unison.

"How about telling us how to destroy her?" Starvros continued.

"Well, not that you mention it, there is a story about a book, or a prophecy, oh I do not remember!" said Mayor Brown.

"The book!" Starvros said as he struggled to remove it from beneath his clothing.

"Is this the book, Mayor Brown," Starvros said as he handed the book to Mayor Brown.

"I-I d-do n-not know, Starvros. The Legend of the Snow Monster told of a book that would destroy the curse, but again it came through our parents and their parents before them, so we thought they were fables to entertain and frighten us," said Mayor Brown.

Starvros handed the book to Mayor Brown and the letters glowed red again They could clearly see the words, "The Book of Prophecy."

"This must be it, Starvros," Mayor Brown said excitedly.

Snarls rent the air near the castle.

The villagers clustered together.

"Be brave men, this is our destiny, said Mayor Brown.

"We have dawdled too long," Starvros said.

"Mayor Brown I am going to put you in the room with Tika and Moira. Use the torch and read the book of the prophecy; try to figure out what we need to do to destroy this double threat on our lives, today." Starvros said handing the Mayor a torch from the wall.

"We will go out to meet the Snow Monster in the flat land before the grotto, to give you time to do this, Mayor Brown, our lives depend on what you do in here," Starvros continued.

"I sense events have already altered his nightly visits to the village, I will do as you say," Mayor Brown said.

Starvros opened the door to the room where Moira and Tika were and ushered the Mayor into the room while quieting the girls. Starvros shut the door and locked it firmly.

Tika ran to the window,

"Starvros, did you find Dirk? I thought I heard his voice. Please tell me, Starvros did you find the man I love?" Tika sobbed.

"I am here, Tika! Stop your crying woman, and get on with reading that book and let men be men!" Dirk said softly to the sobbing Tika.

Tika smiled at Dirk through hers tears and softly said,

"I am sorry, Dirk. I Love you!" She then turned from the window and joined Mayor Brown and Moira.

Mayor Brown came to the window as the men went to the room to retrieve their weapons. It was fortuitous that the Snow Monster's minions did not put their belongings in another place. Starvros went to the Mayor and handed him a knife through the window.

"I do not have to tell you what to do Mayor Brown, if we are not victorious, Starvros spoke quietly.

"Yes Starvros, I know what to do," said Mayor Brown as he pulled the weapon through the slit in the door.

As Starvros turned to leave, the Mayor spoke to them.

"Fight bravely men. The future of your families, you and our village rest upon what you do this day. We are not lost, yet. Ancient traditions and training will guide you and hold you steadfast and unmovable. Ancient warriors are in your blood; allow them to arise in you with a better hope than we have had in the past. We fight for an unchained future, where every man will be judged by what he brings to this life, not how he was born into it. Every man is born to improve his lot in life for self and for others. The Legend had us bound to one way of living, when life offers a full spectrum of venues for our life's flow. The Snow Monster, as our jailer, lived off our substance and sucked the will to live from us, the energy to fight for our lives, and the mindset to unite toward a common purpose, until today. Go now men! Go forth, conquer our enemies and deliver us from the evil, and the greed and the tyranny that has bound us for over 5 centuries. May our ancestors be with you? Do not be afraid, have courage and you will win the battle!" the Mayor said as he spoke quickly to the villagers.

Tika and Moira watched silently as they witnessed the men of their village unite with Starvros and Dirk to fight the greatest battle of their lives.

"Let us go men we will make our stand in the flat land before the grotto. Follow me!" Starvros said, as he led the way from the dungeon to the grotto entrance and beyond.

The men stood before the grotto, waiting for the Snow Monster as his snarls drew closer.

"Wait until they are close men; await my signal and then attack! Fight as you have never fought before, said Starvros as he looked at Dirk who stood beside him, knife in one hand and spear in the other.

Dirk nodded to Starvros, "Well said Little One! he whispered.

Starvros smiled at Dirk and the villagers and then crouched low as he heard another snarl from the Snow Monster reverberate over the mountains, as if he were everywhere at once. The men of the village crouched as low as Starvros and Dirk, awaiting the onslaught coming their way.

"Steady men, steady! Wait for the signal! Starvros said.

CHAPTER 12

ENDINGS

The Snow Monster became aware of his surroundings as he stood on the bridge to Mt RaNanjitsi. He snarled loudly, his displeasure, and then vanished again. When the Snow Monster became aware of his surroundings again, he stood in a small, dark, room, but before he could assess where he was, he began to change again. This time he changed from the Snow Monster to King Hector.

King Hector looked around the small room and chuckled as he saw Gizella.

"Well, well, Gizella, How did you end up here?" King Hector asked, reveling at the sight of the wicked Snow Queen Fairy helplessly tied to the bedposts.

Gizella's eyes snapped, icy blue, and bulging as she mumbled through the gag Dirk had stuffed in her mouth to keep her from cursing him or using magic to release herself.

"F-f-fre m-me, t-tak thi ga of m-me!" Gizella mumble through the gag.

King Hector walked toward Gizella in obedience and removed the gag from her mouth.

"Untie me, you fool!" Gizella stormed.

"That blacksmith tricked me and tied me to the bed' It is good that I can control the Snow Monster with my mind, but it took a lot out of me to get you here and to make the change to King Hector," Gizella ranted.

"So you control when I change to the Snow Monster, too, Gizella," King Hector said quietly.

Does that mean that your powers are limited, Gizella? asked King Hector.

"You mind your business, King Hector. Come! I will look through the orb to find this blacksmith and destroy him and then we will go to your castle and deal with those villagers," Gizella said as King Hector freed her from the bindings.

Back in the great room, Gizella walked toward the orb and stopped when she saw the books in the little room strewn across the worn stone floor.

"What is this? What now?" Gizella said, as she ran toward the shelves. Gizella searched the shelves throwing more books and scrolls onto the floor.

"No! No! No! this cannot be happening! I hate humans! They are nothing but trouble! They will not leave anything untouched by them! Gizella cried out.

King Hector looked at Gizella, puzzled by all the ranting and raging.

"I am human, Gizella. Aside from the curse you have laid upon me, I am Human! said the King.

"I do not want any trouble from you, King Hector. I have had nothing but trouble from you-you humans," Gizella reiterated.

"I was the Fairy Queen of all the fairies in these mountains. I was treated royally and worshipped by the humans who I favored with good crops, wealth, and good health until the day your beautiful daughter was born. You began to shun me, and others followed your example. I tried to win the people back by giving them more crops that are abundant and more animals to hunt. On the day of the Hunters' Ball, your pride grew to its full limit when you did not invite me to the great feast before the hunting season opened. It was my day! It was the day I blessed your hunting season and received my worship, in return. Instead, you lifted your daughter up as my rival! You compared her beauty, no! You claimed her beauty was greater than my beauty! I saw all this through the orb on Mount Ra Nanjitsi. In my fury, I came to the ball and cursed you and Circle Valley for your foolishness, for your pride and for your scorn. I included a way out of the curse. A prophecy that could only happen when the villagers overcame their prideful attitude and united together to solve their problem-the curse of the Snow Monster. If the people of Circle Valley overcame their divisions they would be free from the curse, but they never could, and I saw to that with a few enchantments and your help that kept them afraid. Fear divides. I have been free from you humans for many centuries because of it. I found out I did not need your worship, your adoration. I did not need you humans any longer. You were a lot of work! Now a lad is loose in my mountains, the only clue to the prophecy I overlooked," Gizella said to King Hector.

Gizella spoke to King Hector, "The man who left here has the "Book of the Prophecy," find him before he finds the boy Starvros and kill him. Bing the book back to me. Let us look into the orb to see if it will show us where this human is."

Gizella walked to the orb with the King at her heels and peered into the orb as it began to glow. Gizella waved her hand over the orb spoke five words; "datra, nomna, datra, dimna, matra; the orb cleared and Gizella and the King saw the swirling snow, then Gizella stared and leaned forward closer to the orb. Gizella saw two figures walking away from the bridge and in the hand of the smaller figure, Gizella saw the "Book of the Prophecy!"

Gizella eyes bulged; her mouth opened and closed several times, the blood drained from her pale face. Gizella backed to the carved chair and sat down. Sounds gurgled in her throat, but no words formed.

King Hector looked from Gizella to the orb, puzzled by her reaction.

H-he, h-he has t-the b-book! Gizella whispered. I-I, I-I h-hate h-humans!

"King Hector!" Gizella stormed, pointing at him, "Find them, call the minions, take my guards and find them and get that book before that lad reads it! Go now!"

"Do not try anything, King Hector. I will be watching you and if you do not bring that book back to me I will destroy you! I should have done it long ago, but there are limits to what I can and cannot do and your folly was only pride and arrogance," Gizella continued.

"Go! Go! Gizella said, as she waved her arms and spoke six words;

"Datra, somma, noma, romma datra," and King Hector changed and became the Snow Monster to do her bidding. The guards awakened and vanished from sight. Gizella ran to the orb and saw the minions pouring from the castle of the Snow Monster. They vanished from sight also, as the wicked Snow Queen Fairy looked on with glee and fear; they all reappeared together at the stone pillars before the ravine.

"They are on their trail now, soon the book will be returned to me and I will destroy everyone! The lad, the villagers, those silly lasses, the snow monster, everyone and I will live in peace on my mountains. I do not need anyone! I hate humans!" Gizella said as she relaxed in her carved chair to await the Snow Monster's return to his destruction!

The Curse Unravels

Mayor Brown set about making a small fire in the room on the cold stone floor to light the torch so that they could read the small book Starvros gave him. Soon a small fire was lit and Mayor Brown lit the torch Starvros gave him. Light and heat filtered into the small room. Mayor Brown rose from the cold floor and looked for a place on the wall to place the torch. He found it and then pulled the small bed toward the light.

"Sit girls, we have work to do. Tika dry those tears and help us find the answer to destroy this curse. I do not know what we will find in this book but we have to try. Starvros and Dirk seemed to think it is the key to our freedom from the curse, the Snow Monster and the wicked Snow Queen Fairy, and I trust them," Mayor Brown stated.

"A wicked Snow Queen Fairy?" Moira and Tika asked simultaneously.

"I know you have many questions girls. The moment is critical and we must help Starvros and Dirk as quickly as we can. Our task is to read the "Book of the Prophecy," and discover truths hidden from us long ago," said Mayor Brown briskly as he opened the book with the glowing letters.

"Oh, Oh, Oh," said Moira and Tika, together

211

The scene in the great room continued when Mayor Brown opened the book, and startled by a voice emanating from the book< Mayor Brown juggled the book from one hand to the other to keep from dropping the book. Finally settled, the voice continued when Mayor Brown opened the book to the scene of the feast at the Hunters' Ball.

"Ho! What kind of sorcery is this?" Tika exclaimed and giggled, as Moira stared at her. Both girls realized they heard Starvros say the same phrase on many occasions since starting the quest. Moira's eyes twinkled in merriment as she covered her mouth with her hands to stifle the laughter ready to spill from her.

"Shush! girls," Mayor Brown said sternly.

"Queen Varma, is not our daughter lovely?" asked King Hector.

"Yes King Hector, she is beautiful. The Snow Queen Fairy has blessed us bountifully this year."

"I think she is lovelier than anyone in the whole valley, I think she is more beautiful than the Snow Queen Fairy," King Hector continued, ignoring the Queen's reference to the Snow Queen Fairy.

"Be careful husband," Queen Varma said, looking anxiously around the great room.

"You must know you are not on good terms with the Snow Queen Fairy since you did not invite her to the Hunters' Ball, tonight. What has gotten into you, husband?" Queen Varma asked.

"You are behaving badly and you know the vanity of the Snow Queen Fairy. I hope you do not rue leaving her out of the festivities this season," Queen Varma continued.

"I am tired of bowing to a woman! I am a man, and I do manly things! I run this valley! I call the hunting and growing seasons! I lead the hunt and we are successful because of my skill and training, not because of some woman who lives on a mountain across the valley!" said King Hector.

Suddenly a light flashed in the great room and Mayor Brown almost dropped the book.

The Snow Fairy Queen stood in the midst of the great room clothed in a snow-white gown with crystals embedded in the cloth that resembled snowflakes. Each one, different, reflecting the light from the torches and candles which lit the great room. Her pale hair piled atop her head accentuated the high forehead and thin brows over cold blue eyes and her pointed ears held tiny crystal snowflake earbobs. Her feet, shod in ermine boots peeked beneath the flowing gown. On her shoulders lay a white fur lined cape flowing behind her as Queen Gizella walked through the crowd that parted before her and stood face to face with King Hector. Her blue eyes gleamed in her pale face, the only spot of color. Her lips, thin and straight, trembled in her face; the one sign of the temper she unleashed on King Hector.

"You dare compare your daughter to Queen Gizella! You dare deny Queen Gizella her night! The Hunters' Ball is the one day of all the days, I have blessed you, wherein I required, no; wanted your worship and adoration! You dare state that you are tired of bowing to your Snow Queen Fairy! For that, you have gone too far, King Hector! I have given you, good crops, good health, animals in abundance, children and have favored you with good weather! You dare lift your voice against Gizella, King Hector! The Queen of the fairies!" Gizella raged at the King.

"I-I meant no harm, Queen Gizella. I was overcome…"

"You were overcome with pride you fool, and as your Queen stated you will rue the day of your pride! Do you think you attained all this on your own? We shall see if you can live and, and …

I curse you and Circle Valley and all its inhabitants," Queen Gizella sputtered in her anger.

In an instant, Queen Gizella changed before King Hector as soon as the curse fell from her angry lips. Her hair fell from atop her head, to long pale wisps over ears that grew larger and more pointed. Her white gown changed to a black dress with a long, black, fur lined cape draping her shoulders. Her feet enlarged and the white boots vanished from her feet, leaving her barefooted in the room, before King Hector.

Gizella pointed a long finger with nails blackened by the curse at King Hector as she uttered.

"You fool, you have damned us both with your foolish pride and I in my anger have cursed you and myself as well. I-I hate you humans!" Gizella continued.

"You will no longer see the wealth you enjoyed to this day, neither will you see good crops, health or successful hunting seasons until you are led by one young and humble, not of your bloodline, to overcome the curse of pride and arrogance. Until you as a people unite for the common good of all and see love as more than a fence for your pride; you King Hector, are damned to be the horrible monster you are inside, and I call forth that horrible monster now!" The Snow Queen Fairy said.

"Wait, Queen Gizella, wait! I take back everything I said," King Hector cried fearfully.

"It is too late; this curse will come upon you at the death of your loved ones. You will lose everything you put before Queen Gizella; the daughter you carelessly compared to me in beauty will be lost to you until the prophecy is fulfilled and you come face to face with your descendants," Queen Gizella said.

Queen Varma fainted, and the inhabitants of Circle Valley fled the Castle to their homes.

Mayor Brown and the girls stared at the book seeing the events unfold before them, mouths agape.

"Is that Circle Valley?' Tika asked as the pictures in the enchanted book moved to show the curses' affects as it overtook Circle Valley.

"Yes, that is Circle Valley before and during the curse," Moira stated quietly.

The Hunters' Ball was at the Snow Monster's castle on the night of the curse. King Hector is the reason for the curse on Circle Valley," Moira continued.

"King Hector is the man I saw in the castle when I was captured," Tika said smugly.

"King Hector must become the snow monster when the Snow Queen Fairy dictates," Moira stated thoughtfully.

Tika turned to Moira and spoke harshly, "How do you know these things Moira? You were not around when all this took place. Why are you acting like a know-it-all?"

"I-I d-do not know, Tika, I just know," Moira said.

"S-h-h-h girl, maybe it is part of the enchantment of the book of the prophecy. It imparts knowledge to the reader," said Mayor Brown.

"Then that should be you, not Moira," said Tika.

"Shush! Tika, there is more going on here! Be quiet and let us continue so that we can help Starvros, Dirk and the villagers," said Mayor Brown.

"What does all this mean, Mayor Brown? asked Moira.

"I do not know, lass, let us turn a page and see what else unfolds, Mayor Brown said.

Putting action to his words, Mayor brown carefully turned a page in the worn, aged book. The pages were yellowed, thin and very fragile. The letters on the next page glowed briefly and began to fade before their eyes.

"Oh no! It has faded, how are we going to help Dirk rescue me, now?" Tika wailed.

"Be quiet Tika! Moira snapped. Moira took the book from a puzzled and thoughtful looking Mayor.

Moira walked over to the fire, removed a small glowing ember from the fire and dropped it onto the "Book of Prophecy, at the page that faded in front of their eyes.

Tika jumped to her feet, "Moira are you crazy? You ruined the book!" Tika exclaimed.

Mayor Brown looked at Moira and held his peace.

'How did she know to do that?' Mayor Brown thought as he realized the book did not burn.

Letters began to form on the page as before.

"It has a fire enchantment on it. In case, the wrong people read it, like us. I believe the rest of the book has information the wicked Snow Queen Fairy does not want anyone to see or know," Moira said.

"How do you know that?" Tika asked, looking suspiciously at Moira.

I-I d-do not know Tika, I just seem to know what to do, Moira said puzzled by her own feelings.

The trio looked on as the words formed and read aloud to them repeating the curse as before. Then more words gleamed on the page.

"The child you so carelessly compared to me in beauty will be lost to you. you will never see her again, nor will you see her descendants until the curse is loosed from Circle Valley! You King Hector will live in the castle under an enchantment, a king by day and a horrible monster by night. The inhabitants of Circle Valley who agreed with your folly against me will be cursed to feed the Snow Monster every night until they are loosed from this curse." The words faded again.

"I do not like that book," Tika said.

"Turn another page, Moira. I do not believe we have gotten to the end of this matter," said Mayor Brown.

Moira turned the page and the letters glowed. Moira read them slowly.

"These are the notes of Queen Gizella."

I, Queen Gizella, the last of the Fairy Queens in the realm of the Circle Mountain Range that encircles the valley called Circle Valley, do hereby decree these curses take place in the lives of the inhabitants of Circle Valley until such time that the prophecy comes true. As it is stated, so it is written!

Notation: I have assured that the curse will remain on the King and the inhabitants of Circle Valley, forever. I hate humans!

Because King Hector is a male and such stupidity came through a male, the solution will come through a young male who can overcome the issue of pride with humility and meekness.

The descendants of King Hector will never know who they are. I made sure of that. I coerced my sister to take the babe with her, after I gave her a potion to make her human. She married one of the villagers and the babe became one of them. No one knows who King Hector's descendants are!

My sister did not know the potion I gave her rendered her human and susceptible to death as all humans are. I did not know the potion would also make her capable of producing children and then my descendant married his descendant and now King Hector's descendants are my descendants. I am the only ruling power in Circle Valley and through enchantment; I have closed the valley off to the outside world. Circle Valley is mine! I have secured my place as Queen of the snow fairies! No one can oppose my reign. Only through the prophecy can Maeva's descendants destroy me! I can keep these silly humans out of my mountains forever with the help of the Snow Monster! I hate humans!

Moira gasped as the words faded once again.

"Well, that is the end of it. The wicked Snow Queen Fairy must use the book as a diary. She has noted everything relating to the curse. I see why they call her "wicked," said Mayor Brown.

"We must wait on Starvros, Dirk and the villagers to return so that we can free ourselves from the curse, the Snow Monster and the wicked Snow Queen Fairy, said Mayor Brown. I am sure when the Snow Monster is destroyed the curse will end with his death," Mayor Brown continued.

"But, who is the Snow Monsters descendants? Who is the descendant of King Hector's daughter, Mayor Brown? We need to figure out the curse to end it. That is the only way we can help Starvros and the villagers, is that not true?" Tika questioned.

"I think Moira has the answers we need, Tika!" What do you have to tell us Moira?" Mayor Brown asked.

"I am the descendant of the Snow Monster!" Moira said quietly.

Queen Gizella Uprooted!

Queen Gizella sat in her chair before the orb, eye closed in thoughtful musings, and confident the end to all the humans in her mountains was nearing an end.

'The Snow Monster and my minions and guards will soon return the book to me and I will destroy those meddling humans!' Gizella thought gleefully.

When the Queen opened her eyes and peered into the orb, she saw a very different scene. The orb glowed and cleared showing a small-darkened room. Three people sat by a small fire reading a small book. The queen moved closer to the orb to see better and fell over backwards onto the floor when she recognized the book they were reading.

"H-h-how did they get the book? What has that bumbling Snow Monster done now!" Queen Gizella exclaimed. Gizella got to her feet and peered into the orb again.

Gizella leaned forward, "Who is that girl? How is she able to understand so much about the book?" Gizella whispered.

"How is she able to undo the enchantment in the "Book of the Prophecy"?

Oh! No! Oh! Oh! Oh! It cannot be! I will not allow it! Mt RaNanjitsi, invaded by a human, and now, this, this girl, will destroy everything! I must get to Mt RaNinjitsi as quickly as possible, before that girl undoes everything I schemed hard to build for myself, "Queen Gizella stormed.

The Snow Queen Fairy ran to the middle of the room spoke seven words: "datra, gomma, ramma, somma, tomar, gophar, datra," and waved her hands over her head, when she heard Moira say, "I am the descendent of the Snow Monster." Gizella's screams rent the castle as she vanished.

Defeated Foes

In the clearing before the grotto Starvros, Dirk and the villagers stood in a tight cluster awaiting the Snow Monster and his minions to pour from the castle entrance at the back of the grotto. Each man stood with a spear in one hand, and long, mean-looking knives forged by Dirk in the smithy, in the other hand.

"Stand steady men, stand ready and wait until they are close before you attack, and then make every strike count, every blow must be to the head. The wicked Snow Queen Fairy controls their mind. That is what we must destroy. Do not waste your strength; an enemy must lay before your feet, dead, before you move to the next foe. Fight as you have never fought before. May our ancestors be with you! Go forth and be victorious, free our village from the grip of tyranny and greed!" Starvros said as he heard the snarls of the Snow Monster.

"Well said Little One," Dirk said, smiling at Starvros. Starvros returned Dirk's smile and turned as he heard more than saw the Snow Monster and his minions pour from the grotto. The men crouched lower and an audible gasp arose as they saw the Snow Monster for the first time.

"Do not run men! Starvros said, "his power is limited because he is controlled by the wicked Snow Queen Fairy. If we can keep him fighting a few hours until daybreak he will become King Hector, again, Starvros continued.

The Snow Monster advanced upon the villagers with the host of his minions and the Queen's guards.

The villagers stood their ground, not backing up or running away from the terrible foe before them.

The Snow Monster snarled and roared before them attempting to instill fear in their hearts and minds. Not one man moved. They stood as statues waiting for the battle to begin, waiting for Starvros' signal to fight to the death.

Their eyes were slits in their faces. Their chins thrust out before them as if leading the charge, noses flared as the stench of their foes reached them. Their color, heightened as sweat poured from their faces and their knuckles whitened from the grip on their weapons.

The Snow Monster moved slowly toward the villagers, yet, snarling and growling before them. His fangs dripped saliva and the odor of rotting food issued from him. His matted fur looked more of a mixed bag of colors, including white, brown, black and grey. His claws were as large as his fangs and looked as if they could rip a man to pieces with one blow, yet the villagers held their positions without flinching. He snarled, and roared, and growled before them, but not one man moved from his spot.

Into the mix, every one heard a keening sound as the wicked Snow Queen Fairy appeared in the space between the opposing foes, her head tilted back and her mouth open, screaming.

When the wicked Snow Queen Fairy realized where she was, she advanced toward the Snow Monster, oblivious to everyone else; or what, she interrupted.

"You bumbling fool, you -you -you fool! You horrible- terrible-fool! It is all over! We are defeated! You did the one thing I told you not to do! You allowed the villagers to unite for a common cause, led by this lad. You brought the prophecy to fulfillment. You allowed that child to overcome pride and defeat us, and you uncovered our common descendant after all my careful plans and schemes. If I did not know better, I think you have been working against me all this time," Gizella stormed at the Snow Monster.

"The girl figured out who she is. I was so busy trying to keep the book out of the hands of the lad and all the time it was one of the girls I should have been watching. The prophecy has come true; you and I will be banished to the nether world. I, for my wickedness and you for your silly pride. My magic will cease to rule this land. You will become King Hector for a while and then you must abdicate your throne to our descendant. She is both fairy and human. She will be the new Snow Fairy Queen. I must surrender my crown to she who is King Hector's descendant and descendant of my sister. She will rule over this realm and it will return to the way it was before, when I am gone and my magic will wane and disappear from the land." the Snow Queen Fairy continued, growing calmer after her tirade against the Snow Monster.

Queen Gizella turned to Starvros, Dirk and the villagers.

"It is over! My rule has ended. Put away your weapons. There is nothing to fear anymore. The curse is over. You won! Your courage in the face of the foe you faced today is admirable. however, things beyond our control forged in another realm governed what occurred today. Go and bring the lasses to me. Go, quickly I do not have much time," Queen Gizella stated. Bobbo ran into the grotto entrance to the castle to retrieve Mayor Brown and the girls. The rest of the villager put away their weapons slowly, keeping a wary eye on the Snow Monster, his minions and the wicked Snow Queen Fairy, not ready to trust, that it was over. They were still in fight mode. The men stood tensely, trying to grasp all that Gizella said to them. Some of the villagers talked among themselves, but Starvros and Dirk stood straight and tall before Gizella.

Loose Ends

Mayor Brown asked Moira again. "How do you know all these things, Moira?"

"I am the descendant of the Snow Monster," Moira said quietly.

"W-what is she talking about, Uncle Brown?" Tika said looking at Moira as if she suddenly grew fangs and fur.

"Shush," Tika.

"Go on Moira, how do you know that you are the descendant of the Snow Monster?" Mayor Brown prodded.

"I did not know until I read the name in the "Book of the Prophecy," Moira stated.

"What is going on here, and do not shush me again, Uncle Brown? I have a right to know what is happening. I am in this and have been since the beginning. I am not some silly child, I am a woman and this quest has helped me to see that I must think of myself as a woman too, and I am certainly going to make sure others treat me with dignity and respect, beginning with you, Uncle Brown!" Tika said, heatedly.

"Okay Tika, calm down and let Moira continue so that we can get our answers to this surprising twist on things," Mayor Brown said.

Moira continued, I am the descendant of King Hector and the Snow Queen Fairy. His daughters' name is given to the women in the family for as long as I can remember as noted in our family history. When I was born, my aunt refused to give me my mothers' name when she died giving birth to me. Aunt Jayne's cruelty is the reason I ran away to join Starvros on this quest. If she knew good came out of her meanness and spite, I think she would die," Moira averred

Suddenly they heard someone at the door fumbling with the lock. Mayor Brown signaled to the girls to stand behind him and he pulled the knife Starvros gave him from his waist. Moira bent over, lifted her skirt and removed the knife she had strapped to her thigh.

Mayor Brown's eyes bulged and then he smiled at Moira and signaled for her to get ready.

Tika looked from Mayor Brown to Moira.

"Why you reaching for a knife, Moira You are the newest fairy around here, use some magic to find out who is at the door," she stated daringly at Moira.

"It is me. Bobbo," the muffled voice came through the door, as he burst into the room.

"It is over! We have won! The curse is over! Come! Come! Bobbo babbled.

"She wants to see you girls. She has summoned you! Come quickly. She said she does not have much time, so come along, now!" Bobbo continued grabbing both the girls by the hand and pulling them toward the door.

Tika jerked away from Bobbo.

"I am not going anywhere until I know what is going on! Did I hear you say the curse is over?" Bobbo.

"Yes! yes, said Bobbo, bobbing his head in assent while he spoke.

"You got to come, she wants to see both you girls, one of you is her descendant and she has things to say before she is banished from here. So move it, girl and quit asking so many questions. You will know all in good time. Move I said!" Bobbo said as he grabbed Tika and Moira and headed for the door. Mayor Brown grabbed the "Book of the Prophecy" and followed Bobbo out the door, just as puzzled as Tika and Moira by Bobbo's words. When Moira, Tika and Mayor Brown were hurriedly ushered before Queen Gizella. She looked from one girl to the other.

"Which of you is my descendant?" Queen Gizella commanded. Moira hung back in fear, not knowing if the Queen would harm her or not.

Tika spoke first, "I am not your descendant, and Mayor Brown is my uncle! Tell her Mayor Brown; tell her, you are my uncle. I do not know what this woman will do to me if she thought I was her descendant! I do not trust her!" Tika said.

"Hush lass!" The Queen commanded as she turned from Tika to Moira.

"You are my descendant! What is your name, lass?" Queen Gizella commanded.

"I am Moira; my father is the Shaman of Circle Valley," Moira stated hesitating on every word.

"Ah-h that explains everything. I felt there was other magic at work here. Your father has been working against me. There was no way you three could do this alone. The prophecy has a magic of its own. It was going to come true no matter what I did. I may have delayed it a few centuries, but I could not atop it." Queen Gizella stated.

"You, young woman are the heir to Circle Valley and the Queen of the Snow Fairies. You are both human and fairy. "The land is free from the curse; your people are free from the curse. The land will return to the state it was in before the curse, when I blessed your fields and gave you abundance of animals, crops and great wealth. Passages will open to other lands and you will trade with them and increase in goods. Circle Valley will no longer be a closed off, a land forgotten for centuries. My magic is waning, Hector will tell you what else you must do. He must face his descendant before he is banished.

Queen Gizella faded, her voice faded and the minions and guards faded away. When next Starvros and Dirk, and the villager turned, King Hector stood before them fully clothed in fine clothes.

Ho! What kind of sorcery is this?" Starvros stated, and everyone laughed including King Hector.

EPILOGUE

M oira stood before King Hector in the great room. Moira felt dirty and disheveled before the King, and hungry and thirsty. Moira could not remember how long they have been in the mountains. Moira did not know that her decision to flee her home led her to where she stood. Her past and her future joined in one moment, from one decision. Starvros stood beside her at the request of King Hector and the villagers stood behind them.

King Hector sat on the throne in the great room, as King of Circle Valley. Moira saw the sad replica it had become over the ages. The drapes hung from the windows, tattered and thin, light filtering through in great chunks upon the dust covered furnishings. Cobwebs covered everything in sight. Pelts and animal heads and weapons of all types covered the walls and floors. Two massive fireplaces stood at each end of the room, cold ashes on their hearth. Only a few torches on the walls lit the great room.

"Moira," King Hector said.

Y-Yes, K-King H-Hector, Moira said, and the words sounded strange to her ears. Moira pranced from one foot to the other, uncomfortable before the King.

"Come to me daughter," King Hector commanded.

The villagers gasped. Tika's mouth opened to protest, but no sound came out. Dirk grabbed Tika's hand and smiled at her, lovingly. Starvros stared at Moira, mouth agape.

Moira walked the short distance to the King and bowed before him.

"Do not bow, child. You are descended from my daughter Maeva who I lost because of pride and arrogance. I have only a short time to put things right before I leave you," King Hector stated.

Pride and arrogance often comes with great wealth and power, Moira. It will take over and rule you and you will make poor decisions that can have long term affects on others, including the ones you love. Pride is a destroying emotion and arrogance is its tool. I allowed pride to take everything from me and I was left to face the monster I became every day of my life. Through pride, another gained control of all that I had and through the machinations of the wicked Snow Queen Fairy and her vanity, we have all lost so much," said King Hector.

"Enough of the past. Moira, you should have received your mother's name when you were born; the name Maeva given to every first-born female child is the key to your birthright. You also have lived under the tyranny of another. I do not know whether to thank your aunt or to destroy her, but if the conditions in your home had not been intolerable for you; I would still be the Snow Monster." King Hector averred.

"Yes my King, I recognized my mothers' name in the "Book of Prophecy" written in Queen Gizella's hand. It was then I realized I was your descendant. How am I a descendant of the wicked Snow Queen Fairy, too? I do not understand this and I do not know if I can accept that I am also her descendant," Moira stated.

"Let us do this another way, Moira, the King stated as he saw the ragtag group standing before him.

"Bartoll!" the King shouted and a door to his left opened immediately and Bartoll entered the room. Bartoll eyed Tika and she eyed him as he turned and bowed before King Hector.

Tika opened her mouth to speak, but Dirk squeezed her hand and looked sternly at Tika. Tika closed her mouth and said nothing more.

"Yes, sire, what is your wish?" Bartoll said in his raspy voice.

Bartoll prepare a table for all of us to sit and bring food for us to eat. We have all had to endure very trying circumstances on very little food. Bring water and wine, Bartoll. We need refreshing!" the King commanded.

"As you wish, sire," Bartoll stated and left quickly to do the King's bidding.

"We will wait on Bartoll to do as I asked before I continue, the King stated.

Soon Bartoll returned and ushered the King and the villagers into another room.

The room was smaller and cozier than the great room. A fire burned in the huge fireplace at one end of the room. The heat filled the room with warmth. It was also made of giant boulders with a mantle forged from a giant tree. Candles burned on every table in the room and torches lit the corners of the room. A large table filled the center of the room and food of every kind covered the surface in various dishes made of gold and silver.

Silver candleholders gleamed and reflected light in rainbow hues around the room.

The smell of the food caused the villagers stomach to growl and a low rumble heard by all caused laughter to emanate from all, as the King commanded them to sit and eat.

The villager seated themselves around the table and did not wait for another command from the King, but fell upon the food filling their plates with as much as they could.

"Do not eat too much people; we have been living off very little food for a while. Do not make yourselves sick by eating too much," Dirk stated.

The King allowed the villagers to eat before continuing.

Moira, to answer your question about your dual linage as a descendant of the Snow Queen Fairy and myself. On the night of the Hunters' Ball, after the foolishness and the issuance of the curse which also affected Queen Gizella because Fairies were not to curse their subjects; she changed immediately into the wicked fairy. Queen Gizella took the child that night; Queen Varma fainted and later, locked herself away in her rooms and only Bartoll attended to her. She died of heartbreak and fear a few years later.

Maeva was taken and raised by Queen Gizella's sister, Isabel. She hid Maeva in the only place she could, among the villagers in Circle Valley! Her aim was to hinder or even prevent the prophecy from coming true. Queen Gizella tricked Isabel into taking a potion that rendered her human.

She then sent Isabel to Circle Valley where Isabel married a villager and raised Maeva as their child. They had a son soon after their marriage. Gizella was angry. She did not know the potion would make Isabel human in every way. Time went on and Maeva became an adult, married a villager-The Smythes', and they had a daughter, named Maeva. Isabel told Maeva of her heritage and Maeva determined to keep that heritage alive by naming every first-born female after her.

Isabel's son married and had children. Maeva's granddaughter married one of Isabel's' grandsons and the descendants of Maeva merged with the descendants of the wicked Snow Queen Fairy.

Moira, that is how you became both human and fairy," the King stated as he ended his story.

"I am the descendant of Isabel, a fairy turned human and Maeva, a princess: part human, part fairy. No wonder I always felt odd and out of place, Moira exclaimed when she understood the truth of her heritage.

"That is some story! I always thought I was someone special in our village. Who knew that all this was hidden in our village, in Moira," said Tika.

Tika!" said Dirk looking at her in exasperation.

I mean no harm Dirk, but it is the truth! Tika protested.

"King Hector, where do we go from here?" Starvros asked.

"Good question lad, the curse of the Snow Monster is removed from Circle Valley; the legend of the Snow Monster revealed; the wicked Snow Queen Fairy abdicated her rule to another; banished from this realm, forever I will soon go to the grave that has long awaited my coming. The last enchantments will disappear after I am gone including Bartoll who has been with me since the beginning. His last act is to bring Queen Gizella's crown to place upon the head of her successor,' the King stated.

King Hector rose to his feet and escorted everyone back into the great room. There he sat on the throne and called Moira to stand before him.

I must decree you Moira, as the Princess you are as my descendant and as the new Snow Queen Fairy. King Hector stood and turned to Mayor

Brown and took his hand. He placed Moira's hand in Mayor Browns' hand and spoke to them.

"Mayor Brown, you are the governing body of Circle Valley as its Mayor. I decree and present to Circle Valley, your ruling Queen; Queen Maeva of the realm of Circle Valley in the Circle Mountain Range. I further decree that she is Queen Maeva, Snow Queen Fairy of the Circle Mountain Range and of Circle Valley and its inhabitants.

Mayor Brown and present company, your allegiance to the Snow Monster forced upon you, unwillingly; it is my hope, your allegiance to your new Queen is voluntary and lasting. If you will agree to her allegiance over you, when all is completed you will bow before your Queen," the King averred.

Moira, changes will overtake you if you accept your heritage, do not fear them. You will receive all the power and enchantments of the Snow Queen Fairy. Govern them well. Do not follow the path of your predecessor, Queen Gizella. Use the course of events that shaped your life to provide better for the people you rule. Love them, treat them with mercy and compassion and they will love you in return!

Daughter of royal birth, daughter of Josiah Jerome Hector, 44th heir of Circle Valley, I do hereby decree that by legal birth you are Maeva Linelle Hector, Queen of Circle Valley of the Circle Mountain Range and Snow Queen Fairy; 49th heir of the same realm and its inhabitants.

Queen Maeva bowed before the King. The King stepped aside as he ushered the inhabitants away from Queen Maeva. All were puzzled until lights began to emanate around her. The air began to swirl around and surround her. Queen Maeva looked at the King, fear in her eyes.

Starvros leaped toward Queen Maeva.

"Ho! What sorcery is this? You will not harm the woman I love," Starvros shouted at King Hector.

Starvros stopped in his tracks when he heard the words he spoke to the King.

Queen Maeva looked at Starvros and smiled at him; the love she hid away, shining in her eyes.

Starvros returned her smile, the love he did not know shining in his eyes.

He could not move he could only watch in wonder as the new feelings engulfed him.

"Do not fear daughter, "King Hector said, tears filling his eyes.

"These changes must occur for you to rule two realms. Allow them to take place, child, do not fight them. The curse of the Snow Monster is broken forever. Pride will never be a tool used to destroy a people again. With humbleness of heart you will serve your people and they will serve you," the King continued.

The wind continued to swirl and lights flashed in multicolored hues around Queen Maeva as changes took place in her visage, her hair and her clothing.

The villagers turned away from the lights fearing the worse, Tika turned toward Dirk and leaned her head on Dirk's broad chest. Dirk engulfed Tika in his arms and laid his head atop her head, reveling in the feel of Tika in his arms, watching Starvros, King Hector, Bartoll and Queen Maeva, ever the warrior his eyes roved everywhere.

Starvros did not take his eyes from Queen Maeva even through the blinding lights surrounding her.

When the lights ceased and the wind stopped, Starvros' eyes widened and his mouth opened and the only sound he uttered was a soft "Oh!"

All eyes turned toward Moira, everyone gasped and then they laughed at Starvros. "What? No- Ho! What Kind of sorcery is this? from you, Starvros?" Tika asked laughing.

Queen Maeva stood before them not as the Moira they knew. The transformation left them with a person they did not know standing before them.

Moira stood before the villagers and Starvros in splendid array dressed in a blue satin gown with long flowing sleeves. The dress split up the center revealing golden linen underskirts with yards of ruffles. The many under slips made the dress stand out from Moiré's slim waist, where the gown flowed to the floor of the castle. Over the gown, a blue cape flecked with stardust trailed behind her to the floor as well. Blue booties adorned her feet and sheer blue legging peeped out when Moira moved which was often as the gazes of her friends made her feel uncomfortable.

As their gaze travelled upward, Starvros gasped, Dirk gasped, Mayor Brown gasped and Tika turning to look fully at Moira, gasped. The villagers bowed in awe at the apparition before them that they knew as Moira, the Shaman of Circle Valley's daughter.

Moira was more beautiful than they had ever seen before. Gone was the tall gangly girl with the pale straight tresses.

Before them stood a vision with golden yellow hair trailing down her back in waves and curls almost to her waist. Wisps of yellow hair clung to a heart shaped face. Large eyes with long lashes looked at them. Lips, full and red sat deliciously under an aquiline nose. Dainty pointed ears peered out from the golden tresses studded with blue sapphire ear buds. Her cheeks blushed from her discomfort.

King Hector walked to Moira and took her by the hand.

"Never be uncomfortable about who you are my child. It is who you are meant to be. No one can steal your destiny, child. They may delay it, but it can never be stolen." King Hector said as he turned from Moira to the villagers.

"I present to you, Mayor Brown, Starvros, people of Circle Valley, Your new Snow Fairy Queen, Maeva Linelle Hector!" the King announced in ringing tones.

The villagers bowed lower.

Starvros bowed down before his Queen, wonder in his eyes, love in his heart. The realization almost caused him to topple over, instead, Starvros knelt before Moira too stunned to utter a single word.

His thoughts raced around in his mind, trying to figure out when love came to him for Moira.

Mayor Brown bowed and Dirk bowed before Queen Maeva.

Tika sputtered, "How did this happen? It is only Moira!"

Dirk pulled Tika beside him and spoke to her in a whisper.

"Be quiet woman! She is also Queen of the fairies! Do you want to be the new snow monster? Be quiet I say! Do not say another word! Bow before your Queen! Tika. Bow now! Dirk insisted.

Tika looked at Dirk defiantly.

Tika looked at Queen Maeva.

Queen Maeva returned her look.

"Oh, darn it, Okay, Tika said as she bowed before the Queen. No, I do not want to be the new Snow Monster! Do you think she would do that to me," Tika whispered.

"Yes, if you do not be quiet!" Dirk said.

"I know that I do want to be your wife, Dirk if you will have me?" Tika continued.

"Tika, could you not wait for me to do the asking?" Dirk stated.

"I see you are going to be a handful, woman. I would not love you any better than I do at this moment, Tika. Nevertheless, close your mouth and we will discuss all this later. Now bow and show your Queen, honor," Dirk continued.

Tika turned and bowed to Queen Maeva lowering her eyes before the new Snow Fairy Queen of Circle Valley.

"I do not know what to do, Get up, everyone! Get up! Queen Maeva exclaimed.

"Queen Maeva, do not despair. It will come to you. you were born a princess, it is in you to rule. Rule well with humility. Do not have pride and arrogance like your predecessor. Ruling and reigning well has no place for greed and pride. Arrogance is not the substance of leadership. It will exact a bitter price at the end, Queen Maeva." King Hector stated, Taking her hands and facing her he looked deeply at her as if searing her face in his memory.

Rule well, daughter. Rule well as your domain returns to you in all its past glory and wealth.

Starvros, come here lad, King Hector said as he turned from Queen Maeva to the villagers once again.

You, Starvros are not without merit in all of what has occurred this day. In humbleness of mind you led to the discovery of the Legend of the Snow Monster, the destruction of Circle Valley's greatest enemy and the uncovering of the curse upon the Snow Monster and the village. The prophecy has come true through the united efforts of the villagers themselves. By uniting in your fight against the Snow Monster for your way of life you brought the prophecy to pass through the hands of a youth without pride who led his people to a place they never experienced before-unity! Starvros, you left Circle Valley an untried youth, but through this quest, you have become a man of strength, of character and principles. You lost much because of the curse. You will gain more because of your faith and courage. You have done what no other man has done. I, King Hector, King of Circle Valley, of the Circle Mountain Range, do hereby give Queen Maeva to be your wife! You will no longer know her as Moira- the girl who ran away from Circle Valley. She is Queen Maeva! Queen of two worlds- human and fairy! Rule well beside her, love her, cherish her, and Circle Valley will flourish with you! Keep from pride, arrogance and greed- the formula for destruction!" King Hector continued, stunning everyone in the great room, including Moira, who gasped audibly at the Kings' announcement.

King Hector took Starvros' hand and Queen Maeva's' hand and joined them together in his huge hands. This is your destiny. This is the culmination of the prophecy. The quest was the road to get you here. You did well! Starvros!" the King stated with tears in his eyes.

"Be strong, Be strong King Hector stated as he vanished from their sight leaving Starvros and Queen Maeva facing each other, hand in hand.

"What do we do now, Starvros?" asked Queen Maeva.

Starvros looked into Queen Maeva's eyes, "I love you Maeva and I accept your hand as King Hector commanded!" Starvros stated.

"I accept as well Starvros. I love you, too," Queen Maeva stated softly as she looked deeply into Starvros' eyes.

"Enough, enough, said Tika. Lets open these windows and see our new world. If it is as King Hector said, the effects of the curse upon the land should be disappearing."

"Ho, the watchers are gone and the guards are gone! What kind of sorcery is this?" said Bobbo.

Everyone laughed as Starvros issued orders to open the windows of the great room that opened onto a huge balcony. The villagers set about opening the windows as Starvros led Queen Maeva to sit upon the throne once belonging to her ancestor, King Hector.

Queen Maeva protested, but Starvros was firm.

"Allow your people to serve you with joy of spirit and gladness of heart, Queen Maeva. They are free! Free from years of tyranny and abuse. Allow them to show you their love without restraints. They know what they are doing. Things in motion set us on a course that led to growth in us all, individually and as a people. The quest united a people who are forever changed. Through your guidance, we will rebuild Circle Valley. We will explore all this together, you and I. Come let us go and view our domain, the villagers have opened the windows to the outside," Starvros said as he took Queen Maeva's hand and led her out onto the balcony.

The sunlight flooded the room with its brilliance and warmth. The villagers moved to make room on the balcony for Queen Maeva and Starvros.

They looked out over the countryside and saw the snows receding in record speed. Grass sprang up as the ground revealed itself to the brilliant sunlight. Trees blossomed and leaves appeared on some of the trees and on some of them all manner of fruit trees manifested before their eyes.

"Look! In the woods there are deer!" said Bobbo,

"There are rabbits and other small animals!" Clyde said.

"Look, further out there is that huge herd of elk that almost trampled us, they are returning!" Tika stated.

Flowers and shrubs covered the fields in abundance. Birds filled the sky of multi–

colored hues and sizes. Myriad butterflies and fairies flitted over the flowers and shrubs in flight-like dancing.

"I see squirrels scurrying among the trees," Tika laughed.

"It is a miracle," Queen Maeva, stated

"No, Queen Maeva, it is the end of a terrible era in the lives of the people of Circle Valley. A time of peace, growth and prosperity through rebuilding efforts we initiate from this point on, is the true Miracle, Queen Maeva," Starvros said.

The End!